ASSUME
GUILT

A MATT BARLOW MYSTERY

For Mary!
All Best!,
Go Illini!,
I love Mindy!

PAUL LISNEK

2/19

Praise for *Assume Guilt*

"Assume Guilt is the ultimate courtroom thriller about Murder, Marriage, & Money by lawyer extraordinaire Paul Lisnek. Can our hero unearth the sinister secret of a cold-blooded killer or will it remain entombed forever? Lisnek's debut novel is a fast-paced must read."

—Linda Kenney Baden, Criminal Trial Attorney and Author of *Remains Silent*

"Mix politics with Paul Lisnek's experience as a political TV analyst and his keen legal background, the result: *Assume Guilt* is a recipe for a page turner. Lisnek knows how to tell a compelling story. The combination of politics with the drama of the courtroom produces a riveting story which makes you await the movie version…not to mention the next book!"

—Haskell Pitluck, State of Illinois Retired Circuit Court Judge

"Paul Lisnek slowly peels the onion of his legal mystery, keeping his reader in suspense until the core is revealed. Jury Consultant Matt Barlow is a believable character, and Lisnek breathes life into all of the plot twists of *Assume Guilt.*"

—Charles M. DuPuy, Author of the E.Z. Kelly Mystery Series

"Like the rest of Chicagoland, I've been a long-time fan and admirer of Paul Lisnek's on-air political and legal analysis. And now, I'm a fan of his first work of fiction and the heroic character Matt Barlow! You can't write about politics, law, juries, and how they all interact without knowing it all inside and out; Paul brings all of that and more to the table in this riveting "can't put it down" novel that is filled with twists, turns, and an unexpected ending."

—Tom Skilling, WGN-TV Chief Meteorologist

ASSUME GUILT

GUILT

A MATT BARLOW MYSTERY

PAUL LISNEK

Green Bay, WI 54311

Assume Guilt: **A Matt Barlow Mystery** by Paul Lisnek, copyright © 2018 by Paul M. Lisnek. Paul Lisnek's Author Photo courtesy of WGN-TV.

Publishing Editor: Brittiany Koren
Copy-editors: Jessie Harrison and N.H. Hopp
Cover Art Designer: Barbra Sprangers
Interior Layout Designer: Amanda Dix

Category: Legal Mystery
Description: *In Chicago, a man's world is turned upside down when he's charged with the murder of his wife, and Matt Barlow and his team must find a way to prove his innocence.*
Hard Cover ISBN: 978-1-7326919-1-9
Paperback ISBN: 978-1-7326919-2-6
Ebook ISBN: 978-1-7326919-3-3
LOC Catalogue Data: Applied for.

First Edition published by Written Dreams Publishing in October, 2018.

Green Bay, WI 54311

For my mother, Sandy Lisnek, who left us this summer after a valiant battle with Alzheimer's, and who gave me life and molded me to be the man I am; I shall miss her for the rest of my life.

And for my dad, Seymour Lisnek, for a lifetime of support and believing in me always; my kids Alexandra and Zachary Lisnek, for extending my life through their own; for my 4-legged kids both here and across the rainbow bridge: Mertz, Maude, Matthew, and Myles for providing me with omnipresent spirit; for my brother and sister Rick and Judy Lisnek, who I love dearly and who truly understand the flaws of our judicial system.

Prologue

"Ladies and Gentlemen of the jury, have you reached a verdict?" Judge Jennifer Lyons looked at the jury foreperson over her reading glasses perched on the end of her nose.

I watched Juror 23, a fiftyish woman, pull at the lapels of her crisp, navy blue suit. I didn't like to rely on stereotypes as anything more than a starting point, but like many of the middle-aged female jurors I'd observed over the years, Juror 23 took her civic duty seriously. Every day of the two-week trial, she showed up dressed in a suit almost identical to those worn by the defending and prosecuting attorneys. As befitting a civic-minded woman, she nodded solemnly. "We have, Your Honor."

I recognized number 23's tone. Most judges ate up the deferential but confident voice. Between their black robe and elevated position relative to everyone else in the courtroom, judges had a way of subtly earning, or at least commanding, a juror's respect. Another reason so many jurors tended to dress to impress. But as for lawyers—and politicians? Now they—or we—were a different breed. I often caught jurors in the act of eying us with suspicion. Lawyers and politicians seemed to prove that old saying: familiarity indeed breeds a dose of contempt. Something else I blamed on TV.

I rested my weight against the back wall of the courtroom not far from the door. I drew air deep into my lungs, something I routinely did in moments leading up to a verdict, along with one other critical step in my ritual. In the men's room a few minutes ago, I took a swig of my lifeline, the milky antacid I counted on to quiet the churning in my gut. Some things never change. This time, I was a jury consultant rather than a player at the counsels' table, but my verdict-day symptoms were still the same. And it wasn't pretty.

I filled and emptied my lungs again during the seconds of silence while the judge silently read the verdict. I kept my eyes on Charles Marchand, the defendant, though. He lifted his chin and squared his shoulders, straightening his back. No posture of guilt or acquiescence for him. My old friend and Charles' defense attorney, Kenny Baden, sat equally tall at Charles' side. I couldn't see their faces, but if I'd had a sketch pad and some charcoal I could have produced a fair likeness of their neutral expressions.

Since I was trained to observe, I shifted my focus to the judge's face. I looked for a raised eyebrow, a twist in the mouth—anything that offered a hint of what was to come. But this seasoned judge was hard to read.

Judge Lyons refolded the paper, and turning to address the jury, she said, "I have reviewed the verdict form and it's in order. I'm going to give the verdict form to my clerk and ask the defendant and counsel to please rise… Ms. Foreperson, what say you?"

The foreperson glanced at the judge and at both counsels' tables before glancing down. "In the case of the People vs. Charles Marchand, as to Count One for Murder in the First Degree, we, the jury find the defendant…guilty."

Rising heat, gut to chest, hit me hard, along with the sweat prickling the back of my neck. Despite the sub-zero Chicago temperature outside, the stifling hot, dry air in the courtroom threatened to suffocate me.

I'd had enough. I couldn't stick around to listen to the gasps and buzz sweeping through the courtroom or witness the prosecution's backslapping congratulations. I refused to hang around to watch the sheriff's deputies lead Charles away to the holding area where he'd be searched and processed, then sent to jail for the rest of his days. The likely—and logical—result given the verdict the jury rendered.

As the judge still banged the gavel and called for order in the courtroom, I slipped out the door.

I'd failed. Again.

For nearly a year, I'd lived all day, every day, with each stage of the most intensely followed trial Chicago had seen in decades. From the minute Charles was led out of his Gold Coast townhome, soon arraigned and held without bail, the legal analysts had more work than they could handle, and trial watchers had their fix. Curious folks, not just the regular court-watcher crowds, stood in line and crammed the courtroom to witness the action unfolding minute by minute. Night after endless night, local and national TV commentators took apart the evidence, none more expertly than the renowned lawyer-turned-fulltime legal journalist, Cooper Julien.

Known by his full name to most, a chosen

few—like me—called him Coop. Smirking at the twist of irony that led to good things, Coop had nearly doubled his considerable trial-watching audience during the Marchand case.

Clear and concise, like a good lawyer, Coop never let his audience get too complacent in their stance on guilt or innocence. I admired Coop, sometimes grudgingly. The SOB showed the media world he was willing to challenge every so-called expert on his daily panels.

I smiled to myself, thinking about the many times I'd sparred with the venerable old Coop. The last time our banter played out on TV, I'd come close to ridiculing him for defending the supposedly fair settlement in a civil case over a massive oil spill. *Ha! Bullshit.* A paltry billion or two meant nothing to that multinational energy giant, but Coop wouldn't budge in declaring the verdict and legal fines fair. We laughed about it later. It made for damn good TV.

This or that stance aside, Coop's lasting impression on viewers could be traced to his lack of self-obsession. The guests landed in the spotlight, but then he put them on the spot, too. That's what had turned him into a media legend, admired and feared.

The stars had aligned for Coop. His show had debuted mere weeks before a mass shooting in North Carolina, quickly followed by news of Sandra Marchand's death, presumably a murder and the subject of this case. Coop chose cases wrapped up in frenetic sensationalism that appealed to viewers because he stayed methodical and calm in his coverage. I, more or less, had handed Coop his show's motto: "The thinking person's legal show."

Of course, Cooper Julien wasn't alone in analyzing the Marchand case. Not with the politics inevitably intertwined. A perfect storm for media, new as well as old. Rumor had it that Charles Marchand, the one-time professional chef, Hollywood-handsome—and in the last couple of decades a controversial, but rich real estate developer—had moved beyond the putting-out-feelers stage to give the current governor a run for his money. That was over a year ago, of course, before Charles stood now accused of murdering his stunning socialite, philanthropist wife.

Sandra's popularity in town proved what many of us observed about Chicagoans, namely that we weren't hung up on where our city's citizens were born. Emblematic of the Midwest, we knew everyone was "from away." From away might easily mean Serbia or El Salvador, but it could just as easily mean New Orleans, like Sandra had been. How a person felt about our city was what mattered, and Sandra proved many times over that she had plenty of room in her heart for her adopted Chicago home.

The universe of trial watchers occupied equally divided camps of accusers and supporters. As the jury consultant for the defense, I'd started out suspecting Charles' guilt myself. Over the months, I'd inched my way into the opposite camp. *Damn it*. That only sharpened the pain of failure.

An army of reporters had lined the corridor of the courthouse just outside the packed courtroom, waiting to see whether lawyers would come out of that room alone or if a relieved Charles Marchand might walk alongside his lawyer after a not guilty verdict. The press corps stood with cell phones in hand, rapidly texting and emailing through the spotty wireless network in the building.

I kept my eyes fixed on the exit doors, maybe

twenty feet away. Before I could make my get-away, I had to push past the reporters I'd known for years. They'd all lived the case, too. Some called out my name.

Duffy, a veteran crime reporter from the *Sun-Times* shouted, "Hey Matt, dude, slow down."

I didn't look at him as I waved him off. But Raphael, we all called him Raphie, the new kid on the *Chicago Tribune's* crime beat, fell in step alongside me, his floppy hair all but hiding his eyes. I picked up my breakaway stride. Any other day, I'd have stopped and given these guys the quote they were looking for. Not today, though. Hell, maybe not ever again. I already knew what the headline would be: *"Marchand, Murder One!"* followed by something in the order of "*Murder conviction kills political career.*"

Outside the courthouse, I ignored the shouts of the field reporters and the vans of the local news affiliates. Each shout, each demand for an interview, felt like a slug in my gut.

I raced across the plaza in front of the Daley Center, slowed down only by sliding on a patch of recently fallen snow that covered icy patches the salt hadn't yet melted. I stayed on my feet, managing to teeter to the left and then corrected to regain my balance.

I shoved my hands in my coat pockets. Damn it, I'd left my gloves somewhere. What else was new? Time to buy another cheap pair, the only kind that made sense for me. I could pick 'em up at any drug store. I wished they sold them in bulk so one grand purchase could get me through a brutal Chicago winter.

My thoughts drifted to memories of my mother ribbing me about the trail of lost gloves. That memory clip brought me to my brother, who'd long ago disappeared into the shady world of the current governor's so-called administration. If Zachary saw my hands, stiff from the cold, he'd add his two cents, too.

My jaw relaxed into a smile, allowing for some give in my rigid, negative thoughts. For just a minute, I allowed myself a moment of nostalgia. As kids, Zach had taken the gloves off his own hands so many times after I'd dropped mine somewhere.

I persisted with pushing my way through and finally ended up with a path in the crush of reporters and crowd of curious onlookers willing to stand in the cold for a glimpse. But a glimpse of what? They wouldn't see Charles Marchand today. Maybe not ever.

On a normal day, I didn't pay much attention to trial groupies. Now their presence taunted me.

"Don't you have anything better to do?" I muttered under my breath. "Go home and mind your own business!"

Apparently, trial watchers had fallen under the spell of death—murder style death. I was sick of death; I was even sicker of failure. Hadn't I sworn off this kind of trial because I couldn't handle another failure? Now, here I was, with it staring me in the face.

Chapter One

Fourteen months earlier

From the Twitter feed of Lourdes Ponce, editor-in-chief, *Gold Line,* her online magazine was "dedicated to the residents of the Gold Coast."

8:55 PM: *Arrived Café Brauer 4 no-kill shelter fundraiser. Freezing cold, thin crowd, but dazzling, Sandra Marchand mingling. No sign of handsome husband, Charles, yet.*

9:02 PM: *Sandra heard complaining to shelter director about paltry crowd. Her word. Café elegant as ever. Mayor's wife here with teen kids. Teachers union VP just walked in. Fireworks soon?*

9:25 PM: *Rumor...Gov. Toland on the way. Charles Marchand arrives. Sandra enjoying the champagne and amused by crowd.*

9:38 PM: *Sandra acting strange. Drinking a lot. Loud laughing. Never saw,-heard that be4. Charles trying 2 calm. S stalked away w/angry glare...crowd acting like Marchand is already gov.*

10:02 PM: *Toland arrives w/entourage. Icy in*

here. 2 political rivals face off. Neither blink. To-
land makes speech, says it's not a nite 4 politics.
Ha! Toland breathes politics. Toland whispers to
Sandra. She laughs, but not the nice kind. Toland
outta here.

10: 35 PM: *Sandra looks tipsy. Crowd leaving.*
Bad nite 4 fundraising/ Sandra. Not the story ex-
pected 2nite.

* * *

I skirted around the Please Wait to Be Seated sign
and waved at the cashier, who raised her hand in
greeting. I didn't know Virginia's exact age, but
some years ago I had described her as "just this
side of death and waiting for the final word." I
found it amusing, anyway.

I headed to Table 10, not all the way in the back
of Granny's Pancake House, but close enough to
be far away from the supposedly secret smoking
section that defied the no smoking laws of the
city. I found it funny that all the women getting
their hair styled next door at Adel's Hair Sensation would sneak out in their curlers and smocks
to grab a quick smoke in the pancake house next
door like it was some prohibition-style speakeasy.

Moving the Reserved sign to the side, I settled
in the chair on the far side of the table, where I
had a view of the front door and sidewalk outside
of the restaurant. Ever since a guy got shot in the
back of the head right through Granny's window,
I'd made sure I could keep an eye on what was
going on both inside and outside of the restaurant.
I told myself it gave me a feeling of being in the
know. Really, it was my hedge against danger.

17

Paul Lisnek

I picked up the copy of the *Chicago Tribune* on the table, and, like clockwork, Fernando, a proud green card holder from Bolivia, showed up at my side. He filled my glass with ice water from the pitcher he held in one hand and poured coffee into a mug from the carafe he gripped in the other.

"Hey amigo…como estás?"

"Bien, Fernando, bien," I responded, grinning. "The café es mucho caliente, heh?"

"Si! Your Español is getting better, el Presidente! Much better."

I suppressed a laugh. Fernando never failed to feign delight at my attempt to improve my conversational Spanish, which in the two years Fernando and I had played our game, had expanded to maybe twenty words.

Shaking his head and smiling broadly, Fernando headed to a foursome in a nearby booth, making room for Granny herself, real name Christina, to thread her way through the maze of tables to stop next to mine.

"Mornin', sweetheart. What'll it be?" She snickered. "Let me guess."

As sure as my table was reserved every morning, seven days a week, Christina, who I religiously called Granny, kidded me about my daily deep dish banana pancakes. "So, are we adding an order of scrambled eggs this morning, or how about a side of bacon, crisp?"

"Half a cantaloupe," I said, wanting to mix things up a little with her. What would a morning at Granny's be without some banter with Granny herself?

"Okay, I see we're being healthy eaters today," Christina teased.

She walked away, jotting something down on the order pad. Given that she often got the order wrong, it wasn't likely she was writing down my order at all. More likely, she was picking names for the racetrack later that day.

Long ago, I set aside a special place in my heart for Christina and her daughter, Alexandra, or Alex, as she was known. Twenty-five years ago, Christina had opened her diner on the busy corner of Diversey and Pine Grove. She'd rapidly turned it into a landmark where hard-working folks wolfed down her stacks of specialty pancakes and three-cheese omelets served with a big fat English muffin or scone. Granny often joked that ever since the neighborhood had gone upscale, her new patrons moaned over the carbs and fat, but went ahead and ordered them anyway. They "succumb to temptation," she liked to say.

I understood. I'd sampled my share of city diners. Nothing existed like Granny's filled deep-dish pancakes, doughy and rich, drenched with maple syrup and a heavy dusting of powdered sugar. I'm a creature of habit. So what? Years ago, I'd settled on the banana variety and a day without them wouldn't feel right.

I opened my newspaper, but laughed to myself, knowing I wouldn't get through scanning the first page before Granny ambled over to my table for her daily chat, a cigarette in one hand and a glass of scotch in the other.

"So, how's my Granny this morning?" I flashed my usual grin. Although everyone called her Granny, she liked the loving way I said it.

Long ago, I learned to count on her tolerating my quirky sense of humor. That made it easier for me to put up with that blue-gray smoke curling up from her freshly lit cigarette. I waited to hear her distinctive voice, made gravelly and tough through decades of chain-smoking.

"Not good, Professor, not good."

"No? What's up?" I asked the question with my typical studied smirk when she used that nickname. She usually called me Professor when something had rubbed her the wrong way.

"Too damn many murders," she said, pointing to the TV mounted in the corner.

I squinted to see the closed captioning on the bottom of the screen. The TV was small and far away, and I couldn't see details. I couldn't have read the words if I'd been up close, either. I'd left my distance glasses in the car and wasn't about to retrieve them. Whatever had happened, though, I spotted Cooper Julien's familiar face on the screen. His show aired in the evening, so the network had obviously called him in for special coverage.

"What happened?" I asked. "Was another kid shot down in the street?" Sadly, not an unusual tragedy in the Windy City. "Or, maybe another politician nabbed for bribery?" Also not an unusual happening. Seemed as if a day didn't go by without a state rep, an alderman, or an Illinois Congressman either reporting to prison or being released after serving a sentence for what all commentators lightly called a "white-collar crime."

Granny sighed. "I suppose you didn't have the radio on in the car."

"You know me too well. I can't stomach the news until I order my pancakes." I glanced down at the front page of the newspaper. "I don't see a headline about a murder."

"It's breaking news, Professor. They found her body this morning."

I squinted at the TV again. "Whose body?"

"Sandra Marchand. You know, the one married to that big shot developer, Marchand. I don't remember his first name."

"Charles," I said absently. No wonder they'd called Coop into the studio—and he'd be there all day and evening. But Charles Marchand was no Donald Trump. Where Trump had earned the label of a celebrity on the lightweight side, Charles was too serious, too good looking to ever earn that reputation. Marchand was a big name in keeping up the progress for West Loop development, despite recessions, near depressions, and all kinds of controversy. I'd chosen the area for the offices of Barlow & Associates in a building not far from one of Marchand's projects, a block-long complex that mixed old storefronts with new townhomes.

"How do you know she was murdered?" The lawyer in me kept a certain skeptical distance from the initial pronouncements, declarations, and judgments, even when reporters jumped ahead of themselves and threw around labels they later walked back—usually reluctantly.

Granny took a deep drag off her cigarette and exhaled smoke out of the side of her mouth in a futile attempt to keep it from drifting my way. "They found the body at the bottom of the stairs in their home—you know, one of those big townhouses."

Big jump to conclude murder. As always, I bristled over the vague language. Who was "they," anyway? And how quickly a prominent woman became "the body." I forgave Granny the things that would make me cringe if others said them.

Alex reached around and set the cantaloupe in front of me. "So, I guess you can tell Mom's all worked up over the murder."

"I'm not worked up," Granny said. "Sure, it could have been a robbery gone bad, but I'll bet you dollars to donuts that husband's gonna need a good lawyer."

I gritted my teeth against the knee-jerk mention of the need for a lawyer and wished the pancakes would arrive. Both women clammed up. Alex busied herself straightening up the basket of flavored syrups and Christina drained her glass of scotch before dropping her cigarette butt into it. Irrationally fond of these women, I knew that at one time, I might've been the lawyer they thought of first.

"Maybe so," I said to break the uncomfortable silence. "I don't know anything about what happened, so I'm not speculating about who's going to need what."

"Lack of facts never stopped anyone else," Alex shot back with a grin as she wandered off.

Granny pulled out the chair across from me and sat down. No invitation needed. "Don't you miss the courtroom, Matt? Not even a little? I mean, I know you're a big-time jury expert now, and you bury your nose in research, but don't you miss *being* the trial lawyer and arguing to the jury for freedom or justice, or—"

"Money?" I filled in the blank, deliberately cutting her off. "It's always about money now. I won't touch criminal cases. Not anymore, not after…" I didn't bother finishing the sentence. No need. She knew.

"I'm sorry. I didn't mean to pick at old scabs…" Granny's voice trailed off. She rose and put her hand on my shoulder.

I reached up and patted her hand. Christina knew the truth. I'd never gotten over watching my client die in a government-sanctioned execution. A legal but unjust lethal injection. Too many people, who otherwise didn't fully accept the death penalty, convinced themselves that somehow it was okay to put a fellow human being to death in a so-called humane way. Of course, this couldn't happen anymore in Illinois, not with the death penalty abolished, but it was hard to consider me a victim of the times. Christina and Alex had watched me go through that agonizing death penalty case. For years, they'd seen more of me than anyone else, even my closest friends, because no matter what, I started my day with a trip to Granny's. And since the mother-daughter duo opened around 5:00 AM, no matter what my schedule demanded, I never had to pass up pancakes.

My heart turned to mush whenever I thought about the way the pair stepped in and became my family through those tough months—years, really. Devoid of any meaningful family myself, they'd stepped into the breach. If I could've begged, borrowed, or stolen a few more years, my guy, my client, would have been one of the lucky ones, one of the prisoners who'd have benefited from a previous Governor's wake-up call, at least that moratorium on the death penalty that preceded its abolition. Such was not to be my luck—or my client's.

"Sorry," Granny murmured. "I feel like I kicked you in the nuts."

"Nah, you aren't the one who kicked me," I said softly. "Hell, everyone used to ask how I could represent a guilty person. Why doesn't anyone ask what it feels like to represent an innocent one—and then be forced to watch him die? That's the tough one…that's the…" Once again, I didn't bother finishing my sentence.

"No more of this talk, Mom," Alex said as she approached the table with my pancakes. "We think you're the best, Matt. You make sure the *real* lawyers don't make mistakes. *You* make *them*

23

all winners. And that's all I want to hear about it. Now eat or *I will* kick you in the nuts." It was strange to hear Alex use the label "real lawyers," but as a jury consultant, I was no longer seen as one of *them* anymore. I didn't much mind it.

Christina snorted, and I laughed in spite of myself. I liked Alex's version of tough love with her mother, and with me, too. Not that she'd ever watched an innocent man die, but she had witnessed part of me die during that case. She's watched me transition from a high-profile criminal defense attorney to a quieter life as the owner of Barlow & Associates, Trial Consultants. Civil cases only.

I pushed the bowl with the melon away and pulled the plate forward. Dipping my fork in the warm gooey pancake filling, I counted on finding comfort there. Even Alex and Christina had no way to know how deep my despair went. It lived inside me like something material, tangible. And I'd found no escape hatch.

I swallowed a few bites of the pancake before touching my upper chest. The burning would start soon, but it was worth it. That's what antacids were for. I liked to think of myself as a man who cared about three things: peace of mind, justice, and pancakes. Oh, the sweet smell and taste of that deep dish banana pancake. I couldn't get enough of them. Peace of mind and justice were hard to come by. But pancakes I could have. No one had to die for a pancake.

Chapter Two

I heard the voices and groaned before I opened the office door. Damn it, how could I have forgotten? Wendy, my administrator, someone whose know-how made my firm possible, had a connection—a strong one—with Sandra Marchand. Of course, she'd be glued to the TV. I stood in the doorway of the conference room for a minute before approaching Wendy, who, along with Janet, my office manager, sat facing the wall-mounted television.

Wendy swiveled the chair to glance at me, her face etched with grief, her blue eyes puffy from crying.

"What's the latest?" I asked, walking up behind them. I put my hand on Wendy's shoulder. Maude, my white Sealyham terrier, followed close behind. As I do most days, I'd made a quick swing back to my apartment to pick up Maude and bring her into the office. Why should she hang alone at home all day when she could provide a welcome distraction in the three-person office?

I'd just flipped off the car radio, so I knew there was no late-breaking news. I often learned a lot by listening to the two women's latest interpretation of unfolding events—regardless of the case or the issue.

Judging from the screen, I saw my pair of employees had chosen to stick with CNN, whose morning news team was questioning their Chicago correspondent. She wouldn't be on the story long. CNN had likely sent their crime reporter, Don Menotti, who would show up on location by noon. That famous Picasso sitting on the Daley Plaza was going to get exposure. So would the old Water Tower, even though it had nothing to do with the case. It wouldn't be long before several iconic Chicago images were imbedded in the minds around the country as the trial progressed. Don rarely reported from Atlanta or the Washington bureau, but was often out in the field. Crime and local politics, plus the occasional super-storm or earthquake, were Menotti's TV beat.

The police denied that they had a suspect—or suspects. The investigation was ongoing…blah, blah, blah. Those statements usually fell on deaf ears. Presumption of innocence was a legal concept. Out in the real world, no one swallowed it, especially on the cable stations.

I predicted the rhythm of the day's news. One repeated clip after another showed Sandra breaking ground for a new no-kill shelter, a bejeweled Sandra on her husband's arm at last year's gala for the Lyric Opera, and an old clip of an interview about her advocacy of education for young women. There she was, testifying before a congressional committee on expanding Pell grants, a pet issue for Sandra. It was for Wendy, too, I recalled, and a personal one. The file film would go on and on, running as B-roll or backdrop behind the numerous personal reminiscences from her legion of friends. These men and women would fight to hold back tears over her death while the legal talking heads already theorized about who the killer might be.

Wendy wiped her eyes and pushed her shoulder-length blonde hair off her face. "He did it. I know he did it."

I swallowed the first thought that came to mind. *I know nothing.* My silence sent a signal that wasn't lost on Wendy.

Wendy twisted her shoulders so she could look up at me. "You think I'm jumping to conclusions," she said defensively. "Go ahead and say it, Matt."

"He thinks you're jumping to conclusions, honey," Janet said. She reached into the pocket of her gray blazer and pulled out a dog treat. True to the weekday morning ritual, the dog positioned herself next to Janet's chair. Then Maude lifted her adorable box-like face, with its long white beard, and stared at her benefactor before wagging her short, stubby tail wildly in the air.

"That's a good Maudey," Janet said, holding out her palm. "There's your cookie."

I reached in front of Janet, grabbed the remote and muted the sound on the TV. "Uh, what have I said about calling her *Maudey*," I said with mock disgust. Why was I wasting my time complaining? When it came to Maude, Janet did as she pleased.

I squeezed Wendy's shoulder. "I'm sorry about this. I know how you felt about Sandra. You and Sandra had a real history, more than most people in the city."

She nodded as she dabbed her eyes again. "I knew Sandra was having a fundraiser last night, but we had the focus group for the Thompson case. Marla decided to go anyway. It was at Café Brauer." Wendy twisted in her chair to cast an accusing look my way. "I *told* you I was sorry to miss it. I like her events."

It wasn't the first time Wendy showed her resentiment about needing to repeat something she'd told me at least once. Most of those tidbits went in one ear and out the other, and so did details about Marla, or any of her friends she hung out with. As my administrator, Wendy did fine work for the firm. She kept me—and Janet, too—on schedule and organized. Nothing much got past her. Her outgoing personality made her great at using the tools of the trial consultant trade. She managed the community attitude surveys and skillfully interviewed random people for mirror juries and mock trials. Not to mention that she willingly worked overtime when necessary and always showed up on time.

But, she had a few quirks. Well, one big one. Wendy's fascination with celebrities in general grated on me. Arguably, Sandra Marchand had been one of Chicago's top ten—maybe even among the top three—most-watched women. Wendy had plenty of company as a Sandra-watcher, faithfully following the charities and listening for any news about her. Today, though, I had to squelch my impatience with Wendy and the celebrity sideshow.

Still, during my initial interview with Wendy some years back, I'd been impressed that she'd worked as Sandra Marchand's personal assistant for a few years, hired at age eighteen. That single lucky break had provided a huge leap up for Wendy and changed the course of her life for the better. I reaped some of the benefits of what Wendy had learned working so closely with someone like Sandra, who had encouraged Wendy to start college part-time. Wendy had taken Sandra's suggestion, and as the first person in her family to go to college, she'd been able to forge a career, and just as important, an independent life.

Wendy had a knack for paying attention to details, exactly what I needed in an administrator. In her interview with me, Wendy had said she'd honed that skill working for Sandra, who ran her philanthropic efforts like a business and was far more than just another celebrity to Wendy. A dozen years ago, Sandra had stepped in as a mentor at a time when Wendy needed direction to break away from a family stuck in patterns that kept them in dead-end jobs and near poverty. I understood Wendy all too well. Maybe that's one reason I hired her.

As I witnessed Wendy's shock and sadness at Sandra's death, I became conscious of the stifling air in the windowless conference room. I shrugged out of my coat and threw it over an empty chair. I fought against the urge to go hide out in my office. I owed Wendy a few more minutes of concern.

"Wendy was just saying that Marla called her late last night. Said Sandra and her husband acted kinda weird at the big gala," Janet said, still preoccupied with rubbing Maude's jowls. "And she checked that Twitter gal you both follow, and she said as much."

So, this was all about gossip. Wendy and I both followed Lourdes Ponce on Twitter. Wendy liked all the insider gossip, but I preferred the political tidbits; they were my way of keeping up with the news. I hadn't checked for tweets from Lourdes yet, though.

"For one thing, Sandra gulped down an awful lot of champagne," Wendy said.

"According to Marla?" I inserted.

"I know," Wendy said, smoothing her hair back again, "but Marla is reliable, and Lourdes' tweets said more or less the same thing. It's unbelievable that Sandra would drink too much. I've never known her to have more than one drink, two at the most, and not that often." Wendy got to her feet and turned to face me, perching her hip on the table. "Always has been a light drinker." She jabbed her index finger in the air for emphasis.

I glanced at Janet. Her face wore a studied frown as she watched Wendy, but she continued to give Maude the attention she craved.

"Marla said you could feel the tension in the room. Everyone noticed it, and they'll be talking about it. You wait. And then, Toland arrived and he saw it all, too."

"Toland?" I asked. "Joanie Toland was there?"

"No, not Joanie. *Leo.* The governor himself showed up." Wendy flashed a reproachful side-long glance. "You haven't checked Lourdes' tweets, have you?"

"Nope. I'd rather hear this from you, though."

"Leo Toland flew up from Springfield for Sandra's event."

I hadn't caught that tidbit on the radio.

"Not just for the fundraiser," Janet interjected. "He had meetings with religious leaders over on the West side. But since he spends as little time in Springfield as he can get away with, why shouldn't he show up at Sandra's big bash? Gave him a chance to press the flesh."

I repressed a snicker at Janet's cliché—she'd never met one she didn't like. But then, the woman always got her point across.

Wendy nodded. "I know. Who would have imagined him showing up, especially because of the non-stop buzz about Charles Marchand throwing his hat in the ring next year?"

It had started. That curiosity about everything I was famous for among friend and foe alike. It was like a buzz that grew louder, urging me to find out more. The more gaps in the information, the more of a puzzle it became, and the more driven I was to fit in all the pieces. I didn't know any of the players personally, and I sure hadn't cast my vote for Toland. Scandal just found its way to that guy. Some people attract bad folks to them for some reason. I saw Toland as one shifty bastard who would never get my vote. If I had to put the two men, Marchand and Toland, up against each other, I'd put my money on Marchand. With Toland in the Governor's mansion, it was only a matter of time before someone blew the lid off of the often-squeaky political machine Toland ran. It screamed sleaze and corruption, but so far, Toland had managed to add some oil just in time to keep the investigations at bay. Wendy and Janet didn't know it, but I had a far more personal reason to send my contempt Toland's way.

Wendy looked down and nervously rubbed the thumb of one hand across the palm of the other. "Someone on TV already dropped a story about Sandra and Charles fighting last night." She groaned. "I hate that kind of gossip."

Since when? I thought, cynically. "If anything was different about last night, you can bet the reporters will snoop around looking for it."

"Snooping not required," Wendy said sadly. "Marla said more than 100 people were in the room and saw everything. A small crowd, granted, but Marla said no one could miss how odd Sandra seemed. Apparently, she was agitated and kind of frantic all night. She's *always* at her best at these events. And the Sandra I knew would *never* argue in public. And now she's dead!"

I listened as Wendy provided more details—hearsay details—about Sandra Marchand's strange behavior. Supposedly strange.

My knowledge of Sandra and Charles was limited to superficial impressions based on the same public faces everyone else saw. As fond as I was of Wendy, I didn't necessarily take as gospel her word about what Sandra *always* or *never* did. I might be a jury consultant, but as a former trial attorney, I knew my way around human nature. I was—then and now—paid good money to understand the foibles and inconsistencies that even the most uncomplicated people possess. Delving into what made people tick had motivated me to pursue degrees in law, psychology, and communication.

More tears spilled down Wendy's cheeks. "I'm sorry. I need a minute and then I'll get to work."

"Don't worry about it. Take your time. Go home if you need to." I picked up my coat. "I really am sorry about this. I know you had special feelings for Sandra. A unique history with her. You knew her in a way only a few people did."

Wendy nodded. Then she opened her mouth as if to speak, but apparently changed her mind. Instead, she bit her lower lip and stared into her lap.

Just as well. She was probably going to again declare Charles Marchand the killer.

Once across the reception area and into my office, I closed the door, but not before Maude squeezed in behind and took her place at my feet under the desk. I was relieved to be away from the flashing TV images. Besides, I needed to work on the community attitude survey scheduled for the pharmaceutical safety case that had been eating up all my attention. Wendy ran the survey and trained the staff of callers, and now it was my job to analyze the design and come up with a jury selection strategy for this particular trial. Safety, security, secrecy—this drug company case had it all.

I flipped on my computer and lost myself in tables and charts and comments on demographics from the last drug company case I'd worked on. We'd won that case for the defense by convincing the jury that the drug worked fine for its intended purpose. This time, I was on the other side of the table working with the plaintiff. I enjoyed this part of preparing for trial, especially now that the kind of cases I took on provided a built-in safety net. Wins and losses would be counted in dollars, not lives.

* * *

Except for a few diehard runners, Maude and I had Lincoln Park to ourselves with another hour or so of daylight left. I pulled my truck into the empty lot off Wellington at the edge of the park. I let Maude out of the passenger side and leaned down to snap on the leash.

"Weather not fit for man nor beast...except this man and this beast." I patted Maude's back, and her tail told me she was happy to be in the park again, even if she didn't understand a word I'd said. Then again, maybe she knew exactly what I was talking about—maybe she'd read my mind.

I tossed my cell onto the seat. Unless I was waiting for a call telling me a jury was back with a verdict, I refused to let anything interrupt these walks with Maude. Didn't a person need a few minutes in a day without intrusion? I grabbed my earmuffs and put them on to cover my ears. I had a thing about hats. They made me look like an idiot. I just was not a hat guy. Earmuffs in place, I was braced against the blasts of wind coming from the northwest.

Over the last few days, the city had wrapped itself in a gray cloak of low-hanging clouds, with the ground covered in ice-encrusted dirty patches that refused to melt under the sunless sky or hide under fresh snow.

"You'd like some new snow, wouldn't you, Maude?" I laughed to myself as Maude propelled me down the path.

I'd moved out of the New Town neighborhood a couple of years before, but when I needed to clear my head, I brought Maude back for a jaunt down the winding paths of Lincoln Park, large areas of grass bordered to the east by Lake Michigan and on the west by hi-rise buildings, vintage co-ops, and from time to time, I'd pass the nature museum and the Lincoln Park Zoo. Nice place to live.

I'd been jumpy and unsettled for the last week, and not because of Wendy's reaction to the death of Sandra Marchand—I stubbornly refused to consider it a murder. Not yet. A woman found dead at the bottom of a staircase doesn't add up to a murder. Suspicion, yes, but no conclusions happened without an investigation. It could just as logically be ruled an accident. The media's desire to create presumptions of guilt made for good TV, though, and Wendy had kept her opinions about Charles to herself—or at least out of my earshot. Of course, that meant she'd abruptly stopped talking when I came into the room.

Wendy wasn't alone.

I'd seen it before, especially in these big, high-profile cases that had certain key elements. With Sandra being such a prominent person of society, I could feel belief building, and not only in Wendy, that the handsome, wealthy Charles Marchand had killed his wife. It was palpable, like a train gathering steam and with the ferocity of talking heads on the legal shows and callers on shock-jock radio. Only Cooper Julien refrained from making quick judgments, calling out some of the other analysts for aiming suspicious words at Marchand. Some of those people were too irresponsible to be called analysts.

I'd given Wendy an afternoon off so she could join a few hundred of Sandra's admirers—mostly women—at a public memorial at the Cultural Center, with its intricate tile and mosaics that was once the central library on Randolph Street. According to Wendy, the staff at Sandra's foundation had arranged it quickly. It was a convenient location, secular, and large enough for a public farewell to one of the city's most generous benefactors. Charles hadn't attended, but his spokesperson announced a private funeral and burial for only a couple dozen or so close friends and relatives.

I had to hand it to Wendy—or more to the point, her best pal, Marla, when it came to the details about the Café Brauer benefit on the last night of Sandra's life. Just that morning, Janet had come into my office and said reporters' interviews with others at Sandra's event all sounded much the same, give or take the inherent inconsistencies of eye-witness testimony. Sandra had been loud and agitated, Charles looked angry, Governor Toland spoke with Sandra, she walked away mad, she argued with her husband, and then, looking disgusted, Marchand led her away. Quite a night.

Ironically, other than the tension in the air and the weak number of attendees, the benefit at Café Brauer had been a financial success. Like Wendy, Chicago's most well-known pet expert and blogger, Steve Dale, had trouble containing his emotions when reporters asked about the nearly quarter of a million dollars raised for the shelters—about the same amount raised the year before. That meant hundreds of dogs and cats had been spared. Plus, an army of volunteers worked hard to find the rescued animals new homes.

The insistent tug on the other end of Maude's leash reminded me of the value of at least one of Sandra's causes. Granny was the one who'd steered me to PAWS Chicago to pick out Maude, an older puppy already trained in the important ways. Maude's first owner had died suddenly, and no one stepped forward to take on the abandoned dog. Granny had a hunch about me. She sensed that even though I was still clawing my way up after the case that led to my major fall, I needed a dog as much as a dog needed me.

Before Maude, pets hadn't been a part of my life. I'd never owned so much as a fish. Now I wondered how I'd ever gotten along without her. Once I'd seen PAWS, I couldn't walk away. PAWS had *rooms* for dogs instead of cages, and that step up in care grabbed my heart; I backed that feeling up with regular cash infusions to support their work. In fairness, I also supported the Anti-Cruelty Society located downtown for their great work and for the front of that building designed to look like a puppy's face. I couldn't resist it. Actually, I can't resist helping any charity whose goal was to protect our beloved family pets.

Maude led the way past the deserted playground, where lonely blue and red plastic slides and tunnels sat behind a chain-link fence. In a few months, watchful stay-at-home moms and nannies would line the benches and keep up their small talk in this upscale area, all the while keeping a sharp eye out for any homeless park dwellers who wandered too close to the playground. Without kids to catch her attention—and the other way around—Maude took me down the fork that snaked around the small lagoon, frozen over now. The bare trees and gray-brown landscape should have looked bleak, but I found the familiarity comforting.

For the first time in a couple of days, my gut felt as close to normal as it ever got. That once-a-day pill I popped, along with the antacids, were miracle workers. Maybe the only kind I believed in. I could spread around blame for the burn and the churning. Give the banana pancakes their due. Maybe I'd heap the rest of the blame on Wendy and her empty talk of theories about why Charles Marchand would kill his wife. But that wasn't the whole story. Whenever Governor Toland was part of the conversation, no matter how tangentially, I couldn't avoid thinking about Zach.

Zach, the secret that wasn't really a secret. Mostly, I failed to mention that I had a brother, or rather, a half-brother. We shared a mother, dead for a decade now, along with our respective fathers, neither of whom had hung around for long. Both of our deadbeat dads died before they could grow old and be filled with regrets or anything that would fit a movie ending. When it came down to it, Zach and I hadn't done all that well in the longevity gene lottery.

Wendy and Janet didn't know Zach existed, let alone that he headed private security for Governor Toland. I hated being grateful to an SOB like Toland, but thanks to him, Zach was gainfully employed. Toland had contributed his fair share to the corruption that continued to give outsiders a reason to refer to Illinois politics as a sewer. Many years ago, when Toland was an assistant to a previous governor, he'd helped Zach cut a deal on a fraud charge that kept him out of jail. The details were fuzzy, but Toland's help came with strings I knew nothing about. I assumed a pledge of loyalty was part of it, though. Zach followed Toland into his subsequent offices and finally into the governor's mansion. I never figured out exactly what Zach did for Toland, but I had a feeling security was the least of it.

At one time I wondered why Zach had never come to me for help, but I suppose family pride, and perhaps a bit of embarrassment, may have driven him to someone else for help. We'd never talked about it. Or more accurately, we'd avoided talking about whether Zach's using another lawyer was a matter of pride, or lack of faith in his much younger brother.

I shook my head to clear thoughts of Governor Leo Toland and Zach. When had I last talked to Zach? I couldn't remember, except that I could measure the time in years, not months.

Maude stopped and raised one front paw, as if on high alert, but I knew the signal. She'd stepped on some ice melt and it hurt her paws. She knew Dad would tend to her, though. I dutifully—and gently—rubbed the underside of her paw with my bare hand, knocking any ice and salt from it. Instinctively, Maude knew the stinging pain would be gone, so she picked up her pace again along the edge of the path, urging—or forcing—me to speed up again, triggering a new surge of energy.

My recent malaise wasn't about Toland or Zach, or Sandra Marchand. It was about Haskell, Joey Haskell. In the privacy of my own thoughts, I often referred to the man-I-couldn't't-save by his last name only. If I thought about Joey, that gave my dead client a childhood—buddies, parents, and pickup basketball games at Wells Park.

I pulled Maude to the terraced rocks by the inlet to the lagoon and stopped to stare at the water moving under sheets of ice scraping against the rocks. Maude's ears pricked up at the sound. Sandra's murder aside, what had really bothered me for the last week was Christina's question: *Don't you miss the courtroom?* Her words had sounded more like a challenge than a question.

Granny—and most people I counted in my circle of friends and acquaintances—didn't buy for a second that I, once a sought-after trial lawyer, was through—finished—with being the public face in the courtroom. They were convinced I harbored a secret desire to return to the days that had given me a recognizable name, rather than operating behind the scenes as a jury consultant. Maybe that was fair speculation. But they couldn't see inside my head—or more to the point, my heart. If they could, they'd understand why I'd walked, no, *stalked* away after failing to save an innocent man and then watching him die. *Legally.*

I turned away, coaxing Maude to come along. I assured her that the sound was nothing more than ice crashing up against the rocks that rested so close to the shoreline. Maude seemed to understand the explanation. My voice had a familiar tone that made her willing to refocus her attention back on me. The light was fading fast, and soon the park would be shrouded in winter darkness.

In the end, the failures that continued to haunt me were just as vivid as Joey Haskell's face. Years of appeals had come to nothing, not even my last-ditch effort to get the then-Governor Ehrhart to issue a stay. I smacked my lips, disgusted by the memory even after all these years. I felt no satisfaction in knowing that the same Ehrhart, who'd refused my request, now sat in a cell. One more Illinois governor serving time. If only… if only…I'd spent years finishing that sentence. If only I could have bought Joey Haskell a little more time, I'd not only have saved a life, but I'd have escorted Joey out of the prison as an innocent man.

I tasted the bile rising in my throat. That happened every time thoughts of Joey entered my mind and I couldn't make him head for the exits. The worst of it involved knowing I'd harbored that hair's breadth of doubt about Joey as a truly innocent man, only to see him posthumously exonerated. As if that set things right.

Cold air penetrated the layers of my jacket and sweater. Anyone with any sense had already left the park to the wind and ice. "Come on, Maude, let's head home."

Maude resisted my gentle tug, so I put a little strength behind the next pull. She picked up the signal and broke into a dog trot down the tree- and bench-lined path leading to my truck.

I settled Maude inside and started the engine, then scrolled my cell for messages. One was from a Lutheran Minister-turned-lawyer friend of mine Arnie Pierson, wanting to meet for a drink, the other a dinner invitation from Mike and Jan Wilder, a couple who lived down the block. I swear I could smell the aroma of banana bread that Jan was known for baking regularly. I loved it when she sent over a loaf or two for me. I'd accept both invitations. And then there was one text from Kenneth Baden, an old friend I hadn't heard from in a while. Well, we hadn't spoken in over a year. Kenny handled criminal cases, not civil, so our paths didn't cross anymore inside or outside the courtroom. Eh, whatever Kenny wanted could wait until I got home.

"Okay, what it'll be," I said, backing out of the space and heading west on Wellington. "Thai or Italian?"

Maude answered with a bark.

"Big help you are, you mangy mutt." I laughed out loud and headed for my favorite neighborhood Thai place.

Thirty minutes, one stop, and a couple of slow rush-hour miles later, I turned off Wellington, headed toward Belmont Avenue, and drove down to my new street. At least it would become my new street once the major eyesore of the neighborhood, a boarded-up supermarket, was finally torn down. I'd moved into my loft aware that newly renovated buildings would share space with this yet-to-be either salvaged or demolished structure. The supermarket had turned into one graffiti-laden dump too many, maybe because all twenty feet of my wall-to-wall, floor to ceiling windows gave me a view of the whole monstrosity.

I pulled off my jacket and hung it on the coat tree in the entryway. "First things first," I muttered as I filled Maude's dish.

With the dog occupied, I moved the egg rolls and Thai-style chicken fried rice covered in peanut sauce from their cardboard containers to a plate. A few bites into my dinner, my cell trilled with the theme song from *I Love Lucy*, my favorite TV show growing up. My phone never failed to grab my attention. Kenny again. I'd forgotten all about his call.

"Hey, I was just about to call you." Ok, so it was a lie, but just a little white one.

At first, Kenny seemed a little too interested in how I was doing and what I was up to. My old friend was talking with an awful lot of uhs and ahs. Unlike the articulate guy I knew. But then, he got to the real reason for the call.

Kenny had lost his mind.

Chapter Three

The next morning, I muttered my frustration as I walked up the stairs to my second-floor office. Not that anyone except Maude was listening. "You know, besides you, I've got four important women in my life, and every one of them is going to be glued to the TV all morning." All of them did exactly what they pleased most of the time, too, but that was a different issue.

I had just left Granny's, where I had polished off my pancakes, and noted Christina and Alex staring intently at the TV, which is how I expected to find Janet and Wendy at the office. "Hell, who's the boss around here, anyway?"

No response. Even the dog paid me no mind.

WGN-TV flickered on the conference room TV screen, but Janet sat at her computer at the reception desk. Through the open door of her office, I spotted Wendy talking on the phone. So, the show hadn't started yet. I waved and went straight to my office, while Maude wandered off and plunked herself at Janet's side to get her treat.

Over the last few days, Wendy hadn't wavered from her belief that Charles killed Sandra. The fast pace of the investigation and impending arrest reinforced that belief. She'd flashed her "I told you so" look my way more than once.

For my part, I remained agnostic on the subject of Marchand's guilt. Did I believe it possible
that the King-of-Development pushed his beau-
tiful Queen-of-Worthy-Causes down the stairs?
Sure. I couldn't rule it out. Not even when Kenny Baden had tried to convince me that the state
could never prove Marchand killed his wife. The
evidence wasn't there, he'd said. I'd suppressed
a loud guffaw. It was way too early to make that
kind of claim. Kenny knew as well as anyone that
evidence had a way of turning up along the way.

Did Kenny tell me how much Charles loved
his wife, how devoted he was to her? Not a word
about that. He hadn't discussed guilt or innocence
one way or another when he'd asked me to join
the defense team as jury consultant, *if* the case
went to trial. Kenny claimed to doubt it would.
The arrest was just that, an arrest. Regardless,
Kenny, a respected attorney in this town, was the
guy that someone with money would call. And he
was a friend of a friend of Marchand's; this wasn't
the time to take chances.

It was no mystery why Charles hired Kenny
straight away. Kenny's last high-profile client was
a politician accused of beating up a woman. Kenny knew how to handle an unrelenting press, and
reporters who couldn't stop talking about the politician's penchant for prostitutes and expensive
divorces. An all-around sleazy life. The not-guilty
verdict meant that Kenny's reputation soared or
sank, depending on the observer's point of view.
The woman herself filed a civil suit that would
drag on for years. Still, if I ever found myself the
object of ugly accusations, heck, I'd want Kenny
to defend me, too.

For reciprocal reasons, I was aware of the reasons Kenny called on Barlow & Associates to join the team he was putting together. My firm had an enviable reputation. No point in hiding behind false modesty. I could be humble about my wins without downplaying my skill—and luck. Kenny already had a commitment from his hand-picked DNA expert, Dr. Melanie Grabavoy, a gem of an expert because she was good at explaining the science to juries without making them feel like fourth-graders. No one nodded off in the middle of her testimony, either. Kenny also had his army of investigators waiting for their marching orders.

He should've known better than to call me, though. My old friend knew very well I hadn't taken a criminal case in years. And he knew why. He had never asked me to break my rule before. If I hadn't liked Kenny, I would have resented it even more that my friend tried to call in a couple of small favors in exchange for a big fat one. No, I said, *absolutely not*. End of story.

Still, refusing to be involved hadn't quashed my interest. I picked up the remote and punched the power button. Sure enough, WGN was standing by. Even the national cable stations were waiting to cover the arrest through local affiliates and bureaus. Outside of Chicago, and thanks to a national media hunger for a new trial to latch on to, Marchand was fast becoming a household name. If he'd had political aspirations, being accused of murdering his wife was not the way to endear himself to potential voters.

According to Kenny, Charles had fallen deep into grief over Sandra.

"He's shell-shocked," Kenny claimed. "He can't believe he'd be a suspect, but logically, he knows the police look at the husband or the boyfriend first."

In some murder cases, Kenny and I knew the police looked at both. Boyfriends and girlfriends had a way of turning up in murder investigations, no matter how devoted the spouses appeared.

Charles declared his innocence, as most criminal defendants would, through a statement Kenny delivered to the press. But for all of the carefully crafted words, Marchand couldn't explain what happened to Sandra. He'd found her at the bottom of the stairs just before dawn. The response was "no comment" to the reports of a very public argument and rumors about Sandra's drinking.

I flipped to WGN and watched the split screen bearing the words "Breaking News," scrawled along the lower third of the screen, with one-half showing the door to the townhouse and the other half showing two commentators' faces framed in TV boxes, one on top of the other. I snorted at the phony image. I knew perfectly well the two talking heads were sitting side-by-side in the same studio. Did everything have to be theater? It was bad enough that trials themselves were packed with performance art.

The somber anchor interrupted the talking heads when the townhouse door opened. Kenny emerged first and started down the gray stone stairs with Charles following behind. Two men flanked him as he made his way to the street. Dressed in a dark blue suit, light blue shirt, and solid dark red tie, Charles looked like he was headed for a day at the office. He grimaced, but kept his gaze aimed straight ahead, avoiding the line of reporters shouting questions at him.

It was only a few steps to the car. One of the men at Charles' side slipped on the ice near the curb and struggled not to hit the pavement on one knee. I winced watching it. I'd taken a spill or two myself on Chicago icy sidewalks and they hurt. Sure enough, even that brief slip turned into fodder for comments to fill the silence. Once Charles disappeared inside the gray sedan, the reporters rushed away.

I almost laughed out loud. I could predict the exact movements of the press corps. Taking their own shortcuts, they'd rush to the police station to join a gaggle of photographers and cameramen to catch a live shot of Charles making the short walk into the police station. Those inherently boring shots passed for news. Then, behind closed doors, Charles Marchand would be fingerprinted and booked, no different from some kid getting nabbed for selling a few dollars' worth of crack in an alley.

Ah, but credit where credit is due, and I threw some credit Marchand's way. He managed to look exactly like who he was—or at least who he had been. Tall and broad-shouldered, with wavy dark hair touched with enough gray to give him a distinguished air. He had that Tom Cruise way of aging in years, but not showing it. Seemingly, always ready to do an action movie regardless of the decades creeping up on him. I was a little that way myself, although a version with lighter brown hair and no gray, along with a slighter, more fit frame. But that was to be expected since Charles had a good ten years on me.

Along with most women, Wendy admired Marchand's taller version of Tom Cruise. Anyone could see Marchand was beyond wealthy. He wielded power and knew how to show it in every situation that came his way, even an arrest for murder. I knew this guy's mug shot would be smart—a smile, but not too broad, proud, or ostentatious.

"So what are your secrets," I asked the TV image. "Everybody is hiding something. What tidbit do you fear hearing on the evening news?"

Once Kenny disappeared behind the double glass doors of the police station on screen, I turned off the TV and left my office. My two employees had moved to the conference room. Janet picked up the remote and muted the TV. "I guess things are moving pretty fast, huh?"

"Kenny will work out a deal for bail," I said.

"I...don't...think...so," Janet said, enunciating each word and giving Wendy a sidelong glance, as if asking for backup.

Why had I offered an opinion at all? Janet wasn't above displaying a flash or two of resentment over money and power—or good looks— that too often allowed sidestepping consequences. According to Janet, people like Marchand weren't treated like everyone else. And she could rattle off a dozen examples without missing a beat. I knew that just because Charles *could* pay any amount of bail money didn't mean that a judge would release him. Still, although I didn't say so aloud, chances were good that Charles would spend the next months as a semi-free man.

"Whether Marchand sits in jail or in his living room, Kenny Baden is going to try to force a quick trial," I offered.

Janet frowned. "Really? He won't play for time?"

"Nah, not in this case. He thinks the evidence is flimsy. Demanding a quick trial is the best way to tilt public opinion toward Charles' innocence."

"*Some* of the public," Wendy corrected, folding her arms across her chest. "And the DA didn't waste time bringing an indictment, did he? He must think he's got a good case."

"Hey, Matt, how do you know what Kenny's strategy is?" Janet asked, narrowing her eyes in suspicion.

Damn it, why had I said a word about this?

"He called me." And in the spirit of in for a penny and all that, I added, "He asked me to join his team if they can't clear Charles before trial."

That brought Wendy to her feet. "I assume you said *no way.*"

"Of course, I did," I snapped. "This firm doesn't handle criminal cases, period."

Something about Wendy's attitude irked me. Like I'd asked Maude earlier: Who's the boss around here, anyway? Of course, my bravado didn't necessarily reflect the desired answer to that question.

I rolled my eyes and sighed as I shifted my weight from one foot to the other. "That's the reason I said no." I looked squarely at Wendy. "I recommended Richard Gabriel's Decision Analysis group. He'll do a good job."

Wendy sighed and stepped around me, but stopped at the door of the conference room. "I still can't believe Sandra's gone. I'm thinking there are lessons to be learned from what's happened."

I waited for the rest of her thought.

"Don't keep us in suspense, honey," Janet said, examining her bright red nails. "What do you want us to learn?"

"What's that Latin phrase?" Wendy tapped her temple with her index finger as if activating a memory chip. "You know, the one about seizing the day."

"*Carpe diem*," I said wryly, "as in there's work to do around here, unless of course you don't feel like gettin' paid…" I stood in the doorway and scanned the room. "Or maybe we don't have any business?"

Janet snickered. "Oh, we've got business, all right. But a case about a drug company fudging their research results is kinda dull next to another episode of the Dead Wives Club."

I groaned. "Hey, that boring drug company is *our* client! So watch it! Their money pays your salaries." I tried to hide how much I enjoyed Janet's wisecracking way of sizing up a situation.

Ignoring Janet, Wendy lifted her chin a notch. "You can make fun of me all you want, but when something like this happens, it makes you think. You know, we can be here one day and gone the next. It's making *me* think about what I really want in my life."

We fell into a self-conscious silence. For a brief moment, I couldn't stomach prolonged conversations about the meaning of life—they made me drift into daydreams about pancakes or deep-dish pizza, sure enough getting hungry again. The Marchand story was getting on my nerves. Worse, it invaded my life—completely uninvited. Asking Wendy to drop her interest—or more accurately, obsession—would be like asking Granny to quit smoking. It would never happen. Kenny's call made it worse.

Dull or not, the drug case demanded attention. I was about to order my battalion of two back to work when the office door flung opened and a young guy with long light brown hair tucked into his shirt collar walked in.

"Hi," he said, "I'm here about a job."

"Looks like someone's seizing the day," Janet quipped.

Maybe so, but we didn't have a job to offer. I opened my mouth to say as much, but Wendy stepped forward and held out her hand. "Come into my office," she said, "and we can talk."

What was that I said about who's the boss?

Chapter Four

I frowned at Wendy's closed office door. "What's the deal?" She'd been quick to usher him into her office. To ensure big words were heard on the other side of the door, I yelled, "We don't have any job openings."

Janet, done examining her nails for the moment, gestured toward Wendy's office. "Didn't you see it? She thinks Mr. Shaggy Mane is cute. Looks like he dragged that suit off a hanger at the Salvation Army, maybe yesterday. Whoever wore it last was probably going to his prom—back in 1980."

"You noticed all that in ten seconds?" I asked. Long ago, I'd thought Janet had likely missed her calling. She would've been one helluva detective.

"I didn't need the full ten seconds, boss. Besides, Wendy did that blushing thing that she does. Dead giveaway. No guy with options wears a worn-out puffy nylon jacket, especially one that's putrid olive green, with a navy blue suit."

I shook my head and laughed as I headed to my office. I had said we didn't have job openings, but in fact, we often needed temps to help with our community attitude surveys and mock and mirror juries. The drug case on our calendar was an example. Maybe with a decent haircut, that guy, whoever he was, could fill in somewhere.

Wendy was a great assistant. The best. She kept me organized and on time, but that was the least of it. She was good at analyzing data and coming up with the kind of juror profiles that told us who to look for in a jury pool. She had a knack for reading beyond the data, almost through the numbers, to grasp human nature. Statistics only tell us so much. We needed to factor in human emotion and perspective. Always fascinated by politics and how politicians sell their stories to the public, I knew their ways weren't a far cry from lawyers working and selling their cases to a jury. The worlds of law and politics cross paths in more ways than meets the eye. Both involve artists of the spoken word trying to convince others to behave in a certain way. "Vote for me!" "Vote for her!" "Find the defendant not guilty!" "Ladies and gentlemen, the defendant is guilty as shit!" Ha! Watch the profanity, but the point is obvious. Lawyers and politicians, often one and the same, and often finding themselves defending or being the criminal.

On the other hand, Wendy's taste in men often made her look like she didn't have an ounce of judgment in her brain. Okay, honesty time. She drew losers to her like vultures to road kill. Only later, when they'd stood her up one too many times or ordered one—or three—too many beers and maybe insulted her looks, did she throw in the towel. Oh, and there was the guy who asked her for a loan to start his business. Twenty grand he wanted, and he asked for it on their second date. I was grateful she wasn't gullible enough to fall for that old trick.

Pushing Wendy's bad dating luck out of my

thoughts, I turned my attention to the drug case, going over the notes from the last strategy session, looking at discovery data, and noting the questions that lingered. The case made me nervous, though. It looked too easy.

Maybe that's why my mind wandered to my old pal Kenny Baden. Unlike Wendy's guys, Kenny was no loser. I had to give Marchand credit for not wasting a second bringing him in. Now and then, but not often, I got an old feeling. It was like a signal priming an old pump. Like bubbles rising when something gets stirred up. The Marchand case had it all. Money and power. Glamour and celebrity. Politics and rivalry. A Greek tragedy, or maybe just another dreary marriage gone bad.

I teased Wendy about her celebrity-watching hobby, but I wasn't above politico-watching myself. I didn't care much about what actor was in town filming the latest Chicago-based thriller or firefighter TV show, but I tuned into political rumors. I'd heard the talk about Marchand preparing to challenge Leo Toland, who was just one more corrupt Illinois politician. Marchand had a chance, too, according to the buzz.

Toland couldn't match Charles Marchand for class. I smiled at the thought of the smoother, more articulate Marchand showing Leo up for the fool he was. Maybe that's why I didn't quite buy this Marchand-the-murderer notion, but that didn't mean I could be lured into the case.

I jumped when the phone rang. I glanced at the screen and groaned. No sense ignoring it.

"Hey, Matt. It's...Kenny."

"Yeah, I saw your name on the caller ID. I'm being polite and taking the call. So, what's up?"

"You know what's up," Kenny said, his voice full of reproach.

My old pal was trying to make me feel guilty. No luck on that front. "Nope. I don't know. I figured it had to be something new. Maybe you wanted me to donate to one of your worthy causes. Maybe go to a Bulls game." *Damn, I'm good at sarcasm.*

"Give the Marchand case a second look, Matt. That's all I ask."

I grabbed a pen and turned it over end to end. "I'm serious," I said, keeping my voice low. "I've looked at it. The answer is still no."

"Remember this. I called you because you're the best. Richard Gabriel is great, but you're better."

With that, Kenny ended the call. He could be one stubborn SOB. And he knew how to play on professional vanity, too. I scoffed at that. Vanity? Me? I liked to think I was beyond that. I swiveled the chair to face the window. Breakthrough sunlight flashed off the metal frames on the corner window of the building across the street. We hadn't seen the sun in this neck of the woods in half a dozen days or more. That's why the expanding light surprised me. Wendy might see it as another sign. Of what? Hope? Was I coming down with a case of superstition?

I sat staring out the window for a lot longer than I usually allowed myself. How long I was lost in my thoughts I can't say, but the knock on my office door grabbed my attention.

"Come in," I said in a loud voice.

Still blushing in the typical way of fair-skinned blondes, Wendy approached my desk, legal pad in hand. Trailing behind her was the shaggy-haired guy in the badly fitting suit.

"This is Rick Seymour," she said, making a half turn to indicate the man, who wasn't quite as tall as Wendy, but she was in the typical stilettos she wore in the office for reasons unknown to me.

I stood when Rick approached my desk and shook my outstretched hand. A firm, professional kind of handshake. His hands were warm, but not hot. Friendly smile, intelligent grayish eyes that didn't hesitate to look directly into mine. Educated and smart, but for the moment, an underachiever. The raggedy wool scarf shoved into one sleeve of the jacket showed evidence of being more used to hooks than hangers. Call me shallow. I noticed things. On the other hand, a pair of badly worn out leather gloves told me one of two things. Either the kid bought used gloves at Goodwill or some such place, or he managed to wear gloves out before losing them, in which case I saluted him. And he wasn't a kid. Thirtyish isn't *that* young, unless of course you're sixty.

"We won't keep you," Wendy said, raising the legal pad and scanning her notes. She held out a piece of paper. "Rick's résumé. Strong computer background. I'm thinking data analysis, uh, and data entry." Behind those comments was a puppy-eyed school girl with a crush.

"What made you come to a jury consulting firm looking for a job?" I asked, taking the résumé from Wendy's hand.

"I've been doing temp work," Rick explained.

Maude let out a weak bark, not meant to scare anyone, only to make her presence known. "Don't mind her," I said. "You interrupted her nap."

Rick grinned down at the dog, seeming to understand. My feelings about him rose a notch. He likes dogs; there's hope for this guy.

"Anyway, Robin over at ProTemp suggested I check out jury consulting firms. I can work fulltime, part-time, temporary. Whatever." He squeezed a battered leather portfolio closer to his chest. "I'm good at analyzing information. But more than that, I work like an investigator. Put me in front of a computer and I can find out whatever you need to know about pretty much anything."

Hmm. I scanned his resume. Maybe so, but Rick's last job was medical data entry, not exactly high-level analysis. Not specialized snooping. Still, he'd worked on medical information for a number of companies. Given the drug company cases that drifted our way, he could prove useful.

"Look, I need a job," Rick said matter-of-factly, "and I can't find one in my field. Actually, I can't find one in *any* field. I'm sure I can do whatever you need." He lifted his shoulders in a slow shrug. "Maybe now and again you need someone digging around the Internet, you know, research."

I scanned the page again and frowned. "What *is* your field? I don't see anything referenced."

Rick squared his shoulders. "I work for myself—I'm an entrepreneur," he said proudly. "I create computer games—cool, high-end computer games. From time to time, I do other work to subsidize my income." He stared down at his feet. "Like now."

Time to time? Right, like when he needs rent money or bologna sandwich makings. Oh well, at least he didn't say he was an actor or claim he was writing the Great American Novel. That was something. I didn't exactly see an appearance on *Shark Tank* in his future, either.

"So, Mr. Entrepreneur, you say part-time works for you?"

Rick raised his free hand toward the ceiling. "Sure."

I caught Wendy trying to suppress a smile,

but she did it badly. What a crappy poker player she'd make. Besides I knew the look, the sidelong glance at the not-half-bad-looking guy around her age. She wanted to keep Rick around to find out if he was a sign that her life was headed toward a change—and for the better. Her personal *carpe diem.*

Wendy chewed on her lower lip. "I need help with the focus groups, Matt, and you asked me to be ready to roll out a mock jury. I have a feeling that Rick's medical entry experience could help us in ways I can't quite put my finger on yet."

"If I do say so myself," Rick said, puffing his chest out a little, "I'm not some geek off the street. I'm an information specialist."

I grinned. He might be bragging. Or maybe not. Either way, we didn't need that much creativity to pull together a mock jury.

Wendy slid another piece of paper from between the sheets of the legal pad. "I've got Rick's references here."

I nodded at Wendy and she returned the gesture, which let me know she'd already looked them over.

Would I regret this? After all, Rick had nerd written all over him and had walked in off the street. On the other hand, I wasn't investing any big-time training dollars and maybe this guy was assertive, hungry, and would get things done.

"Okay, if everything checks out, we'll take you on as an independent contractor."

Looking at Wendy, I pointed to the computer screen. "I want you to duplicate the kind of focus group and mock jury we did in the Conviser case." In that setup, the plaintiffs claimed Conviser Pharmaceuticals covered up the side effects of a drug. I'd worked for the defense side and won a big one for Conviser. But with Potash Pharmaceuticals, Inc., I'd been hired by the plaintiffs. "Rick will work with you to recruit within the demographics we want covered. Then we'll see about the mock jury."

All business now, Wendy confirmed the terms and flashed me a self-satisfied grin as she steered the new recruit out of the office. He gave me a brief wave as he left.

I laughed in spite of myself. Once again, Wendy had won me over. Ah hell, better to hire a guy with the initiative to walk through the door rather than round up strangers from the temp agency to recruit our mock jurors.

I sat down again and fiddled with my pen. The sun had disappeared, so dazzling sunlight no longer bounced off the buildings across the street. A couple of years ago, my make-believe Granny, Christina, had questioned my refusal to consider another murder case, especially one that made its way to nightly news and looped on endless cable TV shows.

"Isn't this like falling off a horse and getting back on?" she asked. "Isn't it time for you to jump on the horse again? Get your feet wet?"

I'd avoided a serious answer by laughing at her mixed metaphor. But she—and others who'd known me for a long time—had asked the same question. Swearing off criminal cases had allowed me to avoid that proverbial horse and wet feet, but nothing had cooled the fire in my gut, the fire I needed meds and pink creamy liquid to douse.

I swiveled to face the desk and opened a drawer. I grabbed the bottle of antacid tablets and shook two out of the bottle. They looked like candy, and the new chewable version added to the illusion;

the luck of the draw delivered one yellow and one pink pill into my palm. There was something about this Marchand murder I couldn't banish from my thoughts. It wasn't only that Wendy had jumped to conclusions or that the press had produced an on-air conviction in the court of media junkies. My gut led me in the other direction.

It was more than that, though, and this kid, Rick, stranger off the street as he was, punctuated what was already there. A dead woman, cause of death unknown. Even the police hadn't called it a murder. A pair of rivals, Marchand and Toland. A fundraiser with out-of-character drinking and loud words. And a whole lot more unanswered questions.

I'd been known to boast about taking the long view of things. I could sit with questions for a while. Maybe I'd chew on them and let them simmer. I had more than a glimmer about who Toland was. But Marchand? Not so much.

I stared at the phone…and stared. How long? Long enough for Maude to throw a glance at me, then tuck her paws under her chin, and offer a sigh as she drifted to sleep.

I made my decision and reached for the phone.

Chapter Five

Even in an orange jumpsuit coming over from the county jail, Charles Marchand looked like a regular guy; well, as much as a wealthy developer with an Ivy League pedigree could be called a regular guy. That thought piqued a mental note to myself. *Find out which of the Ivy League schools Charles calls his alma mater.* And dig up some info on his roots—or see what Kenny already had on his background. Was Marchand a homegrown success story, or did he come from somewhere else? Well-known as he was, I didn't know much about him at all.

For years, I'd watched Marchand from afar, in the casual way we all pay attention to familiar faces. The last couple of months I'd listened with both ears instead of one. Political scuttlebutt had a way of holding my attention like nothing else. Next to pancakes and Maude, I reveled in a good ol' style "Chicago ain't ready for reform" political brawl. Toland and Marchand. As good as any current or past political framework can be.

"I'm glad you came," Charles said, holding his gaze steady on me. "Especially since this bail thing…you know…has me down."

I nodded to acknowledge him. "Tough decision."

I stood slightly behind Kenny and until then had kept quiet. In the last couple of days, I'd had some second thoughts about my impulse to cave in to my old friend Kenny. I'd made it conditional, though. I wanted to see if I was still as curious about the case *after* seeing Marchand face-to-face. I'm an old school kind of guy, the kind who likes to get a sense of a person—man or woman—before I put myself on the line. That's why I took on Joey Haskell. I got a read of the man and acted on my hunch. For all the good it had done either one of us.

I didn't need this case, though. Making payroll wouldn't push me into a bad choice. I had plenty of clients and scheduled trials to occupy my time. If I took on Marchand, I'd be squeezed for time. Sure, Marchand's dollars wouldn't hurt, but I didn't need them to balance my books. I've always been a frugal person, and that's what gave me the freedom to walk away if I had a bad reaction to Charles once we were up close and personal.

The three of us pulled out chairs at the rickety table, depressingly dotted with ancient cigarette burns and peeling varnish. I winced against the wooden chair legs scratching across the dull tile floor. My mood sank fast. I hadn't been confined in a room like this since the days I'd visited Joey Haskell. I splayed my hand across my gut. No wonder the acid burn began to gurgle the minute the guard let us in the door.

Marchand looked sad, real sad. The key was figuring out what brought this prisoner down most. Because he'd lost his wife in a tragic accident? Or was he sad because something turned sour between them? Maybe that something led to her death. Maybe that something led to an impulsive shove and down she went. I also considered that Sandra was murdered, but not by her husband. A jealous woman? One of her followers, like Wendy, only the relationship had gone bad, or the woman was a stalker or really crazy. Or, Sandra had a lover and he—or maybe she—killed her. Those scenarios sounded farfetched, but they weren't entirely implausible, either. I'd seen some off-the-wall scenarios, the kind I couldn't make up. I'd keep my mind open in this case, too.

I conceded that the immediate reason for sadness in Marchand's eyes came from the surprising, some said shocking, outcome of the bail hearing. *Bail denied.* Gavel meets wood. *Next case.*

"I'm requesting a second hearing, Charles," Kenny said. "You deserve to get out of here." Kenny quickly pivoted to the police and coroner's reports. "They've corroborated what you told Cox during your interview." Kenny spoke firmly, his voice businesslike and efficient.

I took that to mean that Marchand had told Detective Joe Cox that he and Sandra hadn't struggled at the top of the stairs. I knew Sandra's alcohol level had been high, at least for her, somewhere north of the legal limit.

As if reading my mind, Charles said, "Sandra was a cautious, deliberate drinker—she nursed a single glass of champagne for a couple of hours, then switched to sparkling water." He paused to shake his head and rub his cheek. "She liked feeling like her normal self at these big galas, without too much alcohol clouding her mind. That way, she could pay attention to faces and names and recognize people when she saw them at another one of her gatherings."

The sadness in Marchand's face deepened, and he looked away, as if needing a second to get hold of himself. "My wife had an unusual recall for names. Sandra had a way of making people feel like she'd been waiting for them to arrive and was so glad to see them again. Especially women, I guess. They saw her as their champion."

Were we veering off topic? Not really. I had learned a lot about Sandra over the last few days, but nothing surprised me so far. Everything Charles said corroborated what Wendy had told me about Sandra. I wondered if the first bail denial had something to do with Sandra's odd behavior at the fundraiser, the lack of conclusive cause of death, maybe the celebrity status of both victim and accused. Any or all of those things. The police hadn't had time to track down and interview every guest registered at the fundraiser.

So far, no one had stepped forward with tales of a nasty streak or ruthlessness, even though everyone agreed that Sandra's devotion to her charities was second to none. With no need to make a living, she used her freedom to work for things she cared about and, according to Wendy, hadn't wasted a minute of her life. Wendy repeated that often. Too often. My ace assistant was nothing if not loquacious. Yeah, that was the best word for it.

All Sandra's virtues couldn't shed light on her odd behavior before she died. In my experience, no one suddenly acted against type for no reason. Non-drinkers didn't suddenly get drunk, at least not knowingly. Someone had to spike the proverbial punch. Something—or someone—had rocked her, thrown her off her center. Likewise, mild-tempered people didn't take a life unless something pushed them over the edge. We *all* had that edge lurking around.

"There's something you need to know, Charles." Kenny glanced back at me. "Matt's assistant, Wendy Crosbie, used to work for Sandra. She was a regular at Sandra's events and a big supporter of her causes. Matt's firm had a focus group the night of the fundraiser or Wendy would have been there."

"Wendy?" Charles stared into the distance, scrunching his face in thought.

I figured he was searching through a database of names to match to a face.

"She was Sandra's personal assistant some years back," I said, providing a clue. "I suppose you wouldn't *necessarily* remember her."

Charles shook his head. "I can't say I do." He kneaded his forehead, as if giving himself a minute to try to place Wendy. "Sandra usually hired a young woman and then mentored her on to bigger things, so these assistants weren't around for long."

I nodded. "That's what happened with Wendy. Sandra helped her get into college and move on. Wendy is heartbroken. She thought the world of your wife." I paused before adding, "Just to refresh your memory, Wendy is thirtyish now, tan all-American girl type—classic blue-eyed blonde, taller than average."

Charles frowned. He paused a moment before his frown deepened. "I think I recall a young woman who fits that description—thinking back a decade or so."

I watched his jaw tighten. Hmm...Charles

might have remembered something, and it wasn't a happy thought. I filed that observation away.

I didn't bother adding that Wendy was furious with me, had barely spoken to me over the last few days. The conversation in my office with Rick Seymour was the last pleasant exchange we'd had. Now she sent me texts and emails, or left notes on my desk. This case had already poisoned the atmosphere in the office. Even Janet kept her head down and limited her witty remarks. Thank God for Rick. His arrival had lightened the mood some.

Wendy had a list of reasons why Charles killed his wife, chief among them whatever caused the bizarre scene at the Café Brauer. Wendy's intuition told her that a woman was probably involved somewhere. Considering cold statistics, I couldn't disagree, at least out loud. But my own gut told me it wasn't true, not by a long shot. Trouble in paradise didn't always mean another woman had been sketched into the picture.

"Wendy won't be questioned, by the way, since she wasn't there. Her best friend might be, though," Kenny explained.

Marchand shrugged as he stared at his folded hands resting on the table.

Was that it? Wasn't he going to explain Sandra's anger at him, the way, according to press reports, she almost broke a champagne glass by thrusting it smack into the middle of his chest?

"It won't be long before Wendy's friend comes up on the list of those who attended the shelter's fundraiser," I added. "She saw what she saw. So did others." I paused. "And that includes Leo Toland and his body guards. Apparently, Sandra was angry with him, too. At least it looked that way to bystanders."

At the mention of Toland's name, Marchand tossed a defensive glare my way.

I'd frustrated Charles. That was okay. The tension between Charles and Sandra played out on a stage of more than 100 people. That sure worked against the "she must have fallen in the night" scenario, which sounded too pat to Sandra's supporters. Most of who attended the Café Brauer event were not only shelter supporters but considered themselves Sandra's *fans*.

Charles threw up his hands in a helpless gesture. "I *didn't* kill my wife."

"I didn't ask if you did," I said. "Don't plan to—it doesn't matter to me."

"Look, we'll cross the Café Brauer bridge later," Kenny interjected. "Granted, it's what's driving this case right now."

"Why was she drinking so heavily that night?" I asked. I intentionally toned my voice to sound curious, not suspicious.

"I don't know," Charles said, his eyes shifting down.

Damn it, he's lying. I had a strong feeling that Charles hadn't murdered his wife, but that didn't make him an innocent man. "I'm only asking the question that every man or woman in the jury pool will ask. The state will be prepared to call everyone at Café Brauer, all 100 of them. Hell, they may even call the governor himself." Jurors don't like men with girlfriends in the background or who abused their wives behind closed doors. *Or who kept too many secrets.*

"We'll be prepared, Matt. Don't worry about it." Kenny stood. "I'll be back tomorrow." Looking grim, he knocked on the door for the guard.

"Wait—one quick question," I said. "Someone like you, well connected and prominent, must know the governor. From early reports, Sandra knew him."

Marchand's eyes narrowed again. "I've met Toland on a number of occasions. He used to show up at Sandra's shindigs…wrong word…galas, luncheons, you know what I mean."

"What's your relationship to Toland?" I asked.

"We don't have one," Marchand said quickly, too quickly, with a note of defiance seeping into his voice. But his eyes shifted around.

I decided not to probe further. I'd figure out the lies as we went along. Clients lied usually to avoid looking guilty, whether they were or not. The guilty and innocent alike. Besides, I had my own reasons not to go too deeply into Toland's past or present.

"I don't like Leo Toland. Avoid him if I can," Charles added, shrugging with an awkward show of nonchalance. "As for Sandra, I didn't encourage her to invite him to her events. In fact, over the last six months or so I specifically asked her *not* to do that. Politically, it didn't look good."

Hell, I hadn't needed to probe after all. "Why?"

"I'm sure you know Toland's reputation. Sandra knew I was thinking about making a run for the office myself. Going up against him in the primary. That's why I didn't want Sandra being around him or having him linked to her causes."

Charles had started talking in a low tone, but by the time he got to the end of the sentence, he'd raised his voice a notch or two. So much for nonchalance. Casual tones never lasted unless they were real. I nodded in acknowledgment as I followed Ken out.

"What was all that about?" Kenny asked once we were outside and on our way to the parking deck.

"You have two pillars of the community, who supposedly had a storybook marriage," I said with a shrug. "He sticks his foot in the river of state politics. Next thing you know, she ends up dead at the bottom of the stairs. No sign of a break in. This case is about motive, Kenny. You know that. The state is banking on convincing twelve people that Marchand is hiding something. It's obvious he is." Surely Kenny had figured this out. "And maybe his secret would have blown up as he ran for office."

"I'm glad you came today," Kenny said, apparently preferring not to comment on my not-so-random thoughts.

"You thought I might back out?"

Kenny grinned. "You gave yourself that option."

"No more. I'm in."

We went our separate ways to our cars. I didn't know about Kenny, but I'd always hated cases that weren't about evidence. I had a hunch—no, I'd gone beyond hunches. I *knew* in my gut this case was about secrets, maybe politics, and maybe even vendettas.

* * *

"I didn't expect to see you here." I kept my voice matter-of-fact as I leaned down and unclipped Maude's leash. As soon as she was free, Maude headed straight for Wendy, who was standing with her coat on and pulling on her gloves.

Wendy bent over to affectionately scratch under Maude's chin.

Maude looked up, clearly enjoying the sensation of deep scratching. No one could resist

Maude.

"I was just leaving," she said, glancing up at me as she stated the obvious. "I left the Potash survey update on your desk." She straightened up and brushed past me, heading for the exits, so to speak.

"Wendy, wait."

She stopped and turned, an expectant look on her face.

"This is silly. We can't keep communicating by texts and emails." I exhaled a heavy sigh. She was more than my office manager and assistant. Wendy had become more like a business partner to me. As much as I teased her about living vicariously through the rich and famous, the fact is I relied on her to cover the details, manage our schedules, and all the rest. Besides, I considered her a friend. Someone who normally never questioned my decisions, much less motives. "Let's talk this out."

That sounded good, but we both knew she owned the solution to our problem. I wasn't pulling out of the Marchand case.

"I'm meeting someone for dinner, Matt. That's why I'm hurrying off. Let's leave it alone. We don't need to hash things out, at least not tonight."

Too easy, I thought, skeptical of her quick choice to avoid a conversation. That wasn't part of her nature. I planted my hand on my hip and cocked my head. My digging-in stance. Wendy knew it well.

"Really, Matt, I'm serious." She swept her arm around the room. "This is your firm. You have the right to take on any client you choose. I can be outspoken and emotional sometimes, but I don't make decisions about the clientele." She glanced at her watch. "I really do have to go. I'm meeting Marla at Mi Casa's, that Mexican restaurant on

Belmont." She opened her mouth, as if wanting to say more, but then she closed it again and looked away.

"What?"

"Huh?"

"What were you going to say?" I knew it wasn't about margaritas and enchiladas.

She put her hand on the doorknob. For a minute I thought she wasn't going to answer me. Not a good sign.

"It's just...I don't know. I've been distant because I don't know what I should do next, in life, I mean. It's not about you and Marchand. It's about me. Sandra's death did wake me up. Gave me a lot to think about. I wasn't kidding about seizing the day and all that." She shook her head sadly.

"Then you're okay with this?" I asked, leaving the pronoun vague.

"If you can be okay defending a likely murderer of someone I used to work for, then I'll try to be, too." She shrugged, feigning indifference. "You know how I feel."

I nodded. "I realize it came as a surprise."

She lowered her head, a decisive gesture of agreement. That was it. She turned and left without another word, letting the door click shut behind her.

Now she had me puzzled. I'd never seen Wendy look as contemplative, even somber. Apparently, Sandra's death *had* shifted something in her. The old Wendy, the chatty Wendy, might have gone on and on about lawyers with no morals defending the guilty, something she'd never understand, no matter how long she worked with me. She defended the legal system in general, but loathed that one principle. She understood everyone deserves a fair trial, yet didn't want to risk someone she thought to be guilty walking free.

Back in my office, I mulled over Wendy's special bond with Sandra. I'd been insensitive in expecting her to get my reasons for taking the Marchand case. Especially since I couldn't completely articulate my rationale, either. I'd been grudging in my attempt to understand, acting professorial and patronizing as I spouted my spiel about everyone's right to the best defense. Yeah, I'd been kind of an ass about it. I had to justify it somehow, breaking my own rule. Hadn't I loudly proclaimed I'd never take a criminal case again?

I left the light on for Maude in the front office so she could wander around, but left the door open so she could settle down under my desk when she was ready. I picked up the Potash file, prepared to review the initial data we analyzed from the community attitude survey.

I struggled to focus. Instead, my mind turned to Marchand, and then to Sandra, and back to Charles again. My mind scanned for missing data points. I understood fights between partners, private tiffs, even relationship-threatening hostilities, the kind of stuff both parties masked in public.

Sudden shifts were different, though. Taking once-private moments and playing them out in public? Not so common. A disciplined social drinker choosing to drain champagne glasses, laugh in a shrill, harsh way? Also not so common. Something else puzzled me. This self-contained woman publicly paraded her anger at two men, potential rivals, no less. But, as far as I or Kenny, or Wendy, for that matter, knew, the men had no connection to each other, or did they?

I got out a legal pad and dragged my pen down the middle of the page twice to divide it in thirds. I wrote CM for Charles on the left, SM for Sandra in the middle, and LT for Leo in the right column. I snorted at my feeble start and tossed the pen down. I had nothing. One arrow connecting CM and SM. Big deal. Okay, half an arrow somehow connected Sandra and Toland, and only because of her charity events.

I drew an arrow connecting Charles and Leo and wrote "same age" along the top, adding a question mark. I made an assumption about their age, one easily verified. I couldn't think of much else. If Wendy were here, she could have filled in facts about Charles. I immediately had the urge to head down to Mi Casa, but I knew she was meeting a friend there. Not nice to barge in.

Shaking my head to clear the cobwebs, I realized that all this was nonsense, not worth my time. I had a jury to pick for the Potash case. We'd have a mundane pool of retirees and self-employed and unemployed souls who'd likely cast a jaundiced eye at both sides.

Get on with the case in front of you.

I might have done exactly that, but for the knock, followed by a voice calling through the front door, "Wendy, are you here?"

The top half of Rick was leaning inside our office. He held a plastic carryout box in his hand. Getting to my feet, I approached the door. "She's not here, Rick. Were you supposed to meet with her?"

"Ah, no. I was on my way home. I stopped at that new Mexican place and got some nachos to take home." He lifted the box.

Damned if his face wasn't turning red.

"When I saw the light," he said, "I thought she might be working late." The box went up a notch. "I thought I'd see if she wanted to share."

His face was a study of mixed emotions. A little

73

embarrassment, some disappointment. Self-conscious and awkward, too. His second unexpected walk through my office door had a serendipitous aura around it. I believed in that sort of thing. A question, followed by the appearance of a potential answer, with almost no gap in time.

"As a matter of fact, she's having dinner with a friend there tonight. You missed her by a few minutes."

"Oh, I see." He flashed a rueful grin, a kind of man-to-man "you can't blame me for trying" smile.

"Why don't you come in? You can eat your nachos here."

Rick frowned. Granted, my invitation sounded odd, even to me.

"Actually, I'd like to ask you a couple of questions," I said. "If you don't mind."

His face brightened. "Sure. Maybe you'd like some nachos."

"I ate already," I lied. Unless Rick considered a handful of pretzels and a couple of antacids a meal. "But, thanks anyway."

Rick followed me into my office. I grabbed my iPad, one of those tools I didn't use often because I wasn't a browsing-the-net kinda guy. I didn't play games, always forgot about the blogs I meant to follow, and had zero use for social media. When I wanted diversion, I preferred the shouting matches political TV offered. I almost always tuned into my old friend Cooper.

"Here's the thing," I hesitated. "And this is between us, you and me, no one else. Everything in this office is privileged."

Rick's face clouded as he lifted the lid of the nacho box. He didn't look up. For a second, I wondered if he was afraid of what he'd become involved in.

"I want you to know that what I'm going to ask isn't really about a case. It's more to satisfy my own curiosity."

"I see," Rick said, staring at the iPad.

"When you work for me, nothing leaves this office," I said. "I'm thinking out loud now, covering all the bases." Two clichés in a row. Could I add a third? Even Janet stopped at two.

"Got it, what happens in the office stays in the office," Rick said, picking up a pepper, black olive, and cheese laden clump of nachos. Ah, there was the third cliché. Rick lifted it toward his open mouth, and despite the precarious nature of the maneuver, he managed to slide the food in. He chewed quickly and swallowed. "I've been doing quite a bit of work on the Potash case," he said. "You haven't seen me because I've been doing most everything from home."

True. This was only the second time I'd seen Rick face-to-face.

"If I do say so myself," he said, "the report I drafted was detailed. Ah, I don't want to pat myself on the back or anything, but I'm good at this." He described some data he'd worked with for an insurance company who had found itself in a third-party dispute in a class action suit. "Now in those files of data, I bumped into a trailhead. I could have ignored it, but instead, I took the path." He lifted another chip of nacho glop to his mouth.

I waited. Surely that wasn't the end of the story.

"And you know what it led to?" he asked.

"That's what I'm sitting here waiting to find out," I said with a snorting laugh.

"Okay, then, that trail led me to a pile of fudged data in a big cardiac drug case—a name-brand blood thinner."

"Really?"

Rick thrust his hand out in front of him, as if pointing to the great infinity stretched out before them. Dramatic and effective, because like a little kid listening to a storyteller, I'd have begged him to tell me more.

He tapped the corner of his eye. "They didn't pay me to notice this stuff, but I can see connections, patterns, big picture stuff—the same skills I use to create my games."

"And you saw…?" *Move it along, already.*

"That drug—that company—*killed* people," Rick said. "For real, no hype. They paid me a few bucks an hour, but the plaintiffs made *millions*."

"So, you really *are* a nerd," I teased. I vaguely knew the facts of the case he was talking about. A friend of mine had lost it. Rick was right. It was a bombshell case that led to debates about Big Pharma funding research of its own drugs and all the implications of conflicts of interest.

Rick grinned. "Usually, trials are pretty mundane. But once in a while, they turn into a good-versus-evil epic battle."

"True," I said, leaning forward in my chair. A signal for me to change the subject. "You could do what I'm asking from home, too, but since you happened to stop by, let's get to it. I want to do a little digging. Follow some Google leads and see where they take us. On the clock, of course."

Rick chewed another mouthful of chips and cheese. Then he pushed the box aside and pulled the iPad toward him. He wiggled his fingers in the air, like a maestro warming up. "What do you want to know?"

Good question. How did Sandra die? For starters.

"This firm is working on jury matters for the Marchand case. What I want to know isn't about the case itself." *Maybe.* "I want to know how well Charles Marchand knows Governor Toland. Two prominent guys, around the same age, quickly becoming political rivals. Hours before she died, Sandra Marchand was apparently angry with both her husband and the governor."

Rick tapped on the iPad screen a few times. "What did Marchand say when you asked him about Toland?"

I hesitated, but not for long. "I haven't asked him." Then I evaded. "I want a profile—an impression. For me. Most likely it's insignificant." *Or not.*

"Okay, sure. Hey, by the way, did you see the news about Sandra Marchand's sister? Her name is Jordan Hayes," Rick said. "Half-sister, I guess, and she nearly died on her way home from that private funeral they had."

I nodded. "I saw that on the news. The reporter said the woman collapsed at the airport in Louisville. The EMTs managed to revive her. A massive heart attack, someone reported." I didn't add that the conspiracy nuts were somehow turning the sister's illness into a mafia plot to wipe out Sandra's family. Or, maybe some extraterrestrials were involved. Who knew?

Regardless, the near-death of Sandra's half-sister reinforced Wendy's new attitude. She'd come back from Sandra's public memorial service on fire with determination. *A well-lived life.* That's what people said about Sandra, and that's what she wanted for herself. I knew that feeling, but I've also experienced what it was like when that feeling got snatched away. When Joey died, my hope for doing something significant had died with him. He'd been my ticket to making a difference. That ticket was stamped, and I didn't see others on the horizon.

"Wendy told me Sandra's death made her want her own life to matter," Rick said, as if reading my mind. "I don't know what that means exactly."

A conversation for another day. The old political saw about not letting a good crisis go to waste came to mind, but I kept it to myself.

He glanced down at the screen. "Hmm…nothing comes up with the two of them together, at least not in the first items that pop up."

I watched his fingers fly again, flicking his finger down the screen. He frowned, turned his mouth down, bit his lower lip. I couldn't read his reactions.

"There's a lot to filter out. They both bring close to a million hits." Rick scoffed. "And *The Sopranos* come up, too. Something about Nancy Marchand, the actress? I think she played the mafia kingpin Tony's mom."

"Right," I said with a laugh. "And there's Toland Agrichemicals, too."

"More prominent than the governor." Rick scrunched his face.

"Ah, your body language tells me you're not fond of the governor."

"Oops. I try to hide my true feelings when I think I should." Rick glanced up and grinned sheepishly.

"No need to hide it in this office," I said. "I was rooting for Marchand to jump into the race."

Rick nodded, then frowned. "Here's a little something. We could spend all night reading news accounts where these guys come up. They get around, those two. But sometimes the simple stuff works better."

"And?"

"Well, Marchand went to college, but where he went is never mentioned in his bios. Odd, really. But when I keyed in a search based on his degrees, I get the oddest thing. Donaldstone College?"

"Huh? No Ivy League? No Big Ten?"

Rick shook his head and kept typing. "Donaldstone, a dinky liberal arts school in a tiny town on the river downstate."

I mulled that over while Rick continued scrolling.

"Whoa." Rick jerked his head back. "Here's a photo of a graduation."

He turned the screen and there they were, Marchand at the podium, Toland sitting on the dais behind him and to the right. Decidedly bored, too, from the half-closed eyes—he looked like a toddler fighting sleep and about to lose the battle.

"Toland's about to conk out." Rick pointed at Toland's image and laughed. "Right there in the middle of graduation." His laugh turned to a thoughtful frown. "Let me see something here. I have a hunch." Typing, scrolling, and then a big laugh. "Yup. They went to college together."

That sent my gut rolling over. Marchand lied, all right.

"See?" he said. "Here's their commencement program."

Rick enlarged the image on the screen. The two of us stared at names of graduates listed in that year's class. The two of them in the same backwater school? That was my assessment of a college I'd heard of only in passing. Rick enlarged the image again. Sure enough, Charles Marchand was listed right where he belonged, between Pamela Marcelli and Casey Mark. Opposite him was Toland, wedged between Jackie Spinelli and Danielle Urquhart.

I flopped back in the chair. "So maybe Donaldstone is one of those small, elite schools." There
might be some gold to mine in that part of March-
and's story. Besides the fact he failed to mention
he and Toland were classmates. An odd thing to
leave out.

What other facts were lurking around that
Marchand didn't think were important enough to
mention?

Chapter Six

"Too bad for Potash Pharmaceuticals. Couldn't pull off that change of venue," I said from my seat at the table in the conference room. Leann Almquist, the lead attorney on the team, sat to my right. In the interest of professionalism, Maude was exiled under Janet's desk, but the room didn't feel the same without her.

"I know," Leann said. "They may employ a couple thousand people around here, but their reputation stinks to high heaven, as my mother used to say. No on-site day care, the bare minimum sick leave they can get away with, a couple of weeks' vacation after five years." She let out a sharp laugh. "My politician husband says they need a union over there."

"Right," I said, grinning at Leann's reference. Her husband had gone from union organizer to state senator and had enough talent to seek a bigger turf eventually. "And let's not forget the EPA fines for illegally dumping drugs in the landfill. They're on the wrong side of everything." I pulled my mouth down into an exaggerated look of disgust. "Maybe you should file a second lawsuit just because they're bastards."

I liked working with Leann, especially now, when we had a chance of nailing Potash for doing something bad, not only illegal, but unethical, too. Fudging medical report data always struck me as the worst kind of moral breach. Always done under a cloak of secrecy, greed stood out as its one and only motive.

Leann and I both flipped through the pages of the community attitude survey report, even though I knew the important conclusions.

"Wendy did a great job on the report," Leann said, "not that I'm surprised."

"We have a new guy who's helping us out part-time. He's quite good. When I looked over the report, I could see he has a good sense for interpreting data, same as Wendy." An understatement, especially according to Rick himself. "They see the big picture."

I swallowed the last of the coffee in the mug and then frowned at the sheet in front of me. "I can see these fifty-something guys thinking about their hearts while they get pissed off at the asshole Potash execs on the stand trying to answer your questions. I just hope we get enough of them in the jury pool."

"The unemployment rate might help with that. Lots of blue-collar guys out of work, and I think they have the best nose for right and wrong and what it means to slip around on safety."

"Potash, or rather, Rosenthal and the other attorneys, will be looking for the young guys who think they're invincible and don't much care, unless they have parents with a heart condition. Should be interesting." I patted the report. "With any luck, this thing will settle before trial."

"Yes, luck, and lots of it." Leann stood and gathered her files and put them in her attaché. "I suppose you need extra help around here," she said with a grin, "since I hear you're working on the Marchand case. Kind of a departure for you. In recent years, anyway."

My gut immediately started acting up. I hated rumors, but this wasn't idle gossip. "So, the word is out, huh?"

Leann looked genuinely puzzled. "You think people wouldn't notice?"

"I didn't consider that at all," I said with a laugh.

"We live in such a small world." Leann turned toward the door, but she stopped short of leaving. "So, tell me, is the rumor true? Was Marchand really going to give Leo Toland a run for his money in the next election?"

I hadn't asked Charles that question, wasn't going to; his team had a job to do. But Charles had opened the door on it himself. That piece of information could mean something to the case against Charles. I didn't know what—not yet. Besides, it was Kenny's job to dig around in Marchand's life.

"Hey, I don't know any more than what was in the papers," I said with a bit of a smirk. I liked it when others thought I knew more than I really did.

Flashing me a skeptical look, Leann slipped her heavy bag over her shoulder. "He'd have had my vote. Of course, so would the new baby chimp at the zoo. Anyone but Toland, that's my motto. He always gave me the creeps. It's like he's hiding something. I heard on TV that Toland and Sandra got into a big fight at the fundraiser for the shelter the night before she died."

That intrigued me, too, but in the way little twists and false clues in a mystery novel attracted my attention. Interesting, but not necessarily important.

With her bag hoisted on her shoulder, Leann gripped the attaché in the other hand. "Well, as they say, see you in court—or maybe not. Let's hope we settle before we have to climb those courthouse steps."

As I walked Leann to the door, Maude came out from behind Janet's desk. "Now you come back here, Maude," Janet scolded. "Matt doesn't want you embarrassing him in front of the paying clients."

Obviously recognizing a teasing tone when she heard it, Maude went straight to Leann and sniffed what even I recognized as very expensive boots. Like the ones Wendy teetered around on, Leann's had pencil thin heels.

"Maude, please," I said, leaning down to grab her collar and pull the dog back. "Sniffing people is impolite, especially when the people you're sniffing are lawyers!" Laughing to myself, I mumbled, "They could be hiding something, little girl, and you might just discover something illegal!" I laughed out loud.

Leann frowned. "Honest to God, you are the only office I visit where a dog runs the place." She shrugged. "But, she's so damn cute. Anyway, all of you have a good afternoon." She reached down to give Maude's head a perfunctory pat, then quickly left.

I turned away and headed for my office, but stopped when I heard footsteps getting louder. Maybe Leann left something behind and had come back for it. I turned around. Definitely not Leann.

* * *

Just as well our mother is long gone. Not because Zach looked sick or even especially old for his fifty-plus years, although his dark brown, almost back hair had gone almost completely gray. So was his skin, now that I studied him closer. Our mom would've hated that her oldest son was living his life in the shadow of someone like Leo Toland. I kept those thoughts to myself, although I didn't need to. Zach knew how I felt about Toland. Way back before he was governor, Toland took advantage of Zach's vulnerability—culpability. In return, Zach got drawn into Leo's hidden web of corruption. And that pretty much ended any relationship my older brother and I would ever have.

If only Zach had come to me for help. Just swallowed his pride and not worry about what I'd think. In my days of practicing law, I'd learned to put judgment aside. Just because the system said you've done something wrong doesn't mean it's true. If the feds set their sights on you, that was usually it for you. The truth usually didn't play a role for some prosecutors who can't see the forest through the trees; no, it's conviction at any price. Zach hadn't understood that years ago. He thought I'd judge him. That's how he ended up going to Toland. And the consequences had created a permanent wedge between us.

I closed the office door and pointed to the chairs across from my desk. Without warning, my head began to throb, but I forced myself not to press my temples and make it obvious. As if acid burn weren't bad enough, seeing Zach in my office knocked me off kilter. Worse, it shoved me out of the present and back into the relative past.

With a soft bark, Maude came out from under the desk and approached the stranger. Zach quickly took steps back toward the door. Maude stopped moving forward and stared at the man invading her space.

"It's been a while," I said, recovering myself as I watched apprehension cross Zach's face. It came back to me, Zach's fear—aversion—to dogs. "Over here, Maude."

"Her name's Maude?" Zach asked.

"Uh huh." I offered no explanation how the best companion I'd ever had ended up named Maude. I pointed to her bed in the corner. "Go on, Maude. Now would be a good time to take a nap." I'm not sure Zach would understand my reference to the great Bea Arthur or her Maude character, anyway. In real life, Bea's bark was likely worse than my Maude's bite.

"Not exactly a guard dog, huh?" Zach remarked with a smirk.

Maude went to bed in the corner and curled up. She'd fall asleep in minutes.

"Have a seat," I said. "Maude won't bother you." Because I exerted some effort, my voice sounded normal, but seeing my brother set off waves of emotion I didn't like. I hated admitting the fact that if I'd never saw Zach again—ever—I'd barely notice it. It wouldn't make a ripple. Not bad, not good. I liked to think Zach occupied a place of neutrality in my life. Sometimes, though, I thought of myself as similar to one of those unlucky presidents who had embarrassing brothers. Periodically, these guys crawled out of their caves and made headlines for saying something dumb or pulling a stunt like asking the president-brother to tell the truth about UFOs.

"It's been a few years," Zach said. "You called

when you got back from wherever that was you went."

I wasn't sure if he was chiding me or simply stating the facts. "Europe—that's where I went. I wandered around a lot. I needed a change. Everyone says you can find yourself if you wander around Paris or London. Ya know, that just ain't so." That's as close to an explanation as I'd give as to why I'd left for a long hiatus from law and life after I failed to do right by Joey Haskell.

Zach chuckled at my attempt at humor. "I hear you've done all right since you've been back, though." He pointed to the corner, where Maude breathed rhythmically—and audibly. "Got yourself a dog? That's a surprise. You know, we never had so much as a goldfish in the house. The little mutt snores, too."

Always the teasing brown eyes. That's why I ignored the reference to Maude as a mutt. I'd counted on Zach's gently teasing ways when we were kids. Sometimes he grabbed me by the arm and, promising me a treat, steered me out our apartment door. Only later did I catch on that my big brother wanted to escape one of Mom's boyfriends. To a man, they were dead-end guys and not good to our mother. Zach had made it into a game, though, acting like he'd been planning to take me on a jaunt down the street for ice cream all along.

A good woman, our mother, but foolish as hell when it came to men. She'd picked two losers as fathers for us. Zach's dad drank himself into the ground. Mine had an aversion to work. What a pair.

"Maude's only noisy when she dreams, probably visions of sniffing the dirt in Lincoln Park dancing in her head." Time for a change of subject. "So, how is your family?" Likely happy to be off the topic of dogs, Zach probably wouldn't mind talking about his wife, Judy, and their two kids. I wouldn't recognize any of them if I ran into them on the street.

"The kids aren't kids anymore. Laila is married, and Myles is about to be. Judy has her own beauty shop now."

"Good to hear." I stared at Zach, who tipped the chair back on two legs and laced his fingers behind his head. "So, what are you doing here—and why didn't you call first?"

"I need to make an appointment to see my baby brother?"

Why not? Everyone else does. "Of course not," I lied.

Ever since he narrowly escaped serving time, thanks to Leo Toland, Zach seemed to swim in a pool of secrecy. Shady deals, corruption—and probably worse—lived in the dark beneath the surface.

"Why don't you tell me why you're here?"

For the first time since he'd sat down, Zach's face changed from bemused to thoughtful. He righted the chair with a clunk. "I was just messing around with your head," he said. "I figured you wouldn't know what to make of me showing up unannounced."

I nodded. "You made your point."

"Before I say anything else," Zach said, raking his fingers through his hair, "I need to know for sure you're working on the Marchand case."

"What makes you think so?"

"I hear things…the guys around Leo talk. And Judy, she heard something at the beauty shop. One of the girls, whose name's Toshi, rents a chair and said she heard something from a client about the famous jury guy right here in Chicago. Said he was going to work for Marchand." Zach flashed a lopsided grin. "I figured the famous guy in the city had to be you. Who else?"

"It's no secret—apparently. Why do you ask?"

Zach paused and stared at the floor, looking like he was gathering his thoughts. "I haven't told anyone about my visit to my little brother's office. I mean, no one knows I'm here." He looked up, but said nothing for a moment.

"I suppose I could have called. But I wanted to see you face-to-face." He paused again, folding his arms across his chest. "Here's the thing. One condition. When I leave, you'll come with me. We'll go down the block and grab lunch at the Lakeview Market. Like two brothers catching up—out in the open. Those are my terms."

My gut did a double backflip. "Yeah, okay, Zach, it's about time we had lunch."

Zach glanced over his shoulder at the door, as if checking to make sure it was closed.

"No one can hear you," I said.

"Whaddya know about Marchand's politics?" Zach blurted.

I drew my head back, surprised by the question, or maybe the timing of it. "Nothing from the inside, if that's what you mean," I said. "I heard he was thinking about making a run in the gubernatorial primary, presumably because he wanted your boss' job."

"Wanted? Past tense."

"Even when a guy is innocent, it's hard to campaign from a jail cell," I said, "although this *is* Illinois. That wouldn't stop anybody." I snickered at my own joke. "Seriously, it's safe to say his political aspirations are dead in the water, for this election cycle anyway."

Zach rested his elbows on his knees and tapped his steepled fingertips together. "That's what Leo wanted. The governor got his way," he said with a scoff. "I know things—things you should know."

I opened my hands toward Zach as an invitation to elaborate. I pulled them back quickly, though, conscious that they shook. A fear reaction. I wasn't sure I wanted to hear any of what Zach had to say, yet I didn't want to miss a word of it, either.

"Here it is, straight, Matt. Leo sent me over to Marchand's house to deliver a message." He paused. "On the night of the lady's charity party. The night she died."

That got me out of my chair. Nervous energy pushed me to take a couple of steps to the small fridge and reach inside for two bottles of water. "Okay…look, before you say anything else, do you need a lawyer?" I tossed a bottle toward Zach's open palms. He caught it like the baseball player he'd been in the city's park leagues.

"I don't know," Zach said. "I'm counting on you to keep all of this confidential."

"Absolutely," I said, sure of only that one thing. "What kind of message?" I hadn't hid the impatience in my voice.

Zach laced his fingers. "I had my instructions. Show up around 4:00 AM and ring the bell until Marchand opened the door. If you live in the normal world, you might ask who pays someone a visit at that time of the morning. In my world, everyone keeps weird hours, and some guys show up at the door with a gun in their hands. The idea is to scare 'em some. Like I said, I had my orders. So I was gonna ring the damn bell until he answered."

"Could have been either Marchand, though,

right?" I asked, twisting the cap off the bottle. If Zach hadn't been there, I'd have pressed the chilled bottle to my forehead. Then again, if Zach hadn't been sitting in my office, my head wouldn't feel like it had gotten caught in steel jaws.

"Nope," Zach said, shaking his head. "Geez, not at 4:00 in the goddamn morning. No fuckin' way the lady is coming to the door. It would be Charles."

I was skeptical. Insomniacs or early risers came in both sexes. Maybe Zach's wife wouldn't answer the door, but how could he have been so sure about Sandra? Zach's flat tone revealed zero emotion. On the other hand, that cool seemed feigned. "Did you deliver the message?"

"Nope. Well, not exactly. I hit a snag, a complication. Marchand opened the door wearing his bathrobe." Zach paused to gulp water and swallow. "The body was on the landing at the bottom of the stairs."

"The body? You mean *her* body? Sandra Marchand?"

Zach nodded.

"You know for sure—100 percent—it was Sandra?" Charles hadn't told the police or Kenny that he'd answered that knock on the door. Why wasn't I surprised by this sin of omission? All along, I'd had the feeling Charles was withholding parts of the story.

Zach nodded again. "The lights were on in the entryway. I could see her behind him, crumpled up like this." He curled his shoulders and arms inward. "I saw her blond hair hanging down from the stairs."

Wincing at the image of Sandra's lifeless body on the landing, something didn't add up in my mind. Thinking out loud, I asked, "Why would

Marchand answer the door at that time of the morning?"

"On any other night, I'm not sure. But that night, turns out he had just called 9-1-1." Zach gestured with his open hands, as if stating the obvious. "He opened the door because he thought I was the police or maybe the EMTs."

Talk about complicating things. Not to mention withholding critical facts.

"As it turned out, I got to his door a couple of minutes before the ambulance showed up," Zach said. "Later, I hung around to see what would happen. I went back to the car and scrunched down and waited. When the EMTs left, I left."

I gulped some water to buy time. A part of me wanted to stop Zach from saying any more. How much did I want to know? I wasn't a lawyer at the moment. I was Zach's brother, and he'd come to me. "What did Marchand say when he opened the door?"

"He looked kind of wild, like he was in shock. He pointed to the body and in a panic he said 'my wife—I think she's dead.' Like I said, he must have thought I was with the police."

I mulled the words...*wild, in shock.* "What did you say?"

"I looked him in the eyes and said, 'Hey, you need to listen. Governor Toland sent me'. I stopped almost mid-word and shifted gears. I thought real fast and said, 'But hey, *I didn't see anything here.*' I said it slow. Wanted to be sure he understood me. Then I took off."

"That's all?"

"That's when I hauled my ass to my car to hide out. Two minutes, three at most, the ambulance arrived. I hung around until they brought her out—face covered. Marchand didn't know I was there, watching." Zach shook his head and clicked his tongue in a regretful way. "Damn shame."

"But we don't know what happened," I said. Still, the idea of Marchand holding back information circled in my brain, looking for a place to land. How could it be that Zach was one of the last to see Sandra Marchand? And she might even have been alive at that moment.

"How well do *you* know Marchand?" Zach challenged.

"Barely at all, met him once or twice," I said, perching one hip on my desk. "Like everyone else, I knew *of* him. I've heard what everyone else has heard about his political ambitions." I exhaled with a huff. "Speaking of, what about Toland? That's the question. How well does *he* know Marchand?"

Zach shrugged. "He doesn't say and I don't ask."

I hesitated, asking myself if I wanted to know the answer to the obvious question. Apprehension aside, the answer was yes. "Tell me, then, what was the message you would have delivered?"

Without so much as a subtle flinch, Zach said, "I'd have told Marchand that it would be better for everyone if he stayed out of politics. I'd have reminded him that *stuff* has a way of turning up." He screwed his face up in what I read as disdain. "But that's the kinda shit Toland always talks. He *assumes* guys like Marchand have plenty to hide. These celebrity types are willing to pay a price to keep their secrets hidden. I was supposed to find out what Marchand wanted, but, you know, without really asking." Zach shrugged. "It was simple. Toland didn't like the idea of a rich developer standing in his way."

"What he *wanted*?" I asked, almost yelling the

words. "What? As in a job or an appointment? Money?"

Zach's face fell. "That's the thing about Leo. What he tells you is what you need to know... nothing more."

I groaned. What a way for a fifty-something man to live. I found myself in that middle ground of feeling regret over the years-long rift with my brother and still being angry with him for making such bad choices. "And that's good enough for you?"

Zach opened his mouth as if to speak, but then closed it again. He sighed softly. "It doesn't matter anymore. I got the kids raised. Judy's happy with her shop. That's what counts."

I could almost see Zach's defensive walls falling. Maybe he'd grown weary of the devil's bargain he'd made, staying out of jail for spending his days—and nights—doing the governor's bidding. Political dirty work. I'd seen other politicians go down for making promises for political contributions, but somehow, money still made the world go round and elected officials got to fill positions with appointments. They had to be sure every appointment was followed with a statement like, "This person is eminently qualified, and the contributions and connections had nothing to do with this appointment!" What a bunch of crap... and typical for this state—hell, for the whole country.

Years before, Zach got himself into a swamp of trouble for trying to bribe a couple of aldermen, money in exchange for landing key city renovation projects. He was good at that kind of work, too, and had a nice little construction/restoration business going. Toland, owner of the largest contracting firm in the county, maneuvered himself into a position on the planning board that approved contracts. He'd seen something in Zach, and I guess, thought a guy like him might be useful, especially since Toland pulled strings and kept Zach out of jail. And so that sealed the devil's bargain.

Superficially, Zach's title meant everything from arranging the security detail for campaign rallies to nosing around contracting firms to make sure their deals were clean, or at least looked that way. Apparently, the job required delivering messages at all hours, too.

Guys like Toland always had a Zach-type around, and Zach had moved up right along with Toland, all the way to the state house. A trusted lackey, I surmised, the one keeping his eye on the contracting business and potential political interlopers. Was it possible Zach was getting sick of being one of those glorified gofer guys? Wouldn't that be something?

I weighed that against other realities. Zach had built a life with Judy. On the outside, he'd done all the usual family stuff—parent-teacher conferences and graduations, cleaning the gutters on his northwest side bungalow and grilling in the backyard. He looked like any other guy who worked his way up through a politician's staff. Apparently, he'd found some happiness with his family. I hoped so. It was surprising to me how much I wanted that to be true.

"Were you with Toland earlier, you know, at that fundraiser?" I asked.

Zach shook his head. "Nah, the regular guys covered that. I had to—"

"You had to *what*?" I interrupted, groaning inside.

"Nothing." Zach averted his gaze downward.

He couldn't—or wouldn't—say. That shady secrecy was exactly the kind of situation I imagined as the constant theme running through Zach's life. No wonder Illinois had ended up the butt of political jokes on late-night TV.

"Let me get this straight," I said, my thoughts racing, going from ho-hum business as usual to leftover shock that someone in my family was caught up in the ugly side of Toland's machine. "Marchand had no idea why you showed up at his house, and probably still doesn't. But you told him you didn't see anything and ran."

"Yes, that's right. Toland has me do this kind of thing all the time. He threatens people with state investigations, audits, bogus shit like that. He gets off on his enemies feeling harassed, you know, always looking over their shoulder."

"How far would Toland have gone with Marchand?"

Zach glanced at me, then looked away. "I don't know. Toland has…make that *controls* guys I don't even know about."

Good news or bad news? I couldn't say. *Maybe both.* "Back to the original question. How well do you think Toland knows Marchand?"

Zach bobbed his head and shrugged. "As far as I know, not well. But then, what the fuck do I know? Toland hates him, though, I know that. Once he saw him on TV opening a building downtown and muttered something about him being a little prick, an arrogant son-of-a-bitch. That's about as far as it went."

"Why are you here telling me all this?" I asked. "You don't have to. You could have kept the information to yourself."

"I'm not sure." Zach looked down at his hands. "Maybe I'm a little sick of delivering messages.

And, maybe I'm thinking it will come out any-way. Maybe it's better that you hear it from me."

A hush settled over my office. I stole a glance at Zach, whose shoulders drooped, making him look old and used up. But Zach's funk wasn't my business. Marchand was.

* * *

I walked into the lower door of my office building, phone in hand. Kenny called me before I could get to him.

"I'm heading over to see Charles," Kenny said. "Can you meet me there?"

Wanting to hear Kenny out before revealing what I'd learned, I asked, "Any special reason for today's visit?" I added a bit of inquisitive sarcasm in my voice.

"We have to deal with the Café Brauer night. The prosecutor is using it as an argument against bail. Seems like half the city saw Sandra, Charles, and Toland in the room, and almost everyone says it was a weird atmosphere. It was obvious some-thing was up."

"So what? Something's always up with cases like this. Do they think he'll take off for the Cay-mans or something?" I was half joking.

From the outset I figured bail would be high, but I also assumed Charles would jump through hoops and put up enough cash to be released.

"When they searched his home," Kenny said, "his passport was out in the open on a table not far from the front door."

That seemed a bit strange to me. Who leaves his passport out and open on a table near the door? I'd be keeping it in a safe area, unless I was stressed, not thinking straight and getting ready to run… and fast!

"So he was getting ready for a trip," I said. "I wonder where and why? For a guy like Charles, a passport alone isn't a sign he's going on the run." Most people in Charles' position put their faith in lawyers and juries and figured that if they did run, they'd get caught anyway. They were smart, even if desperate. "Besides, do they think he got his passport at the ready *before* he decided to kill his wife?"

"We've got a different atmosphere going these days," Kenny said. "Regular people don't much like rich guys—the one percenters—throwing money at problems and watching TV on their comfy couches while they wait for trial. Ankle bracelet or not. Right now, I've got a big argument on my hands."

"Well, okay, see you there."

On the drive to the jail, I weighed my options, starting with confronting Marchand. But the wiser part of me decided to be quiet about the early morning visit from a stranger curiously omitted from the police report. I'd wait to see if Marchand volunteered the information, or if I got the right kind of opening to challenge him. Marchand had no idea that the guy who showed up for that 4:00 AM visit was my brother. Why would he? He had enough going on not to make that connection.

Lunch with Zach hadn't been as strained as I'd anticipated, thanks to Zach's pride in his kids. He never tired of talking about them—and the grandkids he hoped he and Judy would have one day. For my part, I bragged about Maude, but mostly filled the time with stories about Janet, who needled me about Maude, usually accusing me of liking the dog more than I liked most people. Janet meant it as a joke, but I knew it was more or less true. I wasn't a loner by any means. I had plenty of friends and acquaintances, but true, my heart and soul ran deep for animals. They're so loyal, so pure, so much of what I wish people could be.

Once lunch was over, though, I admitted that seeing my brother left me unsettled in ways I didn't welcome. It wasn't just the way my brother had overpaid his debt to Toland. Sure, Toland squashed bribery charges against Zach, charges that could have meant a few years behind bars, but how long would it take to pay off that debt? It had been almost twenty years already.

The times in my life, long ago, when Zach was the only person I could rely on kept coming back to me. Our mother had worked two jobs most of the time, especially when she was married to my dad, who managed to get fired from every job he got. Showing up late day after day had a way of building bad will. Sooner or later, my dad was sent home permanently.

Odd... I never put that memory of my dad's failure together with my own rule about my staff coming through the office door every day on time. I could put up with watching trial news on TV as long as Wendy and Janet were in the office when I came in. It was a trust issue. Slacking off on time would signal slacking off on everything. Both women, being responsible types in the first place, never questioned that rule—they didn't push it, either. Only on rare mornings did I make the first appearance in the office. I preferred my morning at Granny's eating pancakes before diving into some research project.

I could call up a vague memory of Zach fixing me oatmeal in the morning topped with brown sugar to match my sweet tooth, and then dragging me along when he hauled our laundry to the coin-op a few blocks away. It wasn't that Mom didn't care. She could only do so much, especially when she waitressed at two different restaurants.

Watching Zach's face soften when he talked about Judy and the kids, I had to admit that no one could love a family more than Zach loved his. What irony. He'd broken a pattern that had plagued our family for a couple of generations. Of course, so had I, only I'd done it by not having a family at all. At least not yet.

I drove through the intersection and turned into the parking deck at the jail, fighting off the sinking feeling that washed over me every time I pulled in there. I went to the third level, since all lower floors were reserved for jurors, judges, and every-body else except lawyers or jury consultants. The air stank of car exhaust and fast food bags stuffed in garbage cans. Worse, I sometimes sensed the gloom in the very concrete of the place, as if the structure itself had absorbed years of stories, dreary at best, unspeakably tragic at worst. Lives gone wrong and twisted, or lost altogether. Survivors and victims struggling to recover. Attorneys, too, who overworked to exhaustion.

I jogged down the ramp, finally entering the well-lit building. Why had I done this—side-stepped into a criminal case? I hadn't thought about how bad I'd feel just pulling my car into an empty spot on the deck.

Kenny nodded grimly when the guard opened the door to the room with small conference room-style chairs, now beaten up old things from the '70s. I stood behind him, sending an unambigu-ous message that Kenny was in charge. Because of Wendy, I had a unique perspective on the Café

Brauer night. Regardless of my differences with Wendy in both style and temperament, I didn't doubt the accuracy of her take on the scene that had unfolded, based on what her friend said. Nothing I'd heard on the news contradicted her every contention about Sandra's behavior. Now, I wanted to hear Charles' side of the story.

Charles looked even worse than before. No surprise there. People in jail turn grayish more from the bad food than from lack of sun and fresh air. That's what I believe, anyway. From the look of Charles, the circles under his eyes, the deepening lines around his mouth, it was clear that money and prestige had no power to prevent a guy from gradually looking less and less vigorous and healthy.

"How are you doing?" Kenny asked, his voice both kind and concerned.

Charles shrugged but the tension was building to a crescendo. "How do you *think* I'm doing? Get me out of this hellhole! I didn't kill her! I didn't kill anyone! Christ, I hate this. I despise this place. My life's going to shit!" He waved his hand in the air. "I'm helpless in here. I can't fight this thing when I'm fucking locked up." He puffed out his cheeks and then blew out the air. Giving me a deep stare and lowering his voice, he said, "I want to *fight*."

Then quit withholding information and stop the petty lies.

I almost wished my hunch, usually pretty reliable, was dead wrong this time. I didn't blame Zach. He had no reason to tell me things that could end up backfiring on him.

"The bail hearing is next week," Kenny said, clicking open his old-fashioned, battered briefcase. "With a little luck, we'll get the judge to let you get out of here and give you some freedom until the trial. That's a lot better than this."

Relief crossed Charles' face, but his voice remained tense. "Yes, please, just please make that happen."

"Look, getting you out isn't a slam dunk," Kenny said. "You need to understand that."

"I know," Charles said, nodding and closing his eyes to acknowledge the truth.

"But you can help yourself, Charles. Give me more details about the fundraiser at Café Brauer. Our investigators are talking to people. The police are busy interviewing, too—they have a big team out digging around. Our people are hearing stories that are consistent."

Charles' features fell in resignation. "I know what they're all saying. I've told you it was a bad night."

"Seems so," Kenny said. "The prosecutors will argue that you were violent and planned this murder—that it was heinous and you're too dangerous, too much a flight risk to let out on bail. But that's what prosecutors do. Reality doesn't matter. They'll focus on the conditions just hours before your wife's death. We haven't found the counterpoint."

"What I've said is that Sandra was drinking more than usual." Charles glanced at me. "I would expect everyone there to verify that—she was drinking *a lot*!"

Annoyed with Charles' defensive tone, especially given what he was withholding, I said, "Again, *why?* By the time she went home—with you—she was tipsy, if we're going to be polite, drunk, if we're not. But a jury, any jury, will want to know what made her *appear* out of control? Why did she allow that to happen?"

Charles jutted his chin defiantly. "And, like I said, I don't know. Sandra was heartbroken over the recent dip in donations to the shelter. They had to take in more and more dogs and cats. She had to lay off a couple of employees and fill in with volunteers." Charles shook his head, visibly sad talking about Sandra and her passion for the shelters. "Sandra knew that they'd be picking up so many abandoned pets because their owners lost jobs and couldn't afford to keep them. It *broke her heart*."

I got it. I agreed with it. You know, dog and pet people get it, they really do. And those that don't understand these feelings, well, they probably never had a pet. Sad for them.

"But why that night?" Kenny asked. "Why did she choose to let her guard down *that night*?"

"Choose? She didn't choose," Charles said. "She hoped for twice as many people at the Café Brauer fundraiser. She hounded her assistant for updates on the number of pre-sold tickets. They couldn't make up the difference at the door. What looked to the press like a big crowd looked paltry to Sandra. She lived for her causes, man. Hell, she loved those animals more than she loved me!"

I nodded. I got that.

"And she'd done this before?" I challenged him in the same tone any prosecutor would at trial, especially if he took the stand, an unlikely event. "When donations were off, you're saying that she drank a lot and got loud and belligerent at her fundraisers or with her staff, but no one ever saw that happen before. Who can back this up?"

"They'll say her behavior was unusual," Charles said, banging his fist on the table. "I concede that. I'm telling you, she was exhausted—burned out. She'd been working too hard, not taking care of herself. She lost it."

"Like a breakdown?" I asked.

Charles frowned and tilted his head, obviously considering the word. "Sort of," he offered.

I wasn't buying the "my-wife-had-a-one-night-breakdown defense," ironically, even if it were true. That's because it wouldn't work. Few jurors would believe it. Besides, I knew Charles was leaving things out. That's what pushed me to be provocative. "And she didn't want you running for governor, did she? Wasn't she against you playing around in politics?"

Kenny shot me a warning look.

I threw up my hands. Anyone who took the witness stand would say this behavior was out of character for Sandra. Charles would either look guilty or, at best, appear to be indifferent. An inebriated, heartbroken woman fell down a flight of stairs to her death while her sober husband slept soundly in their bed. Sure. That's why they had to keep Charles off the stand. As for secrets, I respected the right to keep a secret, except when the secret keeper is charged with murder. Secrets weren't so good then.

"Toland arriving at the event changed the atmosphere," Kenny said. "It looked like the three of you were angry with each other."

Charles put up his hand. "No, that's not true. Leo liked to show up at Sandra's events now and again. Typical politician glad-handing. I don't know what happened that made Sandra go off on him like that."

Again, he doesn't know. "That's when an already bad situation escalated, though, right?" I asked.

"I think so," Charles said, rubbing his forehead, "but I've been over and over that night so many times it's blurred together. I can't remember the details anymore."

"And what's *your* relationship with Toland?" I asked. "How well do you know him?"

Charles narrowed his eyes. "I hardly know him at all. Like clockwork, he shows up for ribbon cuttings at my projects—he likes public appearances to bolster his image as a supporter of economic development. He needs a spotlight like vampires need blood. Mostly, he's full of shit."

"So no history with him, then?" I prodded.

Charles rubbed his nose as if it itched. "No."

"So no photographs of you two together are going to show up in a Google search—not big hugs or handshakes?"

"No—well, maybe some group shots. We end up at the same public events. That sort of thing. That's gonna happen from time to time," Charles said, lowering his gaze. "I didn't support the guy for governor. Plus, my company rarely used his firm. We hired other builders, and sometimes *they* used his company, but we never hired them directly."

Okay, that sounded reasonable. He'd covered his ass. Then why was he hiding the shared college? And that nose scratch he did...a classic liar's gesture. I like to think of myself as a pretty fair reader of body language. Although I was unconvinced the guy was a murderer, I knew he was papering over something. I'd make a point of watching my old pal Cooper Julien that evening. With these journalist types snooping around, maybe he'd have learned something, or at least picked up some hints about where the buzz about Marchard in the press was leading.

Chapter Seven

There were ruts and there were rituals, I thought, amused by the labels I created for the scene going on in front of me. The difference was entirely in the eye of the beholder, as they say.

Granny dragged deeply on her cigarette and blew the smoke sideways, like she did every day of every week. She drained her glass and dropped the cigarette in it. So, rut or ritual? On some days, I admitted it was a rut, but deep inside I needed that sameness, Christina's dull predictability, as a way to kick off the day.

"So, the prince and princess maybe weren't such a fairytale after all. Whaddya think about that, Professor?"

Surprised, I glanced at the newspaper still folded on the table. "You know I don't think anything, Christina. I haven't had my pancake yet. Don't mess with my rituals; could be going through withdrawal."

Granny pointed to the TV mounted in the corner. I expected to see CNN, or maybe even Coop talking, but instead, the local NBC affiliate flashed their breaking news banner, which interrupted the regular programming on *The Today Show*.

What now? I grumbled inside.

I wasn't ready to listen to talking heads commenting and arguing about anything.

"You'll see it sooner or later," Christina said as Alex approached my table through the clatter of plates and silverware clinking in the background. Granny's morning rush in full swing.

"All the stations are reporting that a Marchand divorce may have been in the works," Alex said.

I struggled to keep my facial expression locked in neutral. Another punch in the gut. Charles kept them coming.

"Oh, really?" I said sarcastically. "An anonymous source, I suppose." I glanced at the paper again, refusing to open it until I'd polished off the deep dish banana pancake Alex had set in front of me. My phone was off, but I had no doubt I'd see Kenny Baden's number on the screen when I checked messages.

"Okay, okay," Granny said. Then she downed another glass of scotch. "But, like you lawyers always say, sometimes things aren't what they seem."

I *almost* laughed at the cliché, but even though my mood had turned from neutral to foul, I loved my surrogate Granny and Alex too much to chortle at their expense. Besides, the gooey banana pancake was still hot and the aroma itself acted like a balm…almost. Damn Marchand.

I ate faster than usual, and then popped a couple of those candy-like antacids before opening the paper. Sure enough, the story beneath the fold, reserved for the news a cut below the main headline, *Rumors of Marchand Divorce.*

The opening line said it all: *Anonymous sources indicate that prior to Sandra Marchand's death, the high-profile couple had begun a legal separation after twenty-plus years of marriage.*

What had I said about loathing anonymous

sources? I read on. *Speaking on condition of anonymity, another source reported that Sandra Marchand appeared agitated and preoccupied in the weeks leading up to her death. Another person claiming to be close to the couple confirmed that Sandra had spoken to an attorney about the terms of a separation. Charles Marchand is currently charged with his wife's death. Marchand's attorney, Kenny Baden, had no comment on these rumors.*

Blah, blah, blah. Of course, Kenny said that. I expected no less. I felt a bout of paranoia coming on. What did Kenny know about this? Another trip to the jail was in order.

On the way to the office, I turned on the radio and heard a report from a local radio station, a broadcast from the sidewalk in front of Kenny's office building on LaSalle Street. I especially hated information from anonymous sources when I suspected it was true.

"Come on, Maude, let's make our entrance again with our usual flair," I said, coaxing her out of the car and leading her to the front door. I suppressed a chuckle. There was something about a trial—any trial—that called for sending in a few clowns.

Only the faint sound of Janet clicking her keyboard keys penetrated the otherwise quiet office. No radio, no TV. What a relief.

With her tail wagging, Maude padded around the corner of the desk for her ritual visit to Janet, who never failed to have a dog treat in her palm.

"Good morning," I said, looking beyond Janet to see Wendy at her desk staring at the computer screen.

"Mornin', Matt," Janet said, avoiding my eyes.

I smiled to myself. Whatever the two thought

about the latest Marchand revelations, they'd decided to keep it to themselves. What a novelty. Or, amused with my own reasoning, maybe they hoped I'd reveal the identity of the stranger who'd visited yesterday. But that wasn't going to happen anytime soon. Zach and I had information Marchand still chose to withhold.

I waited to get into my office before I returned Kenny's call.

"I'm sick of this, Kenny, and you must be, too. This guy's past drips out and forms a big stain on the case. He's feeding it to us as he pleases. I know he's powerful and rich and supported his wife's good causes, and a few of his own, but who *is* this guy?"

"I'm setting up the bail hearing," Kenny said, ignoring my question. "We're expecting Dr. Baumgartner's review of the autopsy report later this morning. We'll see if he finds anything we can look into. And we'll have the full toxicology panels, too."

Beneath the terse tone, I detected concern.

"What about the house?" I asked, "Any sign of forced entry?"

Not knowing the answer and thinking of Zach, I added, "Or any signs of a third party lurking around the house—anything left behind—boot prints, fingerprints?"

"Nothing."

"Okay, well, keep me posted. I know you have priorities here, but I'm thinking ahead to juries and how people think," I said. "Secrets, pending divorces…it all looks bad."

I ended the call and slid the phone across my desk. But even if I had trouble shaking the cobwebs of the Marchand case out of my head, Potash Pharmaceuticals awaited.

Wendy and I had a mock trial to plan. Who was I kidding? Wendy, with some help from Rick, had done all the work. All I'd had to do was review the plan and sign off on it.

Chapter Eight

I'd begun wishing I'd never heard of Charles and Sandra Marchand. The specter of divorce hanging over Charles' head, plus what I knew to be secrets he was keeping, left me with a wave of sadness washing over me every time the couple came to mind. And that was often these days.

I had trouble shaking off thoughts of Charles and Sandra on my way to a party, where I'd see some old friends. Part of the cure for what ailed me.

I don't mind admitting that Haskell's death had not only thrown me off my life plan, it had been the one thing that sent me to a shrink. A less than healthy childhood, a louse of a father, and a brother lost to the semi-underground of Illinois corruption hadn't done it. My dead client had. In the years that had passed, I'd more or less weaned off the sleeping pills the shrink had prescribed long ago. If I hadn't, I would have detoured and gone home instead of to a party and slipped into oblivion for a few hours. I'd learned that sleep, while it had its positive side, didn't solve problems. When I woke up, Charles Marchand would still be in jail, and I'd still be wondering what his real deal was. That's the risk—emotional risk—I took when I'd agreed to be part of the Marchand case.

I drove east to Lake Shore Drive and headed north as dusk settled over the city, closing its day under heavy gray clouds. My long-time friends Graeme and Catherine Manzo had renovated a 1920s stucco and brick house, saving it from demolition in Andersonville. Like me, the Manzos lived in an old neighborhood on the rise and on its way to trendy.

After circling the block twice looking for a big enough space for my truck, I gave up and squeezed into a space a couple of blocks west. Even it was large enough by barely an inch or two, only in Chicago would that few feet be considered worthy enough to call a parking place.

I grabbed up the bottle of wine off the passenger seat. Having left Maude at home, I had the perfect excuse to slip out early. Damn it, I hadn't arrived and I was already planning a getaway. Giving my head a quick shake to drive thoughts of Charles away, I picked up my pace and hurried down the street.

Catherine's face lit up when she opened the door and saw me standing on the porch. Rather than greeting me with words, her several years living in Europe led her to affectionately kiss both my cold cheeks before leading me into the foyer. She took the wine from my hand, grinning. "Of course, a Chilean red. You remembered. It's my favorite."

I nodded, all too willing to take credit for intentionally bringing her favorite wine. I remembered nothing. It was all dumb luck. I hung my coat on the single empty hook in a long row. The rest were double laden with coats and jackets.

"You are so lucky you showed up tonight,"

Catherine said, pushing her thick blonde hair behind her ear. "If you hadn't, I told Graeme that we'd have to come banging on your door and demand to see you." She planted one hand on her hip. "So, how have you been, Matt?"

"Busy," I said, nervously rubbing my hands together as if they were cold. "But glad to be here, even if I can't stay long."

"Oh, don't tell me. Let me guess. You have an early meeting."

I chuckled at her long-suffering tone. "Well, that's a given. But really, it's Maude. She's been home alone all day. I have to get back and walk her."

Catherine hooked her arm through mine and led me into the large living and dining room, dominated by the soft light from a large crystal chandelier and candles burning on the mantle where a fire in the fireplace made the room glow. Guests stood in clusters of twos and threes, drinks in hand. The scene should have lifted my spirits, and maybe it did a little.

Scanning the room, determined to be a good guest, I spotted Graeme, who stood at a table that at the moment was set up as a bar. I waved and snaked my way through the groups of people until I reached him. My old law school friend suddenly felt like an oasis in the desert.

"How's it going?" Graeme asked. "Or, maybe I should ask if it's gotten crazy yet."

I shrugged. "More or less crazy. We're working on a big pharmaceutical case." I glanced behind me, making sure that no one was close enough to hear. "And then there's the Marchand situation," I whispered.

"No need to whisper," Graeme said with a laugh. "I doubt there's a person in this room who doesn't know all about the Marchand case."

I grinned, hoping it didn't look as false as it felt. "I bet they all have an opinion, too."

"You bet." Graeme handed me a glass of my favorite red wine, a Charbono, the nearly unheard-of grape from Napa, but the best in my opinion. "In fact, if you mingle in the room, you'll soon see it's a major topic of conversation. Lots of Sandra fans milling about."

I rested one shoulder against the wall and sipped the wine.

"I knew Sandra was admired," Graeme said, shaking his head, "but I've not seen such an outpouring since Princess Diana died." He chuckled. "Okay, I exaggerate. But at the risk of sounding sexist, it seems like this is mostly a women's deal."

I rolled my eyes, but offered no comment. Maybe it was Wendy's influence, but I understood why she and women like her felt the loss of a local champion.

Graeme put his arm on my shoulder and nudged me deeper into the room. "Let me get you some food and introduce you around. We've got some new folks in the house tonight. And you've got an excuse not to say so much as one word about the Marchands."

"That's one advantage to being involved in it," I said, glancing at my watch. "I've got fifteen minutes."

Graeme frowned deeply to show he didn't appreciate my time limit.

"How about you come down my way and we'll have dinner at my favorite neighborhood Thai place? Great peanut sauce there," I said. I wanted to see Graeme and Catherine, I really did. But coming into this crowd had been a mistake. My gut burn told me so.

"You name the time," Graeme said, as he lifted his arm to wave in more guests standing at the door.

"Go, go," I said, "be a host. I'm fine here." I pointed to the buffet. Graeme was quite the chef. "I'll help myself."

In the few minutes since I'd arrived, the number of people in the two rooms had more than doubled, and so had the noise level. I ignored the platters of food on the table and negotiated my way through the crowd, excusing myself as I bumped shoulders and arms on my way to an empty space in the foyer next to the door. Once I got there, though, I kept on going, grabbing my coat and slipping out as others were coming up the stairs. I left without saying goodbye. Somehow, I figured Catherine and Graeme would understand.

* * *

Later that night, after a neighborhood walk with Maude, I picked up a burger at a diner nearby, took a few antacid tablets hoping to take the edge off the certain acid to come, and drove to my office to spend a few hours on trial strategy. Or maybe just to brood. I was way too restless to sleep.

Over the past couple of days, I'd checked Lourdes Ponce's tweets, but she'd been oddly silent on the subject of a Marchand divorce. She'd moved on to another scandal, this one involving an alderman and a connected state senator with whispers of pilfered campaign funds. No big deal.

I parked my car and walked with Maude to the entryway of the buildings, entering the security code to open the lower door after hours.

Halfway in the door, I heard a male voice call my name and spun around, startled. I hadn't seen anyone on the street.

"It's me, Rick." He stepped into the pool of light coming from the door.

"Man, you scared me. What the hell are you doing lurking around in the dark?"

"I found some things you'll want to know about," he said without preamble. "Somebody is going to come up with this stuff—it's not hard to uncover. I'm giving you a heads up."

"Come on up," I said, my heart picking up speed.

Rick followed me into my office and opened his laptop. "I don't have an iPad yet," he said defensively. "I sure liked using yours, though.

Too broke to get one, I'd bet.

"It must be important. Otherwise you wouldn't be hanging around my building this late. Why didn't you call me?"

Rick let out a quick laugh. "I don't have your cell phone number. How's that for a good reason. I communicate through Wendy. I've got the firm's number. If I showed up here during the day, I'd run into Janet and Wendy. As for the reason I couldn't call the firm's number, that's about staying in the background here—like you wanted."

"Got it," I said. "I appreciate it. Have a seat, tell me or show me or whatever." I let Maude loose and she sniffed Rick's shoes in her usual curious dog way.

"This goes back to Donaldstone College. The thing is," Rick said, "it's a weird place."

"I don't know that I'd agree, but I'll leave it to you to explain."

"Even somebody like me," Rick said, "whose

parents work *retail* jobs, managed to help me put together some college loans, work-study programs, and odd jobs to pay for UW-Madison's tuition. For all the good it's done me, I got myself a decent degree. It seems odd that these two guys would end up at the same small college in a backwater town on the Mississippi River."

Rick raised his eyebrows and shrugged. "I'm just saying. If that was all, then so what? But something else came up."

I got that gut flipping feeling again. Fast and hard. I listened to Rick tell me how he'd searched the college yearbooks and archives, refining everything along the way. I waited for the bingo moment. Playing in the same charity basketball game four years running in college wasn't going to do it. Yeah, sure, it was another Marchand lie, at least as far as I was concerned. But failure to disclose didn't make the two men buddies.

The two weren't in the same fraternity. Toland was a big frat boy, Marchand went independent. They were both in the tutoring network for the townies the same year. Rick produced a photo of both guys standing with the group of twelve tutors, eight of them girls—no bingo there, either.

"Rick, are you sure any of this tells us anything about Marchand, other than not wanting to be linked with a corrupt governor he hoped to unseat in the next election?"

"It's the hunch thing, boss," he said with a grin. "Just be patient a little longer."

I managed.

It was funny, though, looking at these pictures. Toland was known to come from money yet all the college photos showed him with a scruffy look, one that didn't look intentional or studied. Marchand, whose background was fuzzier, looked preppy and like a member of the country club set.

"Toland looks like he grew up in my sorry neighborhood," I remarked, never shy about pointing out my humble roots.

"Whatever they look like," Rick said, "Donaldstone isn't a golden-kid college. It's more of a last-chance place, definitely a C-list school."

He frowned.

I understood why, or thought I did. Here was this kid who went to an A-list college but couldn't afford an iPad and worked temp jobs. Toland and Marchand, C-list degrees notwithstanding, lived in mansions and dripped money.

"I figured the school records could only tell me so much, but the school is in Birchwood, Illinois. The college *is* the town. So, I searched there, and this is what I found."

One click and the page popped up.

"This ain't tutoring programs or political demonstrations," he said.

The twice-weekly *Birchwood Citizen*. Rick brought up the index for September. Ho-hum headlines. *Donaldstone Defeats Prescott 17-0... Donaldstone Hosts Economic Symposium...Senator Paul Simon holds Q & A with Students.* I could barely keep my eyes open. I held my tongue.

October, same old stuff. Some girl named Allysa is the homecoming queen. Looks like the only football game Donaldstone won that year was against Prescott. An article about drinking on campus...three kids picked up for DUIs over the previous weekend...alcohol education classes open at the student union, townies welcome. *Another banner month.*

Maybe November would be more exciting. "Uh, Rick, are you sure there's..."

"Wait. I'm showing you what the usual fare is."

"Okay." I clamped my mouth shut.

West Side Story opens at Donaldstone College Theater in the Round...no Marchand or Toland in the cast...*Donaldstone Medical Clinic offers New HIV/AIDS Information Program.* No Toland or Marchand mentioned there, either. Another click.

Student Reported Missing.

"A girl didn't show up for her Monday morning class," Rick said. "Couldn't have been too remarkable, even if no one had seen her...unless..."

Click... *Parents Arrive on Campus as Probe Widens.*

Next headline... *Search for Missing Co-ed Launched in State Park.*

"Holy shit. Is this really what you're hinting at?"

"Right here," Rick said.

Missing Girl's Body Identified.

"Her name was Nancy Bayless and she was found dead at the edge of the river, but that's not where she died. She died of alcohol poisoning earlier."

"And you can link Marchand? Or Toland? To the dead girl?"

"I don't know. Maybe. But like I said, what I did here was amateur hour for research," Rick observed. "How do you know what the state's investigators are uncovering?"

Like I always say, I like evidence, but I don't like secrets.

Chapter Nine

Charles spun around, his eyes wide and fierce. "I loved my wife."

"I never said otherwise," I shot back.

Kenny and I sat across from Charles in the same room where we'd met with him a few days before. The barred windows and cinderblock were depressing enough, but the rickety table added the exclamation point to the dreary scene.

"This latest gossip isn't going to help us get you out of here," Kenny said with a huff.

Charles bounced the side of his closed fist on the table. "Sandra and I would not have divorced." Wham, another hit on the table for emphasis. "It's the truth. All of this garbage is coming from an unnamed source. The judge can't use that, can she?"

"Not all the pieces of information are unnamed," Kenny said. "Some came right from your house. You had an itinerary of a trip to Belize—"

"Reservations for two," Charles blurted. "One for me, one for Sandra."

"Airline reservations make you look like a flight risk, especially when you were due to leave town two days after Sandra died," I interjected. I'd held my fire and let Kenny do the talking, but Charles was smart enough to understand that passports and printed-off copies of their reservation confirmation didn't look good.

Kenny waved him off. "Look, Matt, we can deal with a planned vacation. We've got the person at Charles' firm who's handled travel arrangements for him and Sandra for a decade now. I'm not worried about that." Kenny paused. "It's what the search turned up in Sandra's office that looks bad, real bad."

And Charles claims he knew nothing about any of it.

Ironically, knowing what I did about marriages and secrets, I figured there was about a ninety-percent chance Charles was telling the truth about being in the dark. That left the one-in-ten chance the guy was lying. I scoffed to myself. Only I knew for sure that Charles was still hiding something. His link to Toland for starters, but once the lid was off, I expected more secrets to spill out.

Charles pinched the bridge of his nose, a gesture that emphasized his defeated look. And Marchand was not the type of guy who easily accepted defeat.

"How the hell do you think I felt when Kenny told me about Sandra's schemes, seeing her handwriting in her notebook, the entry in her date book? I tell you, I didn't know about any of it."

I had a hint of sympathy in my gut. Assuming he was telling the truth, it had to be tough to find out that your wife had created a list of her personal assets in a notebook, the account numbers of her own brokerage accounts, the value of her stocks and bonds, even her checkbook balance. She'd flipped the page of the legal pad and listed jointly held assets, and the names of three hotshot divorce lawyers, two men and a woman. It was the woman who made her way into a timeslot in Sandra's datebook, squeezed between a board meeting at the shelter and an afternoon appointment with her personal trainer.

"She never told you she wanted a divorce, never hinted at it, not even once?" Kenny said, pencil poised in the air over his notepad.

"*No!* How many times do I have to tell you that?" Charles raked his fingers through his hair as he flopped back in the chair.

"Well, it goes without saying that if Kenny can get you bail, you won't have a passport and you're less of a flight risk. Sandra's lists and her appointment with a divorce lawyer speak to guilt," I said, "not to mention the public behavior that every newspaper and all the talk shows devote airtime to day in and day out."

"It's not proof of anything," Charles said, shoving the chair back and standing. He went to the window, although the grime and bars blocked the sun from trying to come through. "Besides, that one night was the only incident of questionable public behavior in almost 20 years of marriage. It's absurd to think we'd have divorced."

Charles wasn't the first guy whose wife had blindsided him. I got that, but to claim you never caught a whiff of trouble coming struck me as naïve. Extremely naïve.

"So, you're saying everything was going along fine as always," I said, "and until the night of the fundraiser she'd seemed normal—hadn't changed a bit."

Still staring at the window, Charles said, "Damn it, I told you she'd been tense. Worried about donations, stuff like that." Charles shook his head. "Hell, maybe she was unhappy in ways I didn't know. She could be distant, preoccupied. We were busy all the time."

He turned away from the window, his forehead wrinkled in a thoughtful frown. "Some people could look at us and think we lived separate lives. But that wasn't true." He waved toward the window. "People out there wouldn't have seen it, but we got away by ourselves, more often than people knew. We have a little place over in Michigan where we'd disappear for a weekend now and then. The trip to Belize was all about giving us a chance to unwind—reconnect."

Reconnect? What a word. So loaded with underlying meaning.

We barely talk, so let's take a little trip.

I believed what his troubled expression told me. Oh, sure, he was withholding something—and it was big—but I think the guy believed in his marriage. Loved his wife and all that. The only trouble with my feelings about it was that little bumps here, little secrets there, could lead to the end of Kenny's case, and that would mean failure for Barlow & Associates, Trial Consultants. It would also mean that a stubborn man would end up in jail for the rest of his life. I believed push would eventually come to shove. Few people hung on to their secrets, if giving them up could keep them out of prison.

Kenny sighed as he reached into his briefcase and pulled out a file. "Let's deal with the autopsy."

One piece of mixed news. Sandra's blood alcohol level was just above the legal limit. Not particularly high, but elevated enough to argue for a fall. Kenny could paint a picture of a woman found at the bottom of the stairs, whose death could be explained as caused by a brain hemorrhage resulting from a blow—the fall itself.

True, a higher alcohol level could have provided a stronger argument for accidental death. Now the prosecutors could—and would—argue that being what Charles described as tipsy, right at the line of the legal limit, couldn't account for a dead-weight fall.

"I know this is hard for you to hear, Charles, but the autopsy is inconclusive. Both sides can use it."

"Do you have photos?" Charles asked.

Kenny glanced at his briefcase. "We do, but it isn't necessary for you to see them now."

I watched as Charles stared at Kenny's briefcase. I could almost see the part of Marchand's brain that was catapulting him toward looking at the photos. I'd already seen them in court, plus the crime scene photos. The prosecutors would milk them for everything they were worth. Soon enough, Charles would be forced to look at the photos.

"You'll see them another time," Kenny said, standing. He grabbed his coat, and after telling Charles he'd see him at the bail hearing the next morning, we left.

Once again, I felt like I'd abandoned someone in a cold, dark place.

I fell into step with Kenny, and we walked in silence down the hall. The discordant prison noises, the slamming doors, metal hitting metal, a man hollering to get someone's attention, all made me wince.

Wind whipped through the parking garage, making me even more eager to get to my truck.

"I'll see you tomorrow," I called out as Kenny and I headed in different directions.

Kenny stopped walking and turned to me. "You don't have to be there, Matt. You know that."

"I want to be." I couldn't have explained why, especially since I spent half my time angry with Charles and his secrets, and the other half wishing Kenny had never called me. But once in, I never did anything halfway.

What really bothered me was the knowledge that after talking to Rick, I harbored a few secrets of my own.

Chapter Ten

"I must be crazy," I said, pulling my truck into the lot behind the Birchwood Library. "I should be sitting with Charles in his townhouse at this very moment, drinking good coffee, probably eating deep dish pizza. Engaged in deep thought about the case." And interrogating Marchand, too, maybe asking him about the messenger in the night. I hadn't yet figured out how to bring that up without disclosing more about my brother than I cared to.

"Guess you're glad you got the guy sprung, huh?" Rick said.

"Yes," I said. "It meant a lot to Kenny, too."

In the end, the bail hearing had been anticlimactic, as they often are. The passport, the tickets—for two—somehow didn't seem so sinister to the judge. Besides, it wasn't like he was free to wander the neighborhood, not with an ankle bracelet. Marchand would be running his business—and his case—from the friendly confines of his home. It was all over in less than 30 minutes.

* * *

With the passenger door half open, Rick nodded to the unimpressive—really ugly—square, yellow brick and glass building set back from the street on the north end of the two-block Main Street. Not exactly one of the stately old Carnegie libraries, this facility lacked any distinctive flourishes.

"I guess this is the end of Birchwood's downtown," he said with a laugh.

"Kind of a stretch to call it downtown," I added.

From the time we pulled off the highway and ended up on the two-lane road into town, I fought with regret over agreeing to this trip with Rick. If I hadn't believed we'd uncover facts I could use to confront Marchand, I'd have refused out of hand. All things considered, I didn't think I'd find anything that would tell me much about his guilt or innocence. This was more about avoiding nasty surprises.

Rick wiggled his eyebrows in feigned intrigue. "But there are secrets to be uncovered here. Starting in that ugly library."

"Not exactly the Library of Congress, or even Chicago's Harold Washington Library we're used to," I said. "If you want to know the truth, I never willingly visit little burgs like this. I'm already bored."

"Yeah, well, Birchwood isn't exactly Madison, Wisconsin, either. Now *that's* a campus."

Impressive or not, according to Rick, the building held a collection of local and regional newspaper articles that might hold the clue to whatever happened that bound Toland and Marchand. *If they were bound at all*.

I wasn't as sure as Rick was about that, but a day of snooping around held enough promise that I figured a trip to Birchwood was worth it. Rick agreed to keep it between us and not slip up and mention it to Wendy. From what I could tell, the two were spending some time together outside the office. She described them as friends. Rick went on a little more about her, even using the word *special* to describe her. I didn't think much of it, as long as the work got done. What they did on their own time was none of my business, but I was curious. As for Rick's penchant for investigation, I intended to make use of it.

Rick had logically argued that if he'd found a link between the two men with a few clicks of the mouse, then surely the prosecutors could uncover the same information. I only needed to find out why it would be relevant. I was quite certain that a past relationship between the old college class-mates had nothing to do with Sandra's death.

Five hours in the truck with Rick had worn me out. Something about computer games left me drained, as if I couldn't quite grasp what Rick's imagination conjured up. I wondered if Wendy, more than a decade younger than me, understood the guy.

We walked into the library and went straight to the desk, where Rick introduced himself to the librarian, an older woman with a cap of straight gray hair and a pleasant smile. He pointed to me and said, "And this is Matt. I called the other day and spoke to a librarian named Amy Clausen, and asked if we could have a look at your collection on the Donaldstone co-ed case."

The woman's expression was friendly, but impassive. Apparently, looking at the collection was no big deal.

"I'm Amy. Follow me," she said, signaling to her colleague that she needed to leave the desk. Her low-heeled shoes clunked loudly on the wooden floor in the nearly empty building until she reached a metal door.

"I hope you don't mind basements. We keep the materials on that case in a special collection, viewed in the reading room downstairs. Under our fair use policy, you might be able to make copies of the material—we have a readymade set you can work from."

"We're collaborating on a legal analysis of campus safety programs for women," Rick said when we reached the bottom of the stairs.

I'd come up with that justification for our interest. I deliberately intended to play the role of Rick's sidekick on this venture, not the other way around. Low-profile was my motto on this side trip.

Rick lifted a file from his battered attaché. "I came across this case back when I was in college," he lied, "when I was working on a paper on campus deaths...surprising number of 'em. I'm still interested."

The librarian nodded. "Many people are. Mainly, I suppose, because..." She paused and looked away. "What I mean is, no one has ever come up with an explanation for this tragedy."

She led us past some ancient wooden file cabinets and shelves with glass doors and a state-of-the-art copy machine, and on through another door to a small reading room with only a table and chairs and a row of empty shelves.

Amy pointed through the door. "This is where you can set up your laptops. I'll bring the files." She turned on her heel, but stopped abruptly. "Oh, and by the way, we call it the *Nancy Bayless* matter. The girl had a name." She disappeared into an alcove at the end of the room.

Chastised, I admitted to being so focused on

the link between Marchand and Toland, I'd nearly forgotten that the reports of a missing girl—*Nancy Bayless*—had triggered Rick's suspicions.

"Not exactly the conference room in your office," Rick whispered, glancing around the sparse room.

"No flat-screen TV," I added. No Maude, either. I hated like hell to do it, but I'd left her with a neighbor, an older woman named Samantha with a loft on the other end of the building. Sam, as I called her, picked up a few bucks dog sitting for those of us who worked crazy hours. Much as I felt like I was missing an appendage when Maude wasn't around, I liked knowing a real fan was treating her to some sweet talk and walks in the neighborhood.

Amy came back with a file box and plunked it on the table. "Here you are. All we ask is that you put aside the papers as you use them. We prefer to put them back in order ourselves." With that she turned and headed back up the stairs.

Rick dug into the box, lifting out half a dozen folders. "There's not all that much here, not when you consider this is about a campus murder."

I pulled out the chair across from Rick. "We don't know that. It's a campus disappearance. It's an unexplained death…well, not even that. It's a death with unexplained circumstances. Beyond that, it's all speculation—apparently."

I picked up a file. "Why are we here? How come we couldn't do this online?" I asked, more to myself than to anyone else. The first folder I'd opened contained little more than copies of newspaper and magazine articles.

"Simple." Rick, who had argued strongly and ultimately convinced me that a trip in person was worthwhile, said, "We might find things in the files I hadn't come across on my own online. I'm still convinced we will."

He shuffled through the files and came up with a copy of a paper with handwritten notes. "Bingo! Like this." He pushed the paper across the desk in front of my face.

I studied the sheet, confused, but curious. "It's graph paper, and there's no name on it that tells us who wrote it. So we don't know who created it."

I ran my finger across what looked like a timeline, with names marked on the graph. "First impression, it's a list of about twenty people placed in no particular order on a graph. Suspects? People targeted for interviews, maybe?"

The writing was small and not particularly neat, but two names stood out. "Here's Toland—in a slot labeled Wed. Wednesday," I said, tapping Toland's name, "and whaddya know, here's Marchand's name in a slot labeled Thurs. Thursday."

I pushed the page back across the table, and Rick touched both names, too. "Wonder what it means." He frowned. "One hunch, though. I don't think the graph paper has any significance."

Detective instincts or maybe just a hunch without context. "What do you mean?"

"Just that it looks like someone tore the page out of a notebook because it was handy. These are just notes, not a chart or a graph."

I knew what he meant, but couldn't comment on its importance one way or another. "Let's dig in and see what else is here."

I shuffled through the files, my anger at Marchand growing by the minute. I had to hide it, though. I didn't want Rick getting the wrong impression. Like that maybe I believed Marchand killed his wife. Odd, some of the facts pointed that way. But I didn't buy it.

"These are articles from the local paper," Rick said. "I've looked at most of them online, but I'll sift through them again."

From the pile, I pulled out a soft-cover binder about an inch thick. "This one's marked *The Student Voice*."

"The college paper," Rick said. "They still haven't archived all their past issues online, at least not the ones from decades back. Makes no sense. They've archived the issues from 2000 on, but they're way behind on the other ones—and they go back to the 1920s. Can't figure that out."

I saw Rick's point, but it wasn't relevant to what we wanted to know. Besides, having paper in my hands brought out my old-fashioned streak. I liked the idea of looking through hard copies of the paper. "I'll start with these."

My hands trembled. Fear, a dash of excitement maybe. I hadn't been close to this type of mystery in a case for a long time. A cold case, presumably. The facts and figures of liability cases were interesting in their way, but the sense of mystery was missing. I glanced at Rick. He'd opened his laptop, but I pushed mine to the side in favor of a legal pad and pen.

The student newspaper articles were in chronological order, the world of digitization hadn't yet reached this old-world school, starting with the first day Nancy was reported missing. Rick and I speculated why no one seemed to worry when she wasn't seen around campus for a couple of days. Not that it was surprising the students would be blasé about a girl who didn't come home one night. These kids weren't old folks living in some retirement home. Nancy wouldn't have needed a wellness check. Well, actually, the facts ultimately showed she would have been better off if she'd had someone watching out for her. When a student *did* start to wonder about her whereabouts, they kept it an on-campus issue. By that time, though, it was too late.

I jotted down the names of two student reporters, Aaron Nagasaki and Freddy Prigge. Between the two, they'd eventually interviewed enough students to fill out three distinct camps. One group thought Nancy disappeared because she planned to leave school, but others openly said they smelled foul play. The smallest group claimed no hunches and admitted they didn't know anything. Typical survey results, more or less. Only a small group of people were willing to admit they didn't have enough facts to form an opinion. Ergo, that's why in the previous weeks, only a small number of people polled, maybe fifteen percent, were willing to admit they didn't know whether Charles Marchand killed his wife. Ironic, too, and a little depressing, at least from the point of view of a jury consultant. At that point, no one, not even those of us involved in the Marchand case, had enough evidence one way or another to make any kind of definitive declaration.

As I leafed through the pages and followed the passing of the days, more Donaldstone students moved into the foul-play camp. By the time Nancy Bayless' parents arrived on campus, few students believed the senior had disappeared because of school pressure or a break-up with a boyfriend. She was an A and B student and didn't have a boyfriend—at least not that her roommate or any other friend knew about.

"No mention of a boyfriend anywhere in any of the files," Rick commented, breaking the silence in the room that had begun to make me feel far away from civilization. He glanced at the sheet of graph paper that sat between us in the middle of the table. "Last names only, so we don't know how many are boys."

"Or if they all are." I had no idea. "I can't just write off the idea that Marchand and Toland both show up on a scribbled list of names. And during a missing-person investigation. We ought to start calling it that—an investigation."

"Those two were seniors, too," Rick said with a shrug, "but we don't know if that means anything, or gives us clues about the list."

Turning the page, I saw another piece by the two student reporters. "Look at this headline… *Frat men stick together.* This is where Toland comes in, huh? Didn't you say he was a member of the Pi Delta Alpha fraternity?"

"Exactly. But not Marchand. He never joined one," Rick said. "From what I could tell, he was sort of a loner. I think he was the kind of kid who didn't have money for frat crap." Rick let out a snorting laugh. "Like me. Hey, maybe I've got something in common with Marchand after all." He smirked. "I'm just sayin'."

I snickered. "Right, but Toland? He's a different animal." I didn't want to say it out loud, but I kept thinking of Leo as one of those babies born clutching a gold-plated rattle in one hand, and the other hand stretched out to grab more.

Marchand? Now, he oozed class. Even in a jail jumpsuit, his pallor gray and his hair shaggy, he had presence that money couldn't buy. No doubt that helped him at the second bail hearing. He looked like he'd slipped from the womb with an impressive résumé. But nothing in his background pointed to that. Just the opposite. "Funny, isn't it, that Toland came from money," I said, musing out loud, "and he looks like a typical political hack from the southwest side. Who would guess he started out a preppy boy from Wilmette, Illinois?"

"That's what got to me about this Donaldstone connection in the first place." Rick laced his fingers and stretched his arms out in front of him. "I still can't say what it has to do with a murder charge."

"Nothing," I said, amused at how effortlessly Rick assumed the burden of a detective. Too much CSI, or maybe he was like folks who confused online research with the painstaking work of actually solving a crime. "I can't tell you how many times I've come across this or that isolated fact and can't resist following it down a logical chain." I shrugged. "And what did I uncover? Zero. Nada. No new conspiracy or some nefarious plot. I'm left with nothing but a big, fat coincidence."

"I suppose that could happen here, too," Rick said, not looking up, "but somehow I doubt it."

The kid held his ground. I had to admire him for that.

I went back to turning pages and reading, following the student reporters in their quest for answers. Then I saw it. "Oh man, I can't believe they published this in the student paper."

I turned the paper sideways so Rick could see the photo of Nancy—dead, where they found her. It wasn't that she looked so bad. In fact, she was fully clothed with no obvious wounds, her natural beauty still evident, even in death, and buried in a shallow grave near the river. That made sense since alcohol poisoning was listed as the cause of death. That wasn't the mystery.

"Fucking disrespectful, if you ask me." Rick smirked. "But no one is asking me."

"Shock value," I said, my voice rising, "and that

lights a fire under people. I suspect they wanted to hit hard. A girl on their campus not only died, but someone left her by the river, probably hoping she'd never be found."

Rick grimaced, but quickly shifted back to shuffling through a new file.

"Hey, this might be related to the graph paper," Rick said, breaking the few moments of silence that had settled in. "It's somebody's notes. Take a look." He slid the paper across the table.

I scanned the handwritten lines, a kind of shorthand with quote marks around key sentences and phrases. "I'd guess these are interview notes." I lifted all the pages, one by one, looking for a signature, but none appeared. "Seems amateurish, as if the person didn't think these papers would ever see the light of day. I suppose they could belong to one of the reporters. I'll comb through these and look for Toland and Marchand."

Waving a sheaf of papers in front of me, Rick said, "I'll read the transcript of the girl's journal."

I stared at the pages he held, almost queasy. In cases past, I'd read diaries and journals left behind. Even day planners and ordinary calendars had an aura of privacy around them. Sometimes I felt like a voyeur. I'd found clues and used them when they helped my client and tilted toward exculpatory. I'd kept quiet about the details when they tilted the scale the other way. In both cases, I despised taking apart the private and personal.

"Whatever that girl scribbled on those pages wasn't meant for the likes of us to see," I said. Restless, I stood and took a turn around the table and back again. "It's so easy to forget that cases are about *people*. The drug company cases are about people, too, but while I'm studying the data and Wendy's attitude surveys and piecing together our jury strategy, everybody turns into a number—statistics—or a disease. At least until the lawyers turn the numbers back into men and women."

"I guess juries can't sympathize with numbers, huh?"

"No, they can't." I laughed, but it wasn't that anything struck me as funny. "We've turned the so-called jury-of-our-peers into numbers. We take away their names."

"But that's to protect them. Right?"

I nodded. "Media frenzies and nut cases have demanded we keep these folks anonymous, at least until they decide to reveal themselves. I don't blame them for being fearful."

Pointing to the journal, I said, "Wendy told me that teens and youngish women seldom let high school and college diaries survive. They usually toss them out, happy no one saw their shallow thoughts. At least, that's what Wendy claimed."

"Makes sense to me. Kinda like burning sappy poetry you write to a soon forgotten love when you're a kid."

"Exactly." Thinking back on some bad rhymes of my own, I laughed out loud. I considered my writing some version of haiku. No one ever read them to prove me wrong.

Rick stared at the stack of papers, photocopies of the journal. He winced, as if in pain. "I'll keep that idea in mind when I go through these. You know, I'll remember how young she was."

I nodded and glanced at my watch. "Whoa, we've been here for hours already. We've got a long drive back."

I shook off the need for a nap and dug into the interview notes. I knew little for certain, other than the alcohol poisoning finding from the medical examiner, but she sure as hell hadn't walked to the river—at least according to the report. She died somewhere else, so the question became: who carried her to a secluded cove on the bank of the Mississippi River, kicked aside some dirt and mud, dropped her body, and then scattered a few leaves and twigs over her? Cold bastard, whoever he was...or she, I supposed.

Looking at the notes and comparing them to the names on the graph, I started to make connections. Someone, maybe one of the reporters, had interviewed over twenty students, mostly seniors, about the last night Nancy had been seen alive. Most of it matched what Rick had already gleaned from the local papers. I shuffled through the pages faster until I found the two names I was looking for on pages headed Wednesday and Thursday.

"Here they are, the two pages. Other stuff in the file might be important, but we don't have time today." I read the notes, decoding the abbreviations in the makeshift shorthand. "Toland admits to attending the party, but Marchand denies being there." I looked up at Rick. "Why would that be news? He wasn't a member."

"But Nancy had fallen for the bastard," Rick said, thumping the page in front of him.

"Marchand?"

"No, Toland. Listen to this...it's dated two weeks before the party on the night she died. *I've wanted Leo for almost four years. Now's my chance.* Then, three days later, *Shitty date. I thought he was taking me into town for dinner, or maybe out of town. Unlike me, he's got wheels. Went to the Ritoff Bar instead. I was mad at him, but tried not to show it...drank too much.*"

My stomach churned as Rick turned the pages. "There's more here along the same lines. She sleeps with him in her dorm room, but he leaves right away. She's mad about that, too. And the last entry is that he invites her to the frat party, and she's going, but she says here, *I don't want to stay long...will try to get him away alone and confront him.* That's on Friday. She's last seen at the frat party—we think."

"According to the notes," I said, "we're in sync right up to the point where Toland claims Nancy left without him. He stayed and slept alone in his room. But whoever wrote these notes put brackets around the last sentence about watching Nancy leave and then added two big question marks."

"Too bad that doesn't prove anything," Rick said, his voice raging. "I've always had a feeling that Toland is a fucking crook and now we know he was a son-of-a-bitch with women. I wouldn't put a murder past him. I'm not a lawyer, so I don't have to care about the truth...I know what I need to know in order to confirm why I don't take to the guy."

I raised my hands in a show of surrender. "Okay, okay. I don't like Leo Toland, either, but I didn't come here to convict the guy of murder." Something in me wished I could, though.

"I defended the worst kind of wife beater years ago when I was taking cases. The bastard had served 18 months for breaking her jaw, knocking out her teeth, and leaving her nearly blind in one eye." I sighed. "Three weeks after he's released, the woman is found dead, shot in the ear in a convenience store bathroom. They arrested the guy, ex-husband by then. But not so much as a skin cell of his DNA was found anywhere on her or around her. Then again, no one knew about DNA back then. No witnesses, either. No gun found. But no alibi. Still, the jury acquitted him, and the public turned against defense attorneys—again. Turned out, a guy on the run for manslaughter in Florida shot her." I shook my head in disbelief, mostly at this guy's unlikely bad luck.

"And the moral of the story is?"

"A victim can bump up against more than one bad guy. My client wanted to kill his ex-wife. He wasn't even sorry she was dead." I shrugged. "But someone else fulfilled his wish. He didn't commit the crime, and I didn't have to like him to defend him."

I picked up pages of notes, keeping my eyes on the paper. I didn't enjoy talking to Rick about that case, or any other, from my past. So often the past was too painful to revisit. I could have lectured Rick for hours about what my life had really been like. Or maybe I could've filled him with a collection of entertaining anecdotes. Once I went down that road, I might not have been able to focus on a decades-old college campus tragedy.

In the nearly silent room, Rick went back to the diaries and I dived deeper into the interview notes, scanning each page the old-fashioned way for Toland or Marchand. Minutes later, my gut jumped.

"Bingo." I lifted the page. "Go back way before that party. About a month. See if she mentions Marchand. According to these notes, a couple of people claimed Marchand tried to date Nancy, and she refused to go out with him. And talked about it. That's probably why he was interviewed in the first place."

Rick shuffled through the pages, scanning as he went. Then he stopped and thumped the page with his index finger. "Sure enough. Here it is. Two lines, about two months before she ended up dumped in the mud. *Charlie Marchand is sniffing around again. I said no to a date—I'm setting my sights on Leo. Can't stand Marchand...too boring, a boy scout. Mom would love to see him coming through the front door."*

I flopped back in the chair and clasped my hands around the back of my head. "When you're twenty-two, boring is bad. But, hell, that's beside the point. The only link we found was two lines in a damn journal that matches Marchand's interview notes."

"Toland's don't match. Right?"

"No, Toland claimed he dated Nancy twice," I said, "but denied having sex with her."

"No sign she had sex that night."

"It was a damn sloppy investigation, anyway," I replied. "And they didn't have the investigative techniques then that they have today."

"Not bad for one afternoon." Rick waved at the pile of papers in front of me. "We still have the names of the two journalists."

"I think a Google search is in order."

"Here?" Rick asked.

It had been many long hours since I'd polished off a plate of Granny's pancakes. I needed more fuel, especially for the drive home. "I'm thinking some diner or café with Wi-Fi that also has giant burgers and greasy fries."

Rick grinned. "Okay, time to regroup. But wouldn't it be something if those kid journalists, who would be Toland and Marchand's age now, after all, had some hunches we don't know about?"

"I'm counting on it," I said.

Chapter Eleven

I shook Charles' outstretched hand.

"Thanks for coming the other day," Charles said.

From the warmth in his voice, I knew Marchand meant what he said. The rich Chicago development icon had done a fast turnaround. No longer haggard and gray, his stoop was gone, and now he stood to his full height. He'd brought in a stylist to trim his hair, too.

"I'm glad you're here," he said, "both of you."

I wonder if he'd feel that way if he knew about what I'd uncovered, the facts he was stubbornly hiding.

"We've got some issues to discuss," Kenny said, "but we won't keep Matt here."

We'd agreed that I didn't need to be at every visit with Charles, not with the mock jury soon to start for the Potash pharmaceutical case.

"Why did you come, then?" Charles asked, giving me a pointed look.

Taken aback by the question, I kept my voice casual and said, "No special reason, except wanting to see how you're doing, now that you're back on your home turf."

I had to choke down words that would challenge him, blow a big hole in his secrets, but something kept holding me back. How much did I want to know about my client? I had limits. Besides, I was waiting for Zach to get my message so we could arrange a meeting. I hadn't even talked to Kenny about Nancy Bayless and the Marchand-Toland connection, whatever it was.

Charles' expression softened, almost to the point of sadness. "I was hoping you could tell me what you think my chances are."

"We don't have the case assembled," Kenny interjected. "We're looking into a couple of Sandra's past stalkers. The police have turned over files, and our investigator is following up."

"That's good," Charles said, his voice lighter. It hadn't taken Charles long to press Kenny to look into the two men, and one woman, who, according to Charles, had temporarily turned Sandra's life into a hell of fear, 24-7.

Feeling at loose ends, probably because I didn't like holding back information from Kenny, I drove home to pick up Maude before going to the office. Janet had the day off, and Wendy and Rick would be analyzing the results of the first couple of days of the mock jury for Potash Pharmaceuticals. I'd put in an appearance earlier that day, and I'd do it again tomorrow.

With any luck, I'd still have some time alone in my office to read through very dull drug-testing data reports, compliments of Wendy and Rick, who, I conceded, were a helluva pair. I sensed them getting close, too, at least as friends—pals. The romance side wasn't likely to pan out. I couldn't say exactly why. When it came right down to it, Wendy had a stubborn independent streak. She'd worked hard for me, earning my trust. She knew her way around a case, and she was developing into a jury consultant in her own right. She was certainly worth every penny I paid her. Despite her *carpe diem* talk and celebrity watching, she had her feet firmly planted on dry land.

Rick struck me as bright, good at nosing out facts. Maybe a little quick to jump to conclusions, but there was nothing as valuable as being wrong sometimes to retrain that tendency. I knew enough about Wendy to have figured out that her penniless past held no attraction for her—Rick's hand-to-mouth lifestyle was enough to flash a stop sign in front of her eyes. It shouldn't have mattered to me, but it did. Maybe because Rick had turned into an asset I wanted to expand, not squander.

Once inside my apartment, I scooped up the dog, holding her like a baby and rubbing her stomach. "Come on, Maude, let's get to work. You've been lazing around the apartment all morning."

When I put her down, she tilted her head and stared at me, as if trying to comply with whatever I was asking, if she could only figure it out.

"Hey, my friend. Your main job is keeping me company, so that shouldn't tax you too much."

I settled Maude in the car, or more accurately, she forced her way onto my lap in between my chest and the steering wheel—not a safe position, but some days, it was the only way Maude would have it.

"Okay, Maude, earn your keep. What else is Charles hiding?" I knew about the possible divorce, Donaldstone College, a mutual acquaintance with a girl who died.

Silence. All Maude did was tilt her head.

"Don't be shy. You can speak up anytime." I chuckled, but honestly, I found talking to my dog more entertaining than about eighty percent of the conversations I had with mammals walking on two legs. "We're a good team, Maude," I said, "and that's because you always agree with me."

The office was dead quiet when I opened the door. I considered going directly to my office, except that Maude zipped through the open conference room door. Wendy and Rick sat at opposite sides of the table, Wendy with a yellow legal pad in front of her, Rick scrolling through something on the computer screen.

Wendy looked up and grinned when I knocked lightly on the door. "Hey, Matt. Guess what? Our jurors say your side's winning the case, hands down. How 'bout that?"

Relief. I liked it, but it left me an opening. I don't make a lot of snap decisions, but in that moment I did. "Uh, that's good news." I stepped into the room and although it was completely unnecessary, I closed the door behind me. "We need to talk."

Wendy's face scrunched in concern that bordered on fear.

I immediately regretted my words. I had nothing to report with any certainty. I'd seen enough people for one day. If I'd kept my mouth shut, I could have passed my afternoon interacting with data that couldn't talk back. I could have admired the charts and colorful graphics Potash Pharmaceuticals supplied.

Wendy cleared her throat. "What is it? You sound serious."

I glanced at Rick, who stared at me expectantly. "I assume you haven't said anything about our excursion."

"No, of course not. You asked me to keep the information confidential."

"Excursion? Information? Okay men, what's

going on?" Wendy asked.

"I need to talk to you about the Marchand case. New developments." I paused. "Could be new developments. Uh, but probably not."

"That clears everything up," Wendy said, lifting her hands in the air in a show of exasperation. "Tell me what's on your mind."

I pulled out a chair and motioned for Rick to move from the end of the table and come closer. "This is between all of us now. The three of us, and only us. Understood?"

Wendy's wide-eyed expression had gone from concern to alarm.

"Here it is, straight. Rick and I took a trip to Donaldstone College on Saturday."

Wendy's mouth fell open, but only for a second. Then she leaned to her side and pulled a legal pad from the pocket of her attaché-style handbag sitting on the floor next to her.

"Whoa…no notes. Not yet." My heart thumped fast. As if heartburn wasn't bad enough, now I had palpitations. There I was, in my once fairly orderly office, working with Janet and Wendy to handle civil cases, which, while not exactly riveting, paid the rent, oh and bought the dog food. Now I was nearly crazed with irrational fear that I'd put it all at risk. Because of Marchand and Kenny. Yes. But Toland and Zach figured in, too. All because I'd gone off on what would probably turn out to be a wild goose chase. Or not. And that wasn't good, either.

She slid the pad to the side and looked anywhere but at me. "Force of habit, I guess."

Rick sat impassively, but I changed that by asking him to explain the digging he'd done.

He sat a little straighter in the chair and took Wendy through the facts as we knew them, starting from the curiosity about Charles' background.

Rick shrugged. "I don't know why, but I wondered whether he was Big Ten or Ivy League. It bothered me that he'd gone to a dinky little college, but then I saw Toland went there, too."

Wendy turned to me, her eyes still saucers. "So, our sleazy governor and Mr. Prince Charming were buddies?"

"Wait, we can't jump to that conclusion," I said. "We don't know that."

"We know they were at the same commencement ceremony a few years back," Rick pointed out. "I found the picture of them sitting on the stage in some old newspaper story. Not a big jump to figure they knew—still know—each other."

"Why am I just hearing about this now?" Wendy frowned. "And more to the point, what does it have to do with anything?"

"We don't know," I said quickly, before Rick could start speculating. "Maybe nothing."

"Why did a picture in a newspaper prompt a trip to Donaldstone College?" Wendy asked.

Of course she'd ask that. Any inquiring mind would.

I filled in the blanks, going over the Nancy Bayless case, including the notations in her diary. "For a couple of months, she turned down Marchand for a date. She set her sights on Toland. Then the last time anyone saw her alive was at a frat party where she drank a lot and passed out somewhere in the house—probably never woke up again. The coroner said she died from alcohol poisoning, but no one can say how she ended up on the river bank."

Wendy's wide-eyed look was back. "Are you saying someone moved this girl's body, and no one knows who?"

147

I nodded.

"My money's on Toland," Rick said. "He dated her, acted like a real asshole, too."

Money? What money? Fifty cents? What happened to the starving artist persona?

"Both guys were interviewed by the police," I pointed out, "and no one ever drew any conclusions. At least none that anyone pursued or tried to prove. Seems like the local police dropped it. Nancy's death only got attention because the students themselves kept prodding."

"Did the police, or the reporters, try to implicate Charles?" Wendy asked.

I waved her off. "No. Nothing like that."

"What does Charles say about his connection to Toland?" Wendy asked, a frown forming between her brows.

Rick looked at me expectantly again.

"I haven't asked him," I said.

Wendy's frown deepened. "Why not? I know for a fact that you hate loose ends."

The time had come to spill some beans, much as I didn't want to. "So far, he's had nothing to say. He claims he barely knows Toland. And mostly from Sandra's big charity events."

Wendy nervously fidgeted with the top edge of the legal pad. "So, he hasn't told you the full truth, huh? When do you plan to ask him what the link is?"

I took a couple of seconds to figure out how to answer that. I still hadn't called Zach, and Wendy knew nothing about my brother. Until I talked with him, I wouldn't be dealing with this issue with Charles. Not that I could piece together why that was so important. I just knew it was.

"I will talk to him," I said, shifting in the chair. "Maybe *confront* is a better word. If for no other reason than to find out why he's not opening up about this college connection. He hasn't said anything to Kenny, either."

The look she cast my way bordered on sarcasm.

I tapped my temple. "I know what you're thinking. But Wendy, you have to listen to me on this. I don't think Charles had anything to do with Sandra's death."

"You're consistent. I'll give you that," she said with a one-sided grin.

"Kenny's investigator is looking into the three stalkers, two men and a woman, who threatened Sandra. And those are just a few that got the most attention. Sandra dealt with her share of crazies."

"Really?" she asked.

"You look surprised," Rick said, "but you told me that back when you worked for her, she got hate mail or letters from people asking for money all the time. That there were always a few needy types hanging around trying to impress her and worm their way into her circle. They wanted to have a little of her life rub off on them."

"True." Wendy stared off into space for a second or two. "Why all the secrecy? Wouldn't the prosecution team snoop around Charles' past, hoping to find stuff on him?"

"I assumed so, but I can't see any evidence of a probe that reached down to that little town on the river."

"There was a librarian, Amy, at the public library," Rick said. "She said people study the Bayless case for all kinds of reasons. But of course, she wouldn't have told us if the Cook County prosecutors had contacted her."

"How do you know that?" I asked.

"Because librarians are a lot like lawyers. Their patrons are like clients," Rick said, as if stating the obvious. "They have a code, and one of the rules is they don't talk about who reads what or discuss other people's research."

That sounded weird. I wondered if it was true. "Good observation. I hadn't thought of that, but you're right."

"There's a shitload of data in those library files," Rick said. "It would take days to go through it all."

"Which reminds me," I added, "Rick is going to track down the student journalists. We want to talk to them in case…" I admired those young people—not only for having the guts to put the stark photo of Nancy Bayless on the front page of the student paper, but for continuing to investigate the case long after the national press had lost interest.

I glanced at my watch. I needed to reach Zach. As if on cue, Maude pulled herself up and stretched her front legs, finishing the exercise with a wide yawn.

"One more thing," Wendy said, her eyes on Maude. "Two more things, actually."

I met her eyes. "Okay, shoot."

Wendy raised her eyebrows. "So, what are the divorce rumors all about? Are they true?"

"Marchand denies them. Beyond that, I can truthfully say I know nothing."

Wendy nodded, trusting me to tell her the truth. I might avoid answering a question, but once I agreed to, I told the truth as I knew it.

"Okay, next question, Matt. Are you sure Marchand wasn't at that frat party…you know, maybe hoping to see Nancy?"

I shrugged. "All we can say for sure is that no one interviewed could place Marchand there, and he wasn't a member of a fraternity anyway."

"He didn't seem like a party-guy type," Rick added with a snicker. "He was probably like me in college. Too broke to party."

Wendy grinned, her posture more relaxed now. "You and me both."

"And me," I added with a laugh, surprised by the realization. "Look at us now. Solid citizens contributing to society."

"Well, you guys are," Rick said, quickly adding, "but the jury is still out on me."

All three of us groaned. How many times had I heard that pun?

Chapter Twelve

I smiled to myself as I closed my office door. For the moment, Maude preferred to stay with Wendy and Rick in the conference room. She did that now and then, like a preschooler having a playdate. I was relieved, too, by the tone of the conversation with Wendy. For whatever reason, she'd either put her personal suspicions behind, or she'd come to her senses and admitted to herself that Charles may have been accused, but he sure as hell wasn't convicted. Maybe she harbored doubts herself. I hoped so.

I fished in the top drawer for the number Zach gave me. A private line, he'd said.

I punched in the digits and then listened to the voice mail, puzzled that the number reached Judy's phone. That's what he'd meant by his private line? I identified myself, and said, "Have Zach give me a call, please."

I almost added some words of urgency, but thought better of it. Judy probably had enough worries about her husband. I barely knew her, but as a young woman, she'd stuck by Zach when he'd been caught bribing an alderman for favoritism on a contract. She'd had a good future back then, or thought as much. Zach's contracting firm had gotten off to a great start. When that went bust, she'd had to put up with his secretive life, a flunky...ouch...in a sleazy pol's world. There had been a note of pride in Zach's voice when he talked about her owning a salon now. I was glad for that. Even with all their troubles, the two had stuck together.

Data. Lots of facts and figures. The stats hadn't disappeared while my mind was on Nancy Bayless and her bad fortune. That's what I considered it. Millions of people drank and passed out, only a few died. Of that small number, how many went missing? Nancy Bayless was an exception. Like the rare person who was damaged by the drug in question in the Potash case. Not even one death could be legitimately linked to it. Not that the plaintiffs would concede.

Looking at the graphs, it was easy to see why the mock jury was siding with us, Potash. My pal, Leann, must have been pleased to hear the comments from the handpicked men and women. Lots of positive comments were based on Potash's fancy, eye-catching, attention-holding charts and graphs.

"Okay," I said out loud, "where are the holes? What will the opposition guys say about all the stats?" I knew plaintiffs were determined to show fudged data. That's what the case turned on. I had to take at least one more trip back to the graphs and charts and not just prove that theory wrong, but show Potash as a healthcare company, a community-minded corporation with a mission, not a money-grubbing multinational.

Finally lost in the detail of Wendy's reports, I jumped at the sound of the phone. I glanced at the time. That was fast. Zach had gotten back to me in less than an hour.

"How about grabbing a quick lunch?" I blurted. "Today. At Lakeview Market?" Was I getting paranoid? Toland made me afraid of the phone? New business for me. I feared many things—most notably, another colossal failure. I'd never feared wiretaps or other forms of snooping. Now I wasn't so sure. For all I knew, Toland could have spent taxpayers' money watching my every move during my trip downstate with Rick.

"I could meet you about one o'clock. I gotta finish up a couple of things."

What things? "Sounds good. See you in a couple of hours."

With that, I ended the call, conscious of the hush in my office. I spent so much time in the quiet of my office cave. It was usually all right, but not today.

* * *

I slipped into the booth at the back. For a place called Lakeview Market, it was a dark, grimy sort of place. Wendy once quipped about expecting drunk bodies to be carried out the back door. We'd laughed. Unfortunately, her observation rang true. Zach had been parked in a booth there long enough to have finished half a mug of beer.

"You were hungry, huh?" Zach said, smirking. "Needed lunch right away."

"Very funny." My big brother always did have a sarcastic side. We both did. I never was sure why, but maybe it kept us laughing about our sorry dads and our long-suffering mom.

Zach gulped back a mouthful of beer. He scanned the area around the booth—for all of a second. Then he leaned forward. "Hey, before you say anything, you need to hear something."

My heart picked up speed. "Oh? What's that?"

"Nothing bad…don't be scared. I'm keeping an eye on your girl and the other kid."

"My girl?" It could only be Wendy.

"That gal who works for you, and the kid with the bad suit."

How the hell... "Why? What's up?"

Zach picked up an oversized laminated menu, the kind that was mostly pictures on six or eight pages. He opened it, but instead of pretending to study it, he again looked around him, presumably to peruse who might have been seated near us in the last ten seconds. Then, the waiter headed our way to take our order, delaying his answer.

The Lakeview Market was known for burgers, and Zach ordered one. I knew its corned beef sandwiches were almost as good as the ones the more famous Manny's Deli served up. I asked for mine on dark rye, and decided to be prudent and ordered coffee. Zach pointed to his beer mug.

Zach waited for the waiter to disappear down the next aisle before he spoke. "For one thing, you and that kid are snooping. For another, your girl knew Sandra, and Leo did, too."

Hardly a big deal. I waved off that last bit of information, but still noted it in my brain—kind of transferring it, so I could recall it and see if I was missing something.

"So, you're watching me, too?" Had Zach followed me out of town—on his own or because Toland told him to?

"Yeah, I'm keeping an eye on you," Zach whispered, leaning across the table. "What's up with you going to Birchwood and hanging around Donaldstone?"

Damn it. "Funny thing, Zach, I was about to ask you questions in the same ballpark."

Zach shrugged. "Go head and ask."

"What do *you* know about Leo's time at Donaldstone College? Has your boss said anything about his frat house, his college years? Anything related to that time in the Gov's life?"

Zach frowned and propped his elbow on the table, resting his cheek in his palm. "I was down that way, to that college in the boonies. A few years back. Leo was giving a talk there at graduation."

There went my heart again, thumping harder, making me aware that when it came to Leo and Charles, I went into hyper-alert mode. Maybe, though, we were getting somewhere.

"You went with him?" I asked.

"I was like his body man that day." Zach let out a quick snort. "You know, like Reggie and Obama. I carried his shit around. Made sure he got his coffee and the bag of candy he munches on all day."

Big difference. Reggie was a big-time college basketball guy, who used his job with the president as a stepping stone to something else, like grad school and a book deal. My brother's body man job was all part of the dead end he'd been trapped in for years.

"So, what did the governor say about his alma mater when he was a VIP guest?"

Zach stared off into the restaurant as if gathering his thoughts. When he turned back to me, he said, "Funny thing, for once Leo was kind of quiet that day. Not all bluster and bragging."

I filed that away, with other odd impressions and facts.

"Elaborate," I said, forcing myself not to mention Nancy Bayless. Not yet, and maybe not even that day.

"I remember him calling himself a fuck-up, not that he used that phrase. He admitted he was a rich kid with every privilege he could name, and he still fucked up at college. He went on and on about his own kids, their good grades. He told me once he hoped his kids wouldn't end up at Podunk U., like Donaldstone." Zach scoffed. "He couldn't say that out loud that day on the stage."

"He's got two girls, right?"

"Yeah, and one of 'em is off at some fancy place in Ohio, but it sounds like it ought to be in Florida."

"Miami University," I said.

"Yeah, that's the one."

Zach and I both flopped back against the back of the booth while the waiter put our plates of food in front of us. Hot greasy fries with the corned beef...I shouldn't have, but I did. I was honest with myself. I'd pay later, but used the medication as an excuse for indulging.

"My own kids did okay, too," Zach said, raising his voice back up to normal volume. "They stayed in town. One went to Northwestern, the other is at DePaul."

"That's good," I said, meaning it.

"It sure is." In an instant, the gleam of pride in his eyes was replaced by a subtle darkening.

Regret, I'd bet. Still, whatever he'd done, he'd made his punishment for a stupid mistake count for something.

"Did he say anything about his fraternity...you know, talk about the other guys in the house, the parties, that sort of thing?"

Zach shook his head. "Not that I recall. He was kind of serious."

"Real serious or fake 'I'm a serious public servant' attitude?"

"Ah, I don't know what was in his head—I don't think about it much." Zach grinned. "But even on his best day, I'd never describe him as a public servant. More like an actor on top of his game. He might even believe his own bullshit sometimes."

I couldn't have said it better myself. I'd tried to figure out how to ask the next question, but not be too obvious about what I already knew.

"How did he react when he saw Marchand on that dais with him?"

Zach's brows shot up and his mouth turned down. "Yeah, I figured you knew about that. The best I can tell ya is that Leo acted like he didn't know him. I think I saw him shaking hands with him, as if they'd just met. How do you do, and nice to meet you and all that."

I filed that away. It more or less matched Charles' account.

"But, remember, Matt, I wasn't paying much attention to who he shook hands with—which was everybody." Another Zach smirk. "I was shuffled off to the side with the sound guys. The real security team was nearby. My big job was keeping track of the portfolio that held the speech and his suit jacket. He took it off when he put the robe on."

"You mean, Marchand and Toland didn't talk, stop, exchange a few words, like guys who used to know each other. No back-slapping or big grins."

"Not that I saw. I wondered what Leo thought when Marchand got his honorary degree…for whatever that's worth down in Podunk…and he made a speech. Not half bad, either, you know, about not letting where you came from stand in your way."

"Marchand is kinda like us," I said, certain Zach would get my meaning. We lived in a crummy apartment in the worst housing in an almost middle-class neighborhood. The city was like that. You could own a pretty nice house back in those days on streets that looked good on one end and bad on another. Not that we owned anything. Our mother managed to keep us in a four-room place, a basement apartment, really, although they called it a garden apartment. To be fair, not a bad place all in all.

Zach's eyes flashed with recognition, as if he could picture Marchand as a kid. "I didn't pay much attention, but I remember Leo saying something about getting a good education at public schools and that little place in the boonies. My words, not his."

"Did *you* happen to talk to Marchand?"

Another headshake. "No reason to. I'm serious, little brother, I was along for the damn ride. I kept Leo company in the car going down there. He's a big White Sox guy, da Bears, da Bulls...we talked about small shit. I used to do those trips all the time. Joanie, Toland's wife, was always busy with her own causes and she hated most of that stuff—sitting in the hot sun all afternoon. Ha! Not a chance she'd have come along to sit through a graduation."

There were worse things, I supposed, than keeping Leo company. That didn't sound as dreary as showing up at house doors in the middle of the night to deliver messages. Riding in the governor's limo and holding on to his suit jacket had to have been a much easier day.

Leaning in closer and speaking in a low voice, Zach launched into amusing stories of Joanie Toland—Mrs. Toland to Zach—traipsing through the county fairs all summer as Leo built goodwill and made stump speeches, even in the years he wasn't up for reelection.

"I heard them argue a few times," he said. "She talked about eating fat and sugar crap and sweating in the sun. 'I'm sick of spending my whole summer dehydrated,' she'd yell."

I laughed at the falsetto voice Zach used to imitate Toland's wife.

"You should have heard Joanie on the subject of what she called 'farm animal stink,'" Zach added.

"I can imagine." And I could. I'd been downstate on cases a couple of times when the fairs were in full swing—complete with corn dogs and cotton candy and stuff that was basically as Joanie described it, fried dough and sugar.

"Speaking of wives, what about Sandra? Was she there with Charles?"

Zach laughed. "Oh, yeah, she was there all right. Now there was a woman that made her guy look good. Charles mentioned her and pointed to a row of chairs on the side where she sat. I think people seemed to know who she was, other than being married to him. He smiled big when he talked about her."

I smiled, hearing my wistful tone when I said, "So they *looked* happy?"

"They did, but then, I was used to seeing Joanie and Leo putting on an act for the public, too. I can only tell what I saw, not what happened when they got home."

"Fair enough."

Zach frowned. "What? Did you hear stuff about 'em? Not so happy even back then?"

"No, just the opposite. Up until a couple of weeks before she died and she had separation papers drawn up, no one has said a bad word about them as a couple."

"No prostitutes or girls on the side? Powerful guy like that?"

"Nope." The one area where Charles had no trouble inviting scrutiny was in the area of women. Hell, he wanted his phone records checked. He welcomed his emails combed.

"Something doesn't add up," Zach said. "That's what you're thinking. And he's still not brought up the stranger at his door in the middle of that night."

"Not a word."

"If it means anything, Toland or the other guys, the security folks I rarely even see, have not asked me anything. Once the news broke about Sandra, Toland covered his tracks…plausible deniability and all that."

I took a big bite into my sandwich and Zach concentrated on whittling down his pile of fries. Despite the reason I was there, it was okay, Zach and me sitting together over lunch. Why had I made such a point of avoiding lunches exactly like these? I almost couldn't remember. I still had a few items to cover on my agenda.

"How long has Toland been tailing me—and Wendy and Rick?"

Zach's arms shot up. "Whoa. You got this wrong. Toland doesn't have anything to do with this. *I* know some guys. I've piled up a few favors."

That was almost too easy. By asking the question exactly that way, I'd caught Zach off guard. "You're doing this on your own?"

"I got it in my head to keep track of things after the last time we…" Zach glanced around "…had our brotherly lunch."

Things. "Are you going to keep it up? Keeping track of us, I mean."

"I am, and the less you know the better," Zach said, his tone flat. "You didn't suspect anything before. Pretend you never heard me talk about it now."

I thought of Wendy and Rick. "But you don't *know* anyone is in danger, right?"

He shrugged. "Let's just say I'm being cautious. Maybe overly cautious."

He knew about my trip to Birchwood. He'd once been on the campus with Toland. He was there the day that picture of Marchand and Toland was taken.

"One more question. When you were with Toland that day of the graduation, did he mention a girl? A dead girl."

"No." Zach frowned. "I'd *remember* that."

"But he acted different," I said, confirming what Zach had said earlier. "Expressed some regrets about his life? That sort of thing?"

"That's fair to say." Zach drew his head back and gave me a pointed look. "What dead girl?"

I kept my mouth shut while I weighed how much I should say. It wasn't much of a competition. Zero kept flashing in my head. "Nothing to report at the moment. I'll let you know when, and if, it's important."

Zach's expression turned skeptical, but then he picked up like we were typical brothers out for lunch. "So, how's that mutt of yours?" he asked, a devilish grin spreading across his face.

"Ah, Miss Maude, my favorite subject," I shot back. "Now you're talking!"

Chapter Thirteen

So much for secrets. How did a smart guy like Charles think he could face a trial with his life on the line and believe he had the ability to pick and choose the facts *he* wanted disclosed? Odd, too, that in the end, it was Toland who was caught off guard and forced Charles to talk about a man he obviously loathed.

After lunch with Zach, I considered telling Wendy and Rick they were being tailed and let them know what Zach was doing, on his own, to keep an eye on them. And on me. I thought better of it, though. Zach was a piece of my life too difficult for easy explanations, not to mention why he'd taken it upon himself to keep an eye on me and people associated with me.

Odd, too, that I wanted to keep Zach *for* myself, as well as *to* myself. I hadn't felt comforted in my relationship with Zach since I was boy under the protection of my fearless older brother. That was the thing about the way Zach's life turned out that had always left me sad. The fearless kid had compromised his future out of fear. In terms of pure potential, it hurt to even speculate about what kind of life he and Judy might have had if Toland hadn't permanently planted a boot on

Zach's neck.

But now, that glimmer of the old Zach came back. No matter what happened in the future, I'd already resolved that I'd bring my brother out of the shadows and into my life. Maybe even get to know his kids. Hell, I had friends. I had plenty of people to invite to my house for a potluck Thanksgiving or Christmas dinner. I never wanted for company, because I had a large and interconnected "family," although not by blood. And they were like family, but without the crazy stuff that goes on with relatives who cause trouble or make demands or borrow money they never intend to pay back. When it came to actual family, Zach was it. My only sibling, my only blood relative.

I was thinking about that one morning a few weeks after my last lunch at the Lakeview Market. Chicago had quickly passed from full-blown spring, which had left Janet sneezing and sniffling and griping about pollen and her annual bout with allergies. We'd moved into summer, which had led to Wendy finally perking up. That day, I was due in court, but I'd still taken Maude for a spin through Lincoln Park. Marchand and his troubles had receded, while jury selection for Leann and the Potash case had moved to the front burner.

I opened the office door and let Maude scamper over to Janet, but Rick stuck his head out of the conference room and said, "Hurry up. There's something you should hear."

Toland's image was on the TV screen. Wendy stood to the side with a remote in her hand. From what I could see of Toland, it looked like an ordinary press conference to me. What a contrast, though, between Leo and Charles, essentially two successful men of the same age. Leo had a doughy look—on the big screen his skin looked pasty—and he had the bulbous nose of a guy who drank. Not that I'd ever heard rumors about it, but his rotund body and puffy face didn't serve him well. I had a hunch donuts were more likely to blame for the belly than beer. I laughed inside. Joanie might not have gone for corn dogs and funnel cakes, but I could see Leo laughing in his "just one of the guys" way as he accepted a plate of greasy, dripping state fair fare.

"There's nothing more I can add," Toland said to a reporter named Becky Cianci, a woman I recognized as one of the gaggle who'd covered state politics for years.

Add to what?

"Wait," Rick said, as if reading my mind, "we'll fill you in if he doesn't."

Cianci piped up, "Then to confirm, Governor Toland, you say you have no relationship with the accused Charles Marchand today, and you..." she flipped a page in her notebook... "have only, quote, a passing recollection of Charles as a college classmate, end quote."

So that's how this would finally come up, not through Charles at all.

"That's correct."

"But the night before Sandra Marchand died you attended her fundraiser at Café Brauer? Can you confirm you had no interaction with Marchand that evening?"

"Other than saying hello, I did not have an extended conversation with Mr. Marchand."

Covered his ass there. "Extended" was in the eye of the beholder.

"Were you aware that Mr. Marchand and Sandra Marchand had a public argument?"

"No, I was not." Toland lifted his hand in the air, a gesture meant to prevent another question from intruding. "This is what I noted, no more, no less. And let this be the last of any probing into this area that's of no relevance to any of the critical issues we're dealing with here in Springfield. I observed that Mrs. Marchand seemed agitated and not like herself, at least in the way I had seen her at many public events, her fundraising gatherings in particular. I'd always found Mrs. Marchand charming, generous, and gracious. As I said at the time, her death is a terrible loss to this city and the entire state. That's all I'm going to say."

"What about your campaign, Governor Toland?" a reporter shouted from the back of the pack. "Were you preparing to campaign against Charles Marchand? Who do you believe will be your likely opponent?"

"I'll comment about my campaign when there's something to say, this isn't the appropriate time or place," Toland said, an indulgent grin appearing. "Besides, at this point, no one has announced his or her candidacy, so I'm certainly not going to speculate. That's your job, not mine."

"Give the guy credit," Rick said. "He knows how to respond to a question without answering it."

"He wants his comments about Sandra to be the story," Wendy added. "Makes him look like a gentleman. Not a guy whooping it up because his rival is up on a murder charge."

Good call. I smiled to myself, though. The cat was out of the bag. I groaned. I was channeling Janet again. Now I had every reason to call Charles, who'd been out of the news for several weeks. That was likely to change. Soon.

* * *

Charles—and Sandra—had lived the good life, all right. It wasn't only the townhouse, although that was part of it. I navigated one of the few diagonal streets cutting into a gentrified neighborhood of townhomes on the city's north side. Some of Chicago's most well-known elites lived on those tree-lined streets, although most bought these townhouses to have a place in the city. Many spent most of their time in their estates in one of the North Shore burbs. From what Kenny told me, though, the urbanized Marchands spent most of their time in town in this surprisingly modest place. Modest by the standards of people with their kind of wealth, anyway.

Since Charles knew I was coming, he'd directed me to a designated guest parking spot for my truck in a closed lot behind the row of townhomes. No squeezing into tight, barely legal spots for guests of people like Charles. After listening to Toland, I felt freed up. Now it wasn't Rick's sleuthing that placed Leo and Charles together. Old-fashioned gumshoe journalism had done that job for me.

After Toland's press grilling was over, I'd left the conference room to Rick and Wendy to do their work. I headed straight to my office, where I called Kenny and told him I wanted to see Charles. "Odd omissions, don't you think?"

Kenny responded with a soft grunt.

"I wonder what else he's not telling us." I already knew an item or two, but I kept up my resolve to wait for Charles to reveal himself. Or, until someone else filled in the bits and pieces.

"This Toland connection is a big zero," Kenny said. "Or, it would be, except there's that Café Brauer scene."

"So, you think all the rest slipped his mind?"

167

Kenny was troubled, and so was I, but I also had a secret—namely information—I hadn't disclosed yet. I made arrangements with Kenny to see Charles. On any other day, pre-Charles, I would have stayed put in my office, and come up with the juror profiles for the Potash case, based on the mock trial results. Mock trials could be exciting, and the way Leann's team was presenting our side of the case was, in a word, brilliant. All that could change if we got the jury selection phase wrong.

Kenny had already arrived, and he let me in through the enclosed back patio doors. In the midst of a busy city neighborhood, the high brick enclosure provided a private patio big enough for a dozen or more guests, without a neighbor ever being able to catch a glimpse of the party. Except for some city noise, Charles and Sandra might have been in their vacation home in Michigan. Knowing me well, Kenny poured me a cup of coffee from the fresh pot before we joined Charles at the dining room table.

"Your favorite," Kenny said, "dark roast, and I've added in some chicory, a bit of New Orleans for ya'."

"And no cream and sugar ruining the taste," I added with a grin, following him into the dining room, formal, yet modern, with a long, walnut table and sleek designed chairs. No curlicue carved furniture for the Marchands. The modern look was distinctly not *Downton Abbey*, but Charles and Sandra could comfortably entertain a group of 14 or 16 around that table.

I was certain Charles had a home office. We knew for sure Sandra had one. So why did the dining room table look like Charles' headquarters, and not just for the trial? Two laptops sat open and old-fashioned files were stacked on the table.

Curious, I asked, "Is this where you run your company now?"

Charles shook his head. "I turned day-to-day operations over to my senior architect. Van Owens—he's been with me for years. We're restoring one of the oldest clusters of factory buildings on the north side." He thumped the table for emphasis. "And they're not going to waste as storage lockers or even lofts. A Made-in-the-US clothing company is taking up one site, and a museum exhibit design firm is taking over another spot where a company used to make women's lingerie. We're keeping the sculptures out front...kind of a Venus de Milo look."

"It's good that you've got somebody you can trust to take over for you, at least for a while longer," I said.

My gaze caught a portion of the bottom of the stairs, several yards away on the other side of an arch that broke up space. The back of the house had a family room-den, the kitchen, a smaller eating space, and a cabinet-lined entryway to the formal dining room. The stairs separated the dining room from the large living room with its fireplace and bank of windows and modern ceiling beams. Presumably, bedrooms and offices were located upstairs.

"Right now, I can't do much about my image, but I need my firm to keep a high profile. It's as if my work has to be a stand-in for me." Charles lowered his gray eyes to stare down at the blank legal pad in front of him. "I'm thinking ahead. What's happening now isn't going to define me forever."

"I don't think you're going to escape some link with the governor, no matter how hard you try." I left it there, hoping Charles would fill in the blank.

Instead, he shrugged, as if not surprised that I'd bring up Leo's interview. "I don't have much to add to what Leo himself said when that journalist asked about a connection. So, yeah, we went to the same school. That doesn't make us buddies."

His fingers fidgeted with a pen, and then, as if noticing what he was doing, he abruptly stopped. Covering up his nervousness, I presumed.

"It's not a stretch to ask about you and Toland," I remarked, the picture of Nancy Bayless on the cover of the student newspaper coming unbidden into my mind. It left me resenting him, just a little, for being so…so…self-righteous. I prepared to burst a bubble—a small one. "It might not have mattered much if you hadn't appeared at the same graduation."

Charles scoffed at that and swatted the air, as if waving away an inconsequential fly. "I'd forgotten all about that. In the last twenty-five years, I'd made it a point to avoid Leo. We barely knew each other at Donaldstone."

"Maybe you forgot," I said, thinking of my pal Cooper and his tendency to get personal, "but reporters tend to be a big part of deciding what's relevant and what isn't."

Kenny slapped the table. "And why didn't *you* tell us you and Toland were in school together and turned up at the same graduation ceremony? Did you seriously think that the press wouldn't have gone looking for information about you? They know what appetizers you order at your favorite bistro. They know what kind of wine Sandra had delivered for your holiday parties. They've seen your housekeeper come and go…c'mon, man."

"She won't talk about us. She had experience with people trying to get information about us long before Sandra died."

Died, not *was killed*. Charles had consistently said that every time. If I noticed it, wouldn't the commentators like Coop and others with legal shows on cable TV see it, too? Small details a lot less significant than Charles could imagine filled empty minutes on those shows. Being on so-called verdict watch was the worst.

I once was on Cooper Julien's show while we waited for a verdict on a police manslaughter case, where the officer, an experienced guy with a terrible track record of roughing up kids he arrested, was accused of killing one such guy. Trouble was, the kid had a record as long as any hardened criminal twenty years his senior. I'd stayed at the CNN station in Chicago, prepared to wait out what could go on for days.

By the time we went over the case, we were down to examining the motive for the defendant related to his marine-style buzz. Even for a pro like Coop, the three days were an endurance event.

Kenny's long, guttural sigh brought me back to the present. "They'd hunt up your dry-cleaning bills if they thought it would make a story," he said.

"Sure, they can uncover all that bullshit, but that's about me—well, Sandra and me. But there's no *real* link between me and Toland."

"You were going to run against him," I said, wanting to reinforce Kenny's attitude. "That's link enough to fuel news stories." So far, Kenny had shown admirable patience with a client who had a story and not only stuck to it, but didn't add anything as time passed.

Charles shook his head. "Correction. I was *thinking* about making a run."

171

Who did he think he was talking to? I didn't know why I still liked the guy at all. Talk about benefit of the doubt. I *actually* believed he hadn't killed his wife. "Come on, Charles, it was practically a done deal. Everyone knew that."

"So what?" Charles got to his feet and traveled the few feet to the patio doors, where shrubs and day lilies bordered the edges, but the large terracotta pots at the corners sat empty. I imagined that the previous summer they were overflowing with impatiens and geraniums. Apparently, no one would bother this year. I understood.

"Look, Sandra fell down the stairs," he said, his voice low. "I don't know exactly how it happened. I wasn't there. I woke up, found her and called 9-1-1."

The buzz of Charles' phone grabbed his attention. He studied the screen and frowned. "I can deal with this later."

He didn't sound convincing.

"Are you sure?" I asked.

Nodding, he said, "It's Sandra's sister, half-sister, Jordan. She's recovered from the coronary she had in the airport after the funeral."

I recalled that incident. Wendy or Janet mentioned it. Maybe Rick. "So, she calls to what, check in with you?" Something intrigued me about that call.

"Yeah, we talk once or twice a week."

"Why?" I asked.

Charles' frown deepened. "*Why?* Because she wants to know how things are going in my case."

"Uh, Jordan believes in Charles," Kenny said. "She's coming back here for the trial. Or at least hopes to."

Why hadn't someone thought to tell me this? Why hadn't I asked? I'd allowed myself to go with the assumption that Charles didn't have much family. Now I learned a sister-in-law believed in my client's innocence. It was something.

"That's good," I said. "Unfortunately, that does nothing to change the fact that no one can back up your story about finding Sandra and calling 9-1-1 that night." Well, Zach could add something. But we'd get to that another day. The fact was, if the prosecutor didn't discover a mysterious visitor knocking on the door, the defense was under no obligation to disclose it.

My visit that day was supposed to see what Charles would offer about Leo and the days they were classmates. I was hanging on to the tidbit about Zach's errand on behalf of Toland. I wasn't sure why, but once I disclosed it, I had a link to a potential player in the case that couldn't be overlooked. I didn't like it, but there was nothing I could do, except to keep quiet. But we didn't have to be quiet about Jordan. At least one of Sandra's relatives was on his side.

As the jury consultant and not the attorney responsible for defending a client, I had the privilege of pointing out the obvious in the starkest of terms. Kenny had to be more judicious with his language.

"Great," Charles said with a cynical grin, "but I *do* appreciate your candor."

"Every detail counts," I said. "Somehow, you and Leo at the Café Brauer, Sandra's strange behavior, your shared past with Leo…"

"No! Stop saying that. Leo and I have *no* shared past."

Kenny then spoke the words I was thinking. "Charles, that's naïve. I have no doubt that from where you sit, it's true, but facts aren't unassailable."

Good word. I could almost hear a narrative about a crumbling marriage spoiling a budding political career, and the two men squaring off with Sandra in the middle. The angry husband pleading with his drunken wife not to divorce him and blow up any chance for a detour into politics. Oh, it would be tricky, but I'd seen prosecutors create a domestic disaster out of much thinner threads. Running up a credit card balance, or raiding the family savings account, or too many parking tickets could all end up political gossip that cast doubt on a candidate's character. Those scenarios aren't even that rare.

Charles turned around to stare at Kenny and me. "I can tell my own story."

Kenny shook his head, rolled his eyes, and threw his hands in the air. The whole range of gestures communicating the folly, the sheer stupidity of even imaging such a scenario.

But me? I kept a lid on my emotions on that topic. Trial strategy was, for the most part, between Kenny and Charles, although I knew exactly what Kenny would think of Charles' talk about taking the stand.

I glanced at my watch. I couldn't stay much longer. "Just to be on the safe side, can you write down everything you remember about you and Leo at college, and on that day a few years back when you both gave speeches?"

"You really want to hear this?" Charles asked defiantly. "Here's all you need to know. He was a little prick...the worst stereotype of a frat boy. A sloppy drunk...a lazy bastard doing as little as possible to get a piece of paper in his hand at the end of four years. He had money and connections. That bought him power—and it bought him girls. He collected women. To him, fucking a girl was

174

like ordering a burger. Just one more thing to do in a day. I avoided him if I could."

Now that was more like it. I sensed some energy behind those words, passion driven by contempt. These two public men knew more about each other than either of them liked. That was my assumption. It was a good time for me to leave.

"I've got to get back to the office," I said, "but I wanted to see what, if anything, could be made of you and Leo and the Donaldstone connection."

Charles' face tightened in defensiveness. "You've got it. There is no connection."

As I walked to my truck, the image of Nancy Bayless once again drifted through my mind, and her embarrassingly youthful reflections in her diary. My gut told me it was only a matter of time before a journalist got hold of that interview list with Marchand and Toland on it. Why hadn't the story already seeped out? I knew it was before the days of social media where nothing stays hidden; or, maybe the journalists looked at it and walked away. Could be it was irrelevant. I tried to believe that myself.

Chapter Fourteen

Standing tall and a little wooden, but looking smug, too, Wendy and Rick filed into my office late one afternoon.

"We have news," Wendy said.

Having been preoccupied with the Potash data and juror profiles, I assumed they'd come to talk about the drug company case. I was surprised to hear the names, Aaron Nagasaki and Freddy Prigge. The Donaldstone student journalists.

"We found them," Rick said. "And it wasn't very hard. Freddy runs his own café in Key West, but Aaron Nagasaki is the managing editor of an independent weekly up in Minnesota—he added Hanson to his name a few years back—hyphenated it. Looking at what he's up to these days, it seems his work is a lot tamer now. You know, he writes more about the water quality of a river than finding a body on its banks."

Wendy shot him a look. Not a nice one, either. That image of a body on the river sounded cavalier, whether Rick meant it that way or not. A part of me wondered if writing hard-hitting pieces about water quality was the more revolutionary act.

"And?" Ready to leave for dinner with a couple of friends, I wanted a summary—hit the high points, I'd often tell Wendy, to prevent her from rambling on too much.

"Both of them remember the case...well," Wendy said. "Both called that whole semester unforgettable, but not necessarily in a good way. Every now and again someone tracks them down. They hadn't spoken with each other, but both speculated that a curious journalist or investigator would eventually call them about Marchand."

"Do they remember him specifically?"

"You bet," Wendy said, her expression fixed in almost painful seriousness. "This Bayless case defined them, somehow. It was as you'd expect for young people on a college campus. Traumatic and shocking. It led Aaron to choose a career as a writer, journalist, and newspaper editor. Freddy was a different story. He pivoted. Walked away from journalism for good."

"Freddy has a harder time talking about it, I think," Rick said. "A death from alcohol poisoning was one thing, sad and tragic and scary. But a body turning up was something else again."

"What did he say?" I asked.

Rick tilted his head back and forth as if considering how to explain something complicated. "He hates that someone got away with, not murder necessarily, but a cover up or what he called 'something fishy'. He's a guy whose 'socioeconomic profile,'" Rick said, his fingers crooked in air quotes, "is more like Marchand than Toland. Humble background, rough in some ways. Donaldstone lured him in the name of diversity, and he was a bright kid in his high school in Louisville. He thinks the college is a great place for a kid like him. It kind of sheltered him, too, he says, from the worst kind of prejudice he'd encountered in his life. Writing about Nancy Bayless served him well with other kids on campus, but also in terms of grades and credit hours he earned working on the paper. But he was still turned off to a career in journalism."

Each smiling faintly, Rick and Wendy exchanged another look.

"He confided that he's writing thrillers on the side," Rick said. "Journalism was out, but fiction appealed."

It was easy to see Rick identified with Freddy's creative ambition. I wondered how Rick's fantasy universe game was coming alone. All that aside, I could see he'd accurately assessed what had happened on campus. It must have been traumatic, just on the face of it. Plus, no matter how you examined it, the whole event smelled of secrecy and indifference. "You have notes on these interviews, I assume."

Wendy jumped in and took over. "Of course. Notes. Plenty of pages of them. When Nancy Bayless turned up dead, the campus started dividing into all sorts of camps. They didn't easily recover, and graduation itself was a somber event. Freddy went, but Aaron got in his car and drove back home to Minnesota the day before the ceremony."

"According to Freddy," Rick said, "Marchand was one of many who didn't show up."

"Maybe he couldn't afford the graduation fees," Wendy added. "I barely managed mine. The only reason I went was because my parents wanted to see the cap and gown."

"Me, too," Rick said.

The two stood silent, exchanging pointed glances. I also noted they weren't carrying file folders or their iPads or laptops. So where were the notes?

"What's going on? You have notes, but you

don't have them with you. You're acting like you're harboring a secret."

"We are." Wendy pulled up a chair and sat down.

Rick pulled another chair from the corner.

"It's best we don't show you our notes," Wendy said. "First of all, neither Aaron nor Freddy had hard evidence of anything. They had hunches. Most of what they came up with put Leo in a bad light, but they read the diary—so there's a hint, flimsy though it is, that Charles looks like a spurned lover or something. Maybe suffering the pain of rejection. But that's all speculation…difficult to prove."

I was getting uncomfortably close to an issue I couldn't avoid addressing. "You don't want me talking about the information. Right? You don't want me knowing much, because maybe I could be compromised in some way?"

Wendy nodded.

We'd crossed a border somewhere and had entered new territory. We hadn't been in this situation before.

"But is it important? To this case, I mean?" I asked.

Wendy rubbed her forehead, looking like a person searching for the right word. "That's the thing, we don't know. I'm not privy to what Charles has revealed about any past association with Toland…" she held up her hand "…and I'm aware we have to keep it that way. But we can say, more or less definitively, that Leo Toland lied in that press conference the other day."

Now we were getting somewhere. My gut churned, though, because nothing about this promised good news. "How so?"

"Aaron and Freddy each had a slightly different

take on what happened to Nancy Bayless," Rick said. "They zeroed in on the frat house, and that meant Toland. And the diary pointed to March- and, not as a suspect, but as somebody involved on the fringes. Plus, they talked to everyone listed on the graph paper. Some were long interviews, too. Coincidentally or not, Aaron distinctly re- members Toland and Marchand showing up at the interview site together."

My gut low buzzed on that one. That didn't match what we'd seen in the notes. "What was the site? And did they interview the two of them together?"

"It was a classroom used for the journalism program. They blocked out certain times for the kids to show up. The professor gave them a free hand in this, but there was nothing casual about it. Freddy said they made specific appointments. They guaranteed anonymity. They were trying to be as professional as possible. And from what each of them told us," Rick said, "they didn't do any group interviews. Freddy said he and Aaron went back to talk to both Toland and Marchand a second time—and some others, too. Guys and a couple of girls who were at the frat house where Nancy was last seen."

"Did these students seriously think that either or both of these guys had something to do with Nancy's death?"

Rick smirked. "They didn't suspect Marchand, not in any considered way, but neither ruled out Leo."

"None of it matters," Wendy said, "because no one, not the police or the medical examiner, found evidence that pointed to anything other than alco- hol poisoning as a cause of death. Long and short of it, though, they thought Leo was a lowlife."

I sighed. "He's a member of a very big club." This guy that no one much liked won one election after another. How could he continue fooling so many people?

I slapped the desk and scoffed. "Cause of death, established, but cause of moved body, unknown. Not a single witness stepped up to say how that girl got to the river's edge?"

"Aaron and Freddy believe no one tried very hard," Wendy said. "That's the thing. The police managed to plant a seed that Nancy wandered down to the river on her own two feet. Aaron thought it was easier to accept the death that way. Less scary for the students to implicate Nancy in her own situation than to believe someone in their midst would handle a dead body and hide a death. Bad for the fraternity and all that."

"And she buried herself in leaves, huh?" I asked. Based on what I saw in the reports, that was one hundred percent implausible.

Rick corrected me. "She wasn't covered very much, at least by the time she was found. The spot was remote. It was way off a path along the river, one mostly used by hikers. The idea she wandered off isn't 100 percent nuts."

I nodded, accepting the more accurate picture. "Still seems odd to me that the Bayless case doesn't come up even in casual conversation. Nancy was a senior, so were Toland and Marchand. Wouldn't you think Toland would have mentioned it at some point in his career—in a speech about campus drinking maybe? You know what I mean. *'Every year we have x number of tragic deaths resulting from binge drinking on campuses around the state.'* I can hear Leo's voice in my head making public service announcements. They were students on a tiny campus when a major tragedy occurred to a classmate, a woman they'd known for almost four years."

Wendy's pinched expression reflected the kind of pain that comes from identifying with a story.

"It's a personal connection," I said, "and he never used it, even as a morality tale."

Wendy's personal response made sense. I had no doubt she linked working for Sandra at such a young age with helping to prevent a vulnerable girl, like she surely was, from becoming a Nancy. A girl attracted to a man who didn't treat her well, a girl who took risks, maybe not all of them carefully calculated.

I knew something Wendy and Rick didn't. Like Toland, Marchand also failed to bring up the girl. I had mixed feelings about that.

Since Charles struck me as a decent guy overall, I didn't think he'd killed the girl, any more than he'd killed Sandra. I knew that was naïve, since decent people can be driven to kill. For all kinds of reasons and justifications. I knew about Zach's 4:00 AM visit and the message he was supposed to deliver… *Things have a way of coming out.*

"I think someone should question Toland about Nancy Bayless, even if we admit it probably doesn't mean anything for his election or the Marchand case…or maybe anything else." Wendy tapped the table for emphasis. "I'm conceding that it could all add up to a bunch of coincidences that don't lead any closer to an explanation of what happened to Nancy Bayless—or Sandra. But these kid journalists knew Leo, and they suspected him of being involved."

I nodded, agreeing in principle, but also considering the information we had in front of us. Disconnected facts. "I wonder why the political journalists aren't pursuing the Leo story. Is it

just about the fall of a potential rival for Leo?"
I mused. A rival Leo thought strong enough to
send a messenger to intimidate—and with a not
so veiled threat.

"Someone picked up the photo that put the two
guys on the same stage, but with nothing there,
why dig deeper?" Rick suggested. "The Bayless
case only comes up if you dig for it."

"I think somebody ought to dig deeper," Wendy
said, "but it shouldn't be you, Matt."

"Well, you work for me, so that rules you out.
Talk about conflict of interest."

"Aren't you curious about Toland and the girl,
aside from anything else?" Rick asked.

Thinking of Zach and Leo-the-jailer almost
made me laugh out loud. If Rick only knew how
much I'd yearned to bust up Leo's little power ca-
bal.

"I'm going to think about what to do," I told
them, ignoring Rick's query. Instead, I picked up
my phone and stood, signaling my need to leave.

"But you want to follow up—somehow?" Wendy asked, most likely to get some reassurance.

"I do. And we will. But not by taking any risks.
You have to be protected from any fallout, but so
do Kenny and Charles. Nothing can ever come
back that in any way points to this office. *Ever*."

Snooping around in Charles' past was a case of
violating what every lawyer is told: don't ask a
question you don't know the answer to. And its
corollary: don't ask a question if you're afraid of
the answer. That's where I was when it came to
Marchand, Toland, and both Sandra and Nancy.

"But, how will you…?"

I waved Rick off. The less said the better. "Nothing for you to concern yourself with. You can be
sure I'm going to figure a way to work it out."

An idea was forming.

* * *

Later that day, I sat over dinner at a favorite Lincoln Park restaurant called The Blanchard trying to enjoy a great French meal with old friends, Lauren and Dan. Among my favorite people, they sensed how preoccupied I was. Maybe they saw my forced attention. Could be my fidgety hands gave me away. While I picked at my dinner, I answered questions as I leaned forward, body language meant to indicate that I was paying attention. I fooled no one. Finally, as we waited for our coffee, Lauren gently chided me for my wandering mind.

"Great dinner," I said, meaning it. I'd known this older couple for many years, but I hadn't seen them in months and months.

"You're just saying that," Lauren said, fidgeting with a strand of salt and pepper hair. "We can see you're somewhere else most of the time. Deep in a case, I assume, and likely not one of those dull corporate liability matters you try to convince us that you enjoy."

I grinned. "You know me too well. It's the Potash case you're thinking of. I'm guessing no out-of-court deal is forthcoming, by the way. No settlement on the horizon. We're going to court." That was a safe detour. I tried to hide it, but my idea about dealing with the journalists was racing ahead. Although I was eager to get home, I managed to relax long enough to savor some of the richest tiramisu served anywhere in Chicago.

Dan was preoccupied, too, but I knew that

wasn't personal, any more than what was taking up my mental space was personal. Dan, an activist of the first order, had been ready to go full throttle for Charles in his bid for governor. He'd planned to knock on doors, man phone banks, deliver yard signs, and basically do whatever else was asked of him. Dan had been especially glum over Sandra's death and Charles' indictment, not that he'd known either of them. Dan *believed* Charles could beat Leo.

"Are we allowed to ask about Marchand, or is that case off limits?" Dan asked.

"Why bother, Dan?" Lauren said with a laugh. "You know he won't toss us even one kernel of information."

"Right you are," I said, "but the civil case is going fine. I can tell you that."

"Big news," Dan said in mock disgust.

I drained my coffee cup and glanced at my watch. "I need to cut this short. I have a meeting at seven in the morning," I lied.

I didn't like telling fibs, but at least I wouldn't get caught in my fib this time. Lauren and Dan would have no reason not to believe my claim of a meeting. Sometimes, I actually had meetings that early.

"Okay, duty calls," Lauren said. "We get it. Keep us posted on what you can."

"I will," I promised, sliding out of the booth, with Lauren and Dan following.

Thirty minutes later, I was in the door and staring at the phone, my landline. Right on time, it rang.

"Well, well, my old friend Matt," Cooper said. "I didn't expect to have a message from you. You must be a busy man."

"I see you on TV so often, it seems like I'm

having a conversation with you every day."

"A loyal fan. I like hearing that," Coop said. "You and millions, my friend…"

Coop had built his reputation on focusing on his guests, creating a situation so they could shine, but he could be a *tad* narcissistic.

"You're looking good, too," I said, shamelessly feeding his vanity in my teasing way. All that aside, I trusted him.

"Did you catch the show this evening?" he asked.

"Nope, I was out oiling the wheels of justice… late meeting." Another lie. "Who did you have?"

"Mr. Barry Scheck himself…another innocent man was released from prison earlier this week. Down in Alabama. Guy's been locked up for *twenty-two years*." Coop paused for effect. "Viewers love and hate those stories. Go to my Facebook page. You'll see it's burning up—rage and tears, cheers and relief. You know how it is. Regular citizens demand we lock criminals up for good. Throw away the key, they yell. But then they cry foul when it takes decades to get an innocent guy out."

"Sorry I missed that." Barry Scheck was a stand-up guy. Seeing him talking about a recent release only reminded me of my own failure. Inevitably, those reminders came up now and again. But it was time to pivot away from *delayed* justice. "Let me get to the reason I called. When might you broadcast your show from Chicago?" I asked. "The Marchand trial isn't starting for a while, but it's a hot topic in the city."

"I wish the concept of swift justice was still operating," Coop said dryly. "These long waits for action are hell on ratings. I'm tired of the same old B rolls, too."

I laughed. "We're more like OJ than one of those cases that take years to try. We're doing okay with the timing for Marchand, who, by the way, would take the stand tomorrow—oops, that's off the record, a mere figure of speech."

"You don't want me dropping rumors about Marchand telling his own story in court?"

Since Coop was teasing me, I could afford to laugh at the notion. Not that Charles didn't regularly tell us that he believed in his own power of persuasion. "Some rich guys know people resent the hell out of them, and they're usually right. Charles, on the other hand, had long basked in the good will that bounced off of Sandra and onto him and gave him a golden sheen, too."

"I got that feeling when I talked to people," Coop agreed.

"A couple of years ago, Sandra held a gala to raise funds for a halfway house for veterans dealing with addiction issues. She held it in the ground floor of an old factory in the West Loop. Charles had bid for the contract to renovate the building and that kept the wrecking ball at bay. So, his work to preserve some of the landmarks, both great and minor, while developing the landmarks of tomorrow gave him a good image in his own right. Sandra would then highlight his projects in her own way." I exhaled a heavy sigh. "The fame of one fed the fame of the other. All the more reason interest in the case is running high."

"Why did you ask about my show coming to Chicago, Matt? Can't be idle curiosity. As I recall, the word 'idle' isn't in your vocabulary."

"Can't a guy want to take you out for a Chicago dinner without an ulterior motive?"

"Sure, people can do that, but they usually don't." Coop paused. "They usually have something on their minds. You aren't one to hang out for the helluva it."

"Could be I'm looking at giving more speeches, maybe doing more TV." Was Coop catching on? I hoped so, but just in case, I added, "I wanted to pick your brain about that—the sooner the better."

"I see, you want to make another change. In a rut, huh? Drug cases getting a little dull. How about if I see what's coming down the pike in way of a major oil spill. It's been a while since you've worked one of those."

"Right. Talk about the slow wheels of justice. Nobody has more tricks up their sleeves to delay a trial better than the oil companies." I laughed, in a casual, devil-may-care way. "Let's just say I'm exploring some options, looking to bring in some variety, not necessarily in the cases, but in what I do on air. There's more to it, of course."

Pause. Silence.

"Of course," Coop said softly, "as it happens, I could arrange to meet you tomorrow or Sunday."

That sent a zing through me. I hadn't imagined arranging anything with Coop so quickly. "I'm listening," I said.

"I'm flying out early Saturday morning to Milwaukee to guest lecture at my alma mater, Marquette. There will be a reception, and then I fly back to New York on Sunday. Seems kids are pretty interested in media these days…being mere attorneys isn't enough."

"I get it," I said. It amused me to think of law students picking up pointers from the colorful Cooper Julien. "You name the time and place. I can meet you at the airport coming or going. Or, at the university. It's up to you."

Speaking out loud, Coop ran down his schedule, settling on the idea of an early lunch at the airport. Nothing fancy. Coop, for all his highfalu-tin talk, was probably a pancake and burger guy like me.

"I'm looking forward to our conversation, Matt. It's been a while, and you always have a lot to say."

He didn't know what I was up to, but he sure was aware there was nothing casual in my call. Especially because I hadn't given any hint over the phone of the topic at hand. Coop knew as well as I did that if I wanted a bigger presence in media all I had to do was put some feelers out. I'd had offers, more than a few.

If Coop hadn't been able to come to me, I might have made up an excuse to go to New York. I'd become increasingly paranoid—having Zach's inside view of Leo was enough to make anybody cautious. Something smelled dangerous about ruffling the Nancy Bayless feathers. I didn't know how Charles would react, or Leo, either, knowing that—although I didn't *exactly* have what it took to put two and two together—I had a lot of odd numbers needing to be added up. I had a strong feeling neither man would want the grave of those shared days disturbed. My guess, they'd long ago buried Nancy and any association with her. How often did either one of them think about their classmate?

I didn't like thinking about the likely answer to my own question.

* * *

"Let's grab lunch," Zach said, during an early call on Saturday morning.

"When?" Not this weekend, I repeated a couple

of times in my mind. I was in my office going over notes, and Kenny was coming in to go over some details, loose threads—without Charles present. Unfortunately, I wasn't ready to chat about anything other than the narrow set of facts we had to work with.

"Next week. Monday. Will that work?"

My dance card was filling up, amused by that old expression that had popped into my mind without a formal invitation. Zach and I agreed on the old standby, Lakeview Market. No daylight yet for us.

"Works for me." He paused. "You're working hard, aren't you? I bet you're in your office as we speak—you and the little mutt."

Zach's voice hadn't changed, except for referring to Maude as a mutt, his now customary teasing term, he didn't sound like himself. He didn't comment on things like my work hours.

"I suppose," I responded. "It's nice and quiet in here for now. Maude is snoozing…she does like her naps."

"That staff of yours must be overworked. Are you giving them any time off for good behavior?"

I scrambled to decode the message.

"You know, Wendy," I said, "always on the job. She's busy at home, designing a community attitude survey. My ace assistant is killing me with overtime."

Zach laughed, a bit too heartily. "Oh, I feel so sorry for you, little bro. At least all that work should keep her off the phone and out of trouble."

I laughed back. We sounded like a couple of phonies. But something stood out. *Off the phone.* I pushed the pause button on that phrase. Zach ended the call abruptly, saying something about needing to pick up Judy.

Maude's soft breathing brought me back to the moment. Kenny wasn't due for our meeting for another twenty minutes, and that gave me time to reflect. I wasn't used to speaking in code, or telling little fibs, or being afraid to talk on my phones, cell or landline. I kept secrets when I needed to, of course. I was private about strategy, not one to banter back and forth with colleagues about my cases. It wasn't easy knowing Wendy was engaged in secretive investigations she wouldn't—couldn't—share with me. My brother warned me about the phone, and not just me, but Wendy, too. Zach probably meant for me to extrapolate and include Rick.

Suddenly, a wave came over me…a wave of fatigue. I was beat. And all because I'd waded into waters that were full of sharks, taking risks I'd studiously avoided for years. I leaned back in my office chair and put my feet on the desk. I closed my eyes and promised myself that once the Marchand case was behind me, I was done—again—with this kind of case. It wasn't only about Charles. Nancy Bayless' wasted life bothered me, maybe like my own mother's foolish choices sometimes left me reeling, even as an adult, and despite her being long gone. None of it mattered anymore. Most of us survive our young adult stupidity and either continue with dumb choices, like my mom had, or we grow up some and gain some wisdom along the way.

But for a few extra ounces of alcohol, Nancy might have left Donaldstone and gone about her life, getting a job, an apartment, whatever…just like the rest of us. All the stupid stuff we did in college was usually put aside, written off. We might exchange a few war stories for entertainment value, but that was it. Marchand and Toland likely would have become merely a couple of blokes she met in college.

I smiled to myself. Given Charles' rather public success, she might have kicked herself for turning down a chance to date him, and she'd probably have muttered expletives at the TV when Leo showed his face. No doubt she'd have spent a few minutes feeling bad about herself for being such a fool over a man not worthy to buy her a cup of coffee.

The sound of the outside door closing got my attention. I sat up quickly, but not before Kenny saw me and grinned.

"Having a nap?"

"Resting my eyes," I insisted, "and thinking about things."

I pointed to the chair across from me. "You want to sit in here or go to the conference room?"

Kenny reached into his attaché and pulled out a DVD. "I've got something you need to see. Let's watch it in the conference room."

I knew what it was. Cell phone video from the night at Café Brauer.

"Good news and bad news," Kenny said.

"How much of each?" I asked.

"Truthfully, nothing much either way."

The story of the case…not much one way or the other to prove or disprove.

Leading the way to the conference room, my gut tightened, thinking about what was on that video. "What's our spin?"

"Charles says he was concerned about Sandra. Troubled by her behavior. We'll concede that she wasn't herself, of course. We'll explain everything through the lens of her behavior and Marchand's worries—and his surprise."

"And she was obviously angry enough to have

separation papers drawn up."

"That, too."

"Without Charles to spin his own story, how will you establish that?"

"Witnesses at the shelter. Her personal assistant says she'd been withdrawn over a period of a few weeks before she died."

I kept the legal pad next to me, anticipating notes. The DVD images soon filled the screen. As cell phone videos often are, some images were hazy, even dark. Other video clips added to the DVD were crisp, ready to use as PR and PSAs for the shelter, which is likely what they planned. Most of it was dull as dishwater.

Sandra looked a little agitated in one clip, but all smiles and graciousness in another. She'd known how to work a room. No surprise there. She spent much of her public life working rooms. That night, her blond hair was loosely pulled back, and her red dress was simple, neither sexy nor severe. In jeans or a glittering gown, she had a look all her own.

"Whatever else was going on in her life, Sandra Marchand had class," I observed.

Kenny nodded. "That's what Charles says... over and over. He's mourning more obviously and painfully now that he's home."

"I expected that. Didn't you?"

"Sure. He's wishing his life could go back to exactly the way it was before." Kenny looked at me. "Don't they all, these people who are forced to defend their lives. Losing Sandra seems to be what bothers him most about the whole notion of going to trial. Our client still can't quite grasp that anyone suspects him. Odd, I know."

"Not really." I lifted my shoulders in a slow shrug. "I guess I'd find it odd if he didn't feel that way."

"The other day he was near tears, thinking about the world seeing photos of her in a tangled heap at the bottom of the stairs. It took me a while to get him to understand that the jurors and people in the court would view them, not strangers halfway across the world or even down the street." Sighing, Kenny pointed to the screen. "There are clips coming up that show her with an angry scowl directed at Charles and naked hate in her eyes when she looks at Leo."

"Really? Somebody caught that, huh?"

"Charles groaned when he saw that look she flashed at Leo."

Leo. There he was again, insinuating himself into the case.

"How much of this riveting footage does the prosecution have?" I asked dryly. In truth, most of it was like watching other people's travelogues.

Kenny shrugged. "They've been combing everything, too."

Leo soon came into a frame of a new clip, the fourth or fifth one in. Grinning and waving, typical pol style, he was making his way through the crowd, refusing the champagne glass offered.

"Watch now, something's coming up…right here." Kenny hit pause. There it was.

The Look.

For a couple of seconds, even media savvy Sandra forgot. The viewer watches as Sandra's face goes from troubled, unusual by itself, to a momentary lapse in her social manner. Her eyes narrowed, then flashed as her mouth formed a truly ugly sneer.

And then she remembered.

The person catching her at that angle then smartly turned the lens on the object of her disdain, Leo, who for a split second looked taken aback.

"The bastard doesn't know why she's reacting with such hate," I said.

"He can join the club," Kenny said. "Charles claims he doesn't know, either."

Not possible, I thought. Charles was holding back. From the look of the body language, Leo was genuinely surprised at Sandra's reaction to him.

The clips continued. I'd seen a few already on Facebook and YouTube, as had everyone in the country who cared enough about the case to follow it. Much of the clips showed essentially nothing, except Sandra uncharacteristically gulping back champagne. In one frame, Sandra turned away from Charles, who had hold of her arm, but realized he'd been caught trying to get his wife's attention and waved to the camera. He whispered something to her...inaudible...and then she turned and smiled, too. That was all of three seconds.

"We've seen those little exchanges between people before," I said. "I can't see why they'd show anything more than a couple putting on a public face. And a woman troubled and drinking too much. Nothing revolutionary about any of it."

"This next clip is going to be on the news—and soon."

Someone caught the action of Sandra angrily pushing a champagne glass into Charles' chest. He held on to it, playing it off as if simply accepting something casually handed to him. He glanced furtively around him. Sandra stalked off and he followed her, now smiling, and wearing the face he preferred the world to see. What a photogenic freak of nature, too. I hadn't paid enough attention to Charles before to note how handsome he looked, polished and practiced. His social smile reminded me of Obama at photo ops, always wearing the same grin and looking good, too. The camera doesn't simply love some people, some people love the camera and know in their bones how powerful visual images are. Charles was right up there with the best of them, even better than Sandra.

"Where has this clip been? Why haven't we seen it before?" I asked. "We had witnesses describe that exact moment. The Marchands left immediately after this moment, right?"

"Yes, but not before Sandra does that cackling angry laugh with Leo—pretty close in, too. It's all very odd."

"What's the relevance of Leo?"

"Weaving it all into motive, we think. Or, we're preparing for that angle. The person who took the video wants to remain anonymous, but she sent it to us and to the prosecution team."

"She must have sat on it for an awfully long time."

"Apparently." Kenny frowned. "I think this whole Leo connection is contrived at best. It would be a complete nonissue if Charles hadn't been rumored to be gearing up for a run in the primary to go up against Leo."

"And favored to win," I said.

"Prosecutors will claim Sandra was against it," Kenny, said, frowning, "and threatened him with divorce to make her point."

"Actually, that sounds like a way Charles can brush aside the divorce." That left me a little optimistic. "I wonder if Sandra knew something about Leo, and maybe Charles, that neither man was aware of. You know, something going back to their college days." Might as well let Kenny know, even obtusely, about that vein in the mine.

Kenny stared at the paused clip on the TV. "If Leo hadn't decided to show up at Café Brauer that night, this wouldn't have come up. But you could be right. Whatever it is, we'd want to present it in a way that favors Charles."

"There's something else to consider," I added. "Based on your notes and summaries, you have half a dozen reliable witnesses that claim, consistently, that Sandra wanted nothing more than for Charles to step up and run for office. She was *thrilled.* Her assistant's word, not mine. On the other hand, an assistant isn't going to come off as a credible sounding board." I shrugged. "What would the woman say? She worked for Sandra and isn't likely to contradict her."

"It's not just her, though. We could put twenty or thirty people up there to talk about how much Sandra wanted Charles in public life." Kenny hesitated. "I haven't said this to Charles, but I think she originally liked the idea of that 'first lady' type of role. She thought it would expand her platform—animal welfare, education, homelessness. She was never timid about the kinds of issues she took on."

I ran through the timeframe in my mind. "So, she liked the idea...until she didn't. That's the puzzle." It was also the question Charles refused to answer. "According to the summaries you've sent, the people you've spoken to, potential witnesses or not, all say they heard Sandra praise the idea of Charles running for office—even the senate—as recently as about six weeks before she died. That seems to be the timing of a last *known* comment. She wasn't quiet about it, and in fact, spoke publicly, even joking with him at a holiday reception with a WGN-TV reporter. No ambivalence about it."

I paused and took a breath. "And then, nothing? All of a sudden, she was draining glasses of champagne and shoving the empties at him. She's a thrilled political wife in the making on Christmas and by Valentine's Day she hates the idea."

I shook my head and, internally, again asked the question about Leo and Charles. I couldn't get it out of my head that my own brother had been sent to issue a warning. As things moved forward, and little pieces filled in the puzzle, Sandra's change of heart would have bothered me, even without Zach's involvement.

Kenny and I watched every clip, continuing to stop and restart, examining the faces, the rapidly changing expressions, Sandra's drinking, Charles' perplexed look, a couple of flashes of bewilderment. But, if Leo had been the one on trial for political one-ups-man-ship, we could have easily used his unmistakable expression of pleasure as evidence. Sure, it was only a split second, but it was caught on camera, and occurred precisely at the moment Sandra was shown arguing with Charles, her face screwed up in tight anger—and more, anguish.

I ruled Leo guilty as charged of unholy glee. And then he recovered from that unconscious lapse into satisfaction of watching his opponent being publicly embarrassed. Suddenly, the clip showed him turning away and focusing elsewhere in the room. The big political grin was back.

A few hours later, Zach knocked on the Marchand's door.

Since Charles' arrest, I had to grudgingly give Leo credit. He'd been quiet, wisely so, about the case itself. Never wavering from his "let the process play out" rhetoric when asked about a presumed rival. Savvy, and a political animal to the extreme, he didn't pile on. Instead, he practiced a top-ten rule of Politics 101. *When an opponent is self-destructing, get out of the way.*

And so Leo had. Ha! The bastard even showed sympathy for the Marchands, dead wife and accused husband.

"Well, we'll use this any way we can," Kenny said, a positive tone forced into his voice.

At least I think it was forced. It was like Kenny to keep up a good front. Then again, he'd won cases others would have deemed impossible to win. Fortunately, the trial itself was still a ways off.

* * *

For anyone else, I'd have resented the drive up to Milwaukee's Mitchell International Airport, specifically to the restaurant, Cooler by the Lake. I could have made the drive in my sleep, having represented two men accused of murder in that city that Chicagoans tended to view as their country cousins. Unfairly, if I were inclined to be objective.

Like Chicago, Milwaukee was a city of neighborhoods and ethnic food and summer fests. It, too, had Catholic churches listed on historic registers. It also had a newish and iconic art museum, minus the lions. Sadly, the two cities had a plethora of guns and crime in common as well. One of my cases was a matter of getting the best deal for a killing my client had insisted was accidental, but the other case was a guilt-innocence choice. I won that one, but the man was sent to prison for a petty drug crime two years later. I'd lost track of him after that.

As I pulled off at the airport exit, I realized light traffic had made the trip not half bad. Besides, Marchand and Toland aside, I looked forward to seeing Cooper Julien. The man was a wheel-barrow of contradictions. He was at once both humble and vain as hell, ready to defer to those with greater knowledge and insight, and not give an inch if he believed concessions hadn't been earned. He could play "dumb like Colombo" if that was called for, but effectively showcase his intellectual superiority when necessary. His abil-ity to read the atmosphere and change his stance and attitude when it worked to his advantage were exactly the traits that made his show so effec-tive—and attracted commentators like me.

I met Coop at the check-in counter. Surprised by his appearance, I thought he looked as if he'd aged overnight. Not merely tired from a hasty weekend trip, an expected reaction, he looked drained, exhausted. Unusual for him. Well over sixty-five, Coop usually had the aura and energy of a much younger man. Health concerns aside, he still had the wardrobe of a guy who knew how to choose a tailor.

We walked to the restaurant and settled in at a table in the far corner, fortified with a bloody Mary for Coop and black coffee for me.

I tried to squelch my concern, but at one point I blurted, "Are you feeling all right?"

"I'm fine," he said quickly. "I didn't sleep in the hotel room, that's all. I've come to loathe hotels, all of them."

"If you're sure that's all, I'll drop it," I said with a grin. "Just checking on my old buddy."

"I'm not too tired to be immensely curious about what you couldn't talk to me about on the phone."

I did a quick scan of the space around us, and satisfied no one could hear us, I started the story with, "I need a favor. I need a public discussion opened up about Leo Toland and Marchand's past, a shared past."

I brought Coop up-to-date on what Rick and Wendy had discovered, and the way in which both men acted as if they barely knew each other.

"Seems to you like silent collusion, does it?" Coop asked.

I nodded. "Neither man seems to want anything out in the open. The thing is, and this is where you come in, there's a cold case in Birchwood that both men were aware of, and could have been at least tangentially involved in."

Coop's eyebrows shot up. He hadn't seen that coming, but then, I knew he'd long ago trained himself not to second guess anyone or anything. He had the ability to listen for data and clues, only asking questions when he wanted a clarification. He didn't lead conversations in directions he assumed they were meant to go. I'd long admired his patience to let something unfold on its own.

I spilled the rest of the story, from the discovery of Nancy Bayless' body to the way the list of interviews had appeared on a piece of graph paper. Without going into detail, I explained that I knew the whereabouts of the former student journalists.

"Rick and Wendy tracked down the two kids who kept the story alive on campus. They interviewed them, got them talking. The information about the case is all there. A couple of boxes of files tell a story, but we don't know why it ended as it did. Even the girl's diary takes us only so far."

I glanced around again. "And believe me, our

corrupt governor comes off as an asshole, even for a kid of, what twenty-one or twenty-two."

"And this involves your client how?"

I knew exactly how trivial the information sounded, at least at first, but I plunged in anyway.

"Marchand asked the girl out. She said no. In her diary she describes him as a boy scout—she liked Leo more, you know, women and the bad boy thing. After she died and her body was found, Leo and Charles showed up together to be interviewed. Walked in the building together, even though they'd been scheduled on different days." That still nagged at me. Why had the original schedule changed?

"That's nothing in itself," Coop said, waving me off with a quick flick of his hand. "No matter, really. So, today, you're telling me they claim no link at all."

"That's right, but it's not true. To hear them talk, they're almost a couple of strangers to each other. Charles has made no secret of disliking Leo, to put it mildly. Called him an 'arrogant prick', an accurate observation, by the way." I lifted my hands in frustration over what appeared to be too many missing pieces of these two men's lives.

"There's a photo of them sitting on the dais at the same graduation ceremony a few years back. Neither Leo or Charles thought it was important enough to mention. Leo was asked outright by a couple of journalists about how well the two of them knew each other, but he deftly changed the subject from Marchand to Sandra. He started his whole prepared spiel about respecting her work in the community."

Coop narrowed his eyes. "And this has to do with me because…"

"Order your lunch. Then I'll explain," I said,

watching a waiter approach the table.

Coop glanced at the menu and looked up. "When in Rome," he said, pointing to a brat platter.

"Two brat platters," I said to the waiter, making quick work of our order.

"I'm watching the time, Matt. I can't miss my flight. I've got a dinner thing tonight."

Maybe, maybe not, I thought, knowing I was being a little cynical. But I understood. Even people who lived our work the way Coop and I did had our limits and wanted to talk about something else. I pulled a folded-up piece of paper from my jacket pocket and slid it across the table. "Two names and phone numbers. Aaron Nagasaki-Hanson and Freddy Prigge, the student journalists. I can't go public, and Rick and Wendy sure can't. But a savvy TV reporter could call them and see if they'll agree to an interview."

"Hmm…let's see. It could be quite a get *if* there's a connection that means something. *If* they have anything relevant to say. And they're willing to go public, be on camera. If they can expose some lies, I'm in. So, what's the hook?"

I grinned. "How about this for a point of interest? The two men were classmates, one a frat boy, the other independent. Both their names turn up in a dead girl's diary. No big surprise, necessarily. But what did these student journalists think?"

"I have to decide if I care," Coop said, his tone flat. "Do you believe Leo killed the girl?"

"I don't know. I think it's a matter of who moved the body. I'm willing to stipulate on the alcohol poisoning. But the point is, Marchand sure didn't kill her—I'm as close to 100 percent on that as I can get."

"And I assume," Coop said, "that if you did believe Charles was involved, you wouldn't be trying to make this old cold case public." Coop gave me a long look, studying me, obviously skeptical, maybe even confused. "What's your theory of the Marchand case?"

"Off the record."

A quick nod. "Understood."

"Accidental death. She'd been drinking, which was way out of character for her. Blood alcohol wasn't especially high, but she was known for nursing one drink all night at her events. So, maybe she couldn't sleep, and got up. Maybe she was thirsty. Hungry? Could have had a headache. Anyway, for whatever reason, she was up and tripped, or took a misstep and tumbled down the stairs."

"Hard to prove," Coop said, "but hard to claim otherwise. From what I gather, the medical evidence supports the claim."

"It does, but Sandra's unusual drinking, the public anger with Charles, the separation papers—Sandra's apparent intention to divorce Charles. Take that away, they've got nothing. With it, they think they have motive."

"What aren't you telling me? What do I care about a cold case and a diary, Leo Toland, and a couple of kid journalists?"

I stared at him, realizing that I had to let one more person in on the missing piece no one knew about except for me—and Zach. Great, telling a guy with his own TV show information that could bring down a governor if all came out.

Of course, that wouldn't be so bad.

"Hear me out," I said.

With that, I told Coop about my brother and all about the reasons I hadn't seen him for years. I took him right up to the day Zach showed up at my office, and how I learned about Leo's message. Zach seeing Sandra at the bottom of the stairs, Charles' assumption that Zach was with the police or an EMT. The not quite delivered message—a warning that was never stated. *Things have a way of coming out.* Zach's actual words, "I didn't see anything here."

"Zach told me Charles looked distressed, shocked...kind of wildly so."

"Wild, not a good word," Coop said. "It can be misunderstood...real easily."

"I know, but Zach seemed to come away with the impression Charles was in shock. He didn't know how long Sandra was on that landing. Charles could have been frantic waiting for the EMTs." I paused, thinking of how deeply I believed my brother's observations and Charles' claims. "Nothing Zach said contradicted anything Charles himself claimed about how he felt in those moments."

We fell silent as the waiter came with the two platters, showing off typical Wisconsin-style excess. The fries and onion rings were heaped in piles so high they were ready to topple. The aromas mixed and made my mouth water. No kidding. I hadn't eaten since my deep dish banana pancake at Granny's about 7:30 that morning.

Coop turned his head and watched the waiter retreat before he said, "So, how is your guy, Kenny, going to use the middle-of-the-night visitor at trial? How will he make it fit?"

"What?" I leaned in to the middle of the table. "Man, I've been sitting on this. Could be good, could be bad. But no matter what the past tells us about the present, Leo sent one of his guys to warn Charles off a candidacy." *If it had been anybody other than Zach, I'd have called the messen-*

ger a goon.

"And on the night after they were face-to-face at Café Brauer." Coop turned his mouth down in thought. Restating the obvious, he said, "And you're sitting on the information."

I dipped an onion ring in ketchup. "I have asked Charles about his relationship with Leo, and to this day, he insists there isn't one."

"And from what you've told me, the governor tells the same story?"

I nodded. "They omit the same information, if that's what you're saying. That's what's got me cautious about this."

"Let me think about this," Coop said, before taking a big bite out of the brat. He smiled, appreciating the taste.

For a minute, Leo and Charles and all the little lies and inconsistencies disappeared and our lunch moved up to the front of the line.

It didn't take Coop long to chime in again.

"Maybe your client didn't kill his wife, but he sure isn't helping himself, is he? He's more or less kept a lid on everything."

I nodded. "That's exactly why I'm here. Maybe you can shake that up."

Chapter Fifteen

On Monday, I was once again dipping fries into ketchup, popping one of my stomach pills, and hoping for the best. After hearing from Coop earlier in the morning, I had news for Zach. And an assignment. Plus a confession. A triple-header. I assumed Zach had news for me.

"You first," he said.

"You ever watch Cooper Julien's show on CNN?"

Zach shrugged. "Sure. Judy turns it on when one of her crime shows isn't on."

I smiled at that. Judy liking crime shows seemed kind of funny to me. "Good. Start paying attention. He's looked around the Marchand case a little. It's possible he's going to interview a man from Minnesota who owns a daily paper."

Zach pretended to yawn. "Get to the real shit, willya?"

I grinned. "Sorry to bore you, bro, but this man went to school with your boss and with Marchand. He was the editor of the paper when the Nancy Bayless' body was found on the river bank."

"And you're thinkin' what?"

I was certain he could put that easy two and two together, but from what I'd seen, my big brother had learned that caution made a difference between him having a job and being thrown outside of Leo's circle.

"Let's just say that message you were meant to deliver was all about the past. It was a political message, just as you thought. I think it links the two men. They've both tried hard to pretend they barely know each other. I know otherwise."

"You gonna tell me."

"Not right now. But here's what I want you to do. I'll let you know when Cooper books the journalist. His name is Aaron Nagasaki-Hanson, but don't tell anyone about it. This is all off the record and I had nothing to do with him being on the show."

Zach rolled his eyes. "I'm as dumb as shit."

I burst out laughing, as old memories flooded back. He used to say that endlessly as a kid. Bad grades, overloading the trash bin, being late for work. It was his one-line response.

"What's the point?" Zach asked.

"The point is, you're going to watch the show. Then you're going to listen to see what Leo's reaction is. What does he say about Aaron? How does he blow the whole thing off?" I stopped to consider what came next.

"What's Leo gonna do about the journalist? That's what you want me to find out. Right?"

"Exactly. I went into this knowing the risk. My people first found him and talked to him. I went to Cooper...Coop. So, if the interview ruffles some feathers, and if one threatening phone call is made, we'll know who to blame. And Coop might warn him."

"I'm thinkin' I'll be the guy with the message," Zach said. "Know what I mean? And why would the guy put himself out there like that?"

I was the one who was stupid as shit. I hadn't thought of that. "Maybe I didn't think that through."

"Yeah, well. Could be he sends someone else," Zach pointed out.

"We'll cross that bridge…" I stopped myself and let out a hoot. "If I didn't love Janet, I'd have to fire her. She's turned me into a cliché machine."

"But it's true. I gotta figure out what I'm going to do." Zach plunked his elbows on the table and tapped his steepled fingers in that way I'd seen him do before when something weighed upon him.

I'd said what needed to be said. Zach responded. I put this situation in motion, and I had no choice but to let it play out.

* * *

Days passed. The Potash case would soon enter *voir dire*, selection of the jurors. It was the only part of the damn case that really had to do with me. The mock trial showed holes in the case, although the jurors found in our favor. Leann knew better than to take the positive response to 80 percent as good enough. Meanwhile, the days grew hot and sticky in that greenhouse kind of way Chicago is famous for.

Coop left coded messages on my landline voice mail, the first time to thank me for lunch, which I took to mean that he'd made the contact. He sent another message telling me that he was working on bringing the show to Chicago. His third message said he hoped to see me soon, that maybe he'd fly in on Thursday. Bingo, he'd booked Aaron.

The next afternoon, I stood at the door to my office and called out my suggestion that we needed ice cream, maybe two kinds, peppermint stick and chocolate-marshmallow-chunk. Janet and I were partial to peppermint, but Wendy was a fan of any variety that included chocolate. I had a feeling Rick would take whatever flavor was available.

On the other hand, his scruffy, struggling creative guy image was gradually being polished up a bit. Nothing like earning steady money to perk up his lifestyle. At some point during the mock trial, I'd noticed the baggy excuse for pants and the plaid shirts had been replaced by a navy sport jacket and khakis. A little preppy, but definitely an improvement over the jeans and the outdated suit. By the time winter set in again, the kid might even have a topcoat.

Janet peered over her red sparkly reading specs. "What's the occasion, boss?"

I shrugged. "It's hot."

"Well, well…that's good enough for me," she said, standing up and grabbing her purse. "Like I always say, 'any port in a storm'."

Wendy laughed out loud from her office. Rick came to the door of the conference room to say he was in.

"Bring enough so we can have some in the freezer," I said, handing her some cash.

Maude came out of my office and pattered over to sniff Janet's shoes.

"Want me to take Maudey?" Janet asked.

I shook my head. "Nah, you'd end up buying her a cone or something." I tried to keep up a teasing tone, but I didn't want Maude eating the human table food Janet assumed dogs would prefer anyway.

"See you in a few minutes." Janet left and

closed the door behind her.

"Wendy? Rick? Conference room." I gestured in a way they'd know meant hurry.

When they followed me inside, I closed the door and started right in. "Overtime tonight. Cooper Julien is going to interview Aaron Nagasaki on his show. I want us all here watching it together. That's why I sent Janet out for ice cream." I grinned. "I don't want her knowing any of this. I'm not saying it's dangerous, but I've got someone who can watch out for you two. And, I had a yen for ice cream."

Wendy's mouth hung slightly open. Rick's deep frown added five or ten years.

"Yes," I said. "I made the Cooper-Aaron interview happen, more or less."

"When?" Wendy asked, puzzled.

"After you told me you'd contacted Aaron. Look, I couldn't risk calling him, for obvious reasons. But Coop is a different story."

"Uh, why now?" Wendy asked. "What's the deal?"

"It's hard to explain," I said. "Just plan to be here. You can go home and come back. Or we'll order Chinese and eat in the office."

Wendy and Rick exchanged a look. I thought I owed them a little tidbit more. "All this could add up to exactly zero, but I want to see what happens when someone in a position to know puts Leo and Charles together."

"What happens?" Rick repeated.

"Exactly...now get to work and when Janet comes back, we'll all sit in here and shoot the breeze about Potash. I know I sound paranoid, but you're already in this pretty deep. Janet isn't, and I want to keep it that way."

"Got it," Wendy said with a grin. "Plenty of

work is piled on my desk, so I'll just stay here. I vote for Chinese."

Somehow, amidst the dilemma of Charles on trial for murder and what I considered a cold case a couple of hundred miles away, we were marking the occasion with ice cream and takeout. I went to my office and took a pill. My gut was beginning to burn already.

Chapter Sixteen

Coop had a courtly way about him. An old-fashioned word, but it had never surprised me that he'd adopted an old-world persona to match. Slow speech, devoid of slang. Always provocative, Coop rarely raised his voice.

"So, Mr. Nagasaki-Hanson," Coop said slowly, "let's clear something up before we delve into the past. Is it fair to say that you have no knowledge of a relationship between Illinois' Governor Leo Toland and the well-known developer, Charles Marchand, now awaiting trial for the murder of his wife, the philanthropist Sandra Marchand?"

"Yes, and call me Aaron, please."

Coop nodded formally, but didn't offer his own name in return.

"My association with both the governor and the accused was brief, and took place during our years as students at Donaldstone College."

"Are you aware that when asked, the governor has said he knew Mr. Marchand only in passing?" Coop asked.

"Yes, I'm aware of that."

That's all he said.

Like a well-prepped witness, he answered the question and didn't elaborate. Or maybe it was his journalism training coming through. He wasn't there to ask the questions, after all. Something about his agreeing to appear surprised me. Maybe he wanted more for his career than running a small local weekly. He was in the Minneapolis studio. In the talking head box, he was well-dressed, attractive in middle-age, not unlike Sandra and Charles, although without the benefit of what money can buy to enhance good looks. Like them, he was the exact opposite of a doughy Leo—my new name to sum him up.

"Then in your own words, tell our viewers how you came to connect the two men."

"Well, Mr. Julien, as I said, I was acquainted with both the governor and Charles when we were students at Donaldstone, a small college in Illinois. During my senior year, I was the editor of the school paper." Aaron paused to clear his throat. "It's almost forgotten now, but we had a tragedy on our campus the fall of that year. One of our students was missing for several days."

"I imagine this was traumatic for students on your campus, something completely unexpected."

"Exactly. There had never been this kind of case on our campus. Of course, for a few days, it was assumed this female student decided to go home for some reason, and the administration and the police told us there was no reason for alarm."

"But the puzzle pieces finally fit together, did they not?" Coop asked.

"Partially," Aaron said. "The student's body was found on the banks of the Mississippi River."

Coop chose—of course—to break for a commercial, making it more or less impossible to turn the channel.

I muted the TV and looked at Wendy and Rick.

"So far, so good?"

Wendy narrowed her eyes in thought. "He's giving him time to set it up. I can almost visualize the sequence. I'm already thinking about what Leo will think about all this."

"And Charles," Rick said. "This is dragging the two of them out from under their covers."

"It's risky," I said, as images of an ad for a drug flickered on the screen. "I'm betting that the focus is on Leo. He's the one who dated the girl. The contents of the diary speak to his behavior, not Charles'."

Only I had a hunch those things that had a way of coming out would damage Leo far more than Charles.

The commercial break over, Coop wasted no time to turn the page to let the viewers find out what happened next.

"There weren't many leads, Mr. Julien, but it wasn't too long before the student's body was found on the bank of the Mississippi River." Aaron left that statement hanging there.

Julien quickly followed with, "So, the investigation switched to an inquiry into murder, I assume."

"That's right, but not for long," Aaron said. "When the medical examiner released the report, the cause of death was listed as alcohol poisoning."

"I see. Then what is the mystery, Aaron?"

"It was determined that the way the foliage appeared around the body, and other factors, that the student didn't die by the river." Aaron paused. "She was brought there after her death occurred."

In a tone filled with empathy, Coop asked, "Then, tell our viewers about the atmosphere on campus when these facts were revealed?"

"It was nightmarish, start to finish," Aaron said. "You see, while the student was still missing, the police had already questioned everyone who had attended the party at the fraternity house where the student was last seen."

Coop announced another break, again at a place in the story where a viewer would sit through more commercials in order not to miss what came next.

"So far, everything matches what we discovered," Rick said. "No big revelations."

I picked up an almost empty carton of sweet and sour shrimp, and for a second or two considered if I wanted to polish it off before putting it down again. "To us, but remember, we found this information, looking for a connection between Leo and Charles."

"But don't *you* want Leo to come up looking bad," Wendy asked. "He dated her, after all. Charles didn't. Just because his name turned up in the diary, they really didn't have much to do with each other. Charles asked her out, she said no. Granted, the language was a little different."

"There's a missing piece," I said. "I keep coming back to Sandra, agitated and hostile to both her husband and Leo." That flash of hatred in her eyes when she looked at Leo on the video clip was hard to miss.

My phone buzzed. Kenny.

It buzzed again. Charles.

I let it go. I'd call them back later. I hadn't alerted them to the program, although I'd recorded it.

As if reading my mind, Coop started the interview with Aaron, exactly where I expected him to pick up the story.

"Well, getting back to the point at which we began, Aaron, how did the death of this student relate to either Leo Toland or Charles Marchand?"

"I interviewed both men back to back. I remember because one of them, can't recall who, rescheduled his appointment with us. They were seniors at the time, like me. Then, at one point, the other editor and I interviewed them again, but together," Aaron said. "Here's the issue. Leo Toland was dating, or had dated, this student. Charles Marchand also asked her out, but we know from her private…uh… papers that she didn't care to go out with him. She was pretty stuck on Leo."

"Papers?"

"A diary…the diary is in the collection at the public library in Birchwood, Illinois, and many people have gone over the public information in this unsolved case." Aaron put his hand on his chest. "I…I don't like the idea that a very young woman's private ruminations are in the public domain. But that's how I learned some of this information."

"I see," Coop said, "so we can assume both men had attended the frat party."

"No. Based on what we know, Leo Toland was at the party, although it's unclear if he spent time with the student who died. It was hosted by Leo's fraternity, you see. No one saw her leave the fraternity house, although she was definitively placed there."

Aaron stopped to take a quick breath. "Charles didn't belong to a fraternity and was not ever seen at or linked to that party. However, Leo and Charles were in the tutoring program and in some other student events and programs."

Aaron filled in the rest, including the detectives' interest in all who attended the party, as well as Charles, because his name came up in the diary. "The important part of this story is that its ending has never been discovered or told. This young woman, who would be the same age I am now, was dumped on the banks of the river and no one knows who put her there."

"Yes, I hope that as a result of your presence here tonight someone watching will be able to shed light on what happened on the night of that fraternity party." Coop pivoted to the heart of the issue, at least as far as I was concerned. "Is it fair to say that Governor Toland's claim that he barely knew Charles and had no prior relationship with him came as a surprise to you?"

"It did," Aaron said, "especially because I had read that Charles Marchand was planning a run against Leo Toland. Neither man said anything about their years together on that campus, as acquaintances if not close friends. And in all these years, the governor has never mentioned so much as one word about what happened on the Donaldstone campus his senior year." Aaron shrugged. "Besides, they were seen together the night Sandra died. And apparently, she was pretty upset with both men."

Bingo. Coop and his producers had filled him in, if he hadn't already been up-to-date on the story.

Commercial break.

My phone buzzed. Charles. Would Kenny be far behind?

Nope. A text…a simple one: *WTF?*

Good question? What the fuck had I put in motion?

"What now?" Rick said, suddenly looking troubled. "I mean, all this seemed intriguing when we tripped over it, but how does this help you prove anything about Marchand's innocence?"

"I can't say," I shot back. "I have absolutely no

idea."

"Then what's next, Matt?" Wendy asked.

I reached down and scratched Maude's back, thinking. I'd wanted to blow the lid off, and I had. "I think I better return these calls."

"Do you want us to wait?" Rick asked.

I shook my head. "At this point, I don't want either one of you to know anything beyond what we just heard, which is essentially what we already knew. We could get calls at the office…I don't know exactly why, but I don't trust Leo." Of course, I had my personal reasons, but I was still hiding them.

Feeling paranoid, and a little foolish, I reached for my wallet. "You two always take the train home. Not tonight. I want you to take a cab. Share one, and tell the driver to drop Wendy off first. Then, Wendy, you send Rick a text when you're in your apartment with the door locked."

Wendy's blue eyes opened wide in clear alarm. "Geez, Matt, you're scaring me."

I rested my hand on her forearm. "No, no, don't worry. I'm being super cautious."

True, but Leo had sent Zach to Marchand's door. That's the part they still didn't know.

Chapter Seventeen

I expected to have Zach with me when I went face-to-face with Charles. Instead, I had to settle for Kenny alone, but that was okay. Zach returned my call, but in cryptic language that made it clear he was doing the governor's business, leading me to believe Leo himself wasn't far away from wherever Zach was. The tone Zach used reminded me of a husband reassuring his wife that he wouldn't forget to pick up milk on the way home. But, on my end, the message was clear. He couldn't talk freely.

I'd not wasted time, either. I waited to be sure that Wendy and Rick were on their way home and called Charles to let him know I'd be coming by that night. He started to protest, using the lateness of the hour and all that, but I cut him off. Then I called Kenny, telling him that some missing pieces would now be on the table.

I parked my truck down the street from March-and's townhouse and waited for Kenny to arrive. I wanted him to hear it all. Mostly, I fumed, angry with myself over getting involved in this case in the first place. I had my fill of the privilege and entitlement, an underlying theme of this entire story. At the same time, figuratively speaking, I rapped my knuckles against my temple. Was I re-

ally so surprised that Charles and Leo would protect each other even in their mutual loathing. My
dad's favorite epithet had been "fuckin' big-shot,"
which was muttered in his boozy way whenever
someone acted from a sense of privilege—at least
from where he sat. Well, for once in my life, I
was inclined to agree with my otherwise sorry-
excuse-for-a-man dad. But, in spite of my disgust
with what I considered a sin of omission, I still
didn't believe Charles had killed his wife. Call
me naïve.

I got out of my truck in the guest parking area,
and Kenny pulled in right behind me.

The houses on the street were mostly dark, but
for a few flashing TV screens casting a blue-gray
haze in living rooms or dens in the homes whose
windows we could see from the lot.

Charles opened the door before we had a chance
to ring the bell. His expression grim, he looked
tired again, defeated. Not surprisingly, Kenny
looked like I'd dragged him out of bed with barely enough time to throw on jeans and a polo shirt.

"This better be good, Matt," Kenny said, his
mouth curling up in a lop-sided smile.

"That's going to be up to Charles," I blurted.
"No more stonewalling, not after—"

"You don't have to say anything more. I get it."

"It's about time." I glanced at Kenny, who
maintained a neutral expression, despite his client's foray into primetime national news. "You
know, this is going to be the buzz all over the *Trib*
and the *Sun Times*."

Charles raised his hands in the air, exasperated,
but helpless, too. "Nothing that was said has anything to do…"

We were still standing in the foyer, three tall,
male bodies, hands planted on hips, the pall per-

ceptible in the energy in the small space.

Finally, Charles gestured for us to come deeper into the house. He led us to what was a small room, more or less an old-fashioned den, rather than having us talk in the large formal living room.

"I can explain the whole ugly thing." He pointed to the bar. "Let's have a drink."

He ate up a few minutes filling three tumblers with ice and bourbon. He hadn't asked what we wanted. If he had, I'd have asked for mine neat. But at that point, I wasn't about to quibble over a drink.

"So, everything I say here is privileged, right?" Charles asked.

"Absolutely everything," Kenny replied. "That said, I want the whole story of how an unknown journalist running a two-bit paper in Minnesota, no offense to his weekly publication, ends up on a national TV show talking about something you failed to mention."

Kenny glanced my way, prompting Charles to do the same.

But on this point, I'd remain mum. I wasn't coming clean about anything. It was Charles' turn to do that. I had my reasons for holding back.

Charles took a big gulp of his drink and swallowed hard. "I don't know how Aaron Nagasaki ended up on that Cooper guy's show. Beats the hell out of me."

Aaron Nagasaki. He spoke his name with a certain familiarity.

"Start at the beginning, Charles," Kenny said, "and keep in mind the story Aaron told may have absolutely nothing to do with your case."

"No 'may have' about it. The whole thing, tragic as it was, is irrelevant to what happened to Sandra—whatever that was." He glanced down quickly, shaking his glass to make the ice clink against the side of the tumbler.

He's lying. I kept that thought to myself.

"We've been asking you for months to tell us about you and Leo," I said, "and you refused. You lied to us about your relationship with Leo. Enemies or friends, you knew each other."

"Not really. But something happened that linked us." Another gulp. Charles flopped back in the chair and tilted his head back, as if the ceiling had become the most interesting thing in the room. "I made one stupid mistake…no, two. First, I helped Leo out, made a bad decision. Then, not long before she died, I finally told Sandra about it."

I held back questions. I had dozens of them. Instead, I watched the body language, the anguish within Charles that came out on his face, his slumping shoulders and nervous hands. I figured he'd tell us in his own way in his own time. But I wasn't in an especially patient mood.

"Here's what happened," Charles said, leaning forward again. "The girl, Nancy, dated Leo a few times. Sleazy Leo, who never met a woman he wouldn't fuck. And abuse, if he could. He was—and is—a first-rate asshole. Sandra tolerated him, barely." He glanced at me. "You know, he gave cash to her causes and showed up when she needed him. So did his wife, another prize. They deserve each other."

"Charles…get to the point," Kenny said. "We know what Leo is, which is why I was inclined to believe you when you said you barely knew him."

Charles barked a cynical laugh. "I wasn't lying. I do barely know him."

"There's got to be more to the story than the two of you dating the same girl."

"He dated her, I tried to." He shook his head. "I'd give a lot, everything I own if I could have gotten her to go out with me instead of Leo. She might be alive today and having a normal life if I'd taken her out that night."

Kenny began to jump in, but I held up my hand to stop him. "Go on."

"So little to tell. I mean, so little to tell before… you know, before she died. I knew she'd been after that son-of-a-bitch Leo, and managed to get him to ask her out. But she looked miserable most of the time. I don't think she went out with him for long. I got the feeling he was sniffing at other doors all the time."

No, it wasn't long, not according to the diary.

Once again, I held my tongue, careful not to give anything away.

"What do you mean by miserable?" Kenny asked. He lifted his glass and took a small sip.

Of the three of us, Kenny had barely touched his. Driving, like me.

"She was unhappy. I remember thinking that she always looked like she'd been crying. She'd show up in class with puffy, red eyes." Charles set his drink on the end table and rested his forearms on his knees. "I recall one morning in our poli-sci seminar, she kind of stumbled in, her hair all messed up. I had the idea she'd been out drinking the night before and had a bad hangover." He rubbed his closed eyes with his thumb and index finger. "I wish I could wipe away that image."

"Because?" I asked.

"It was the last time I saw her alive."

Holy shit, we were finally getting somewhere.

"Because?" I asked again.

"Because she died of alcohol poisoning that very night. Only a few hours after I saw her at the seminar."

"Did that image come back to you in the days that followed?" Kenny asked, his voice low, almost gentle.

Kenny saw what I saw. Our client looked much the way he had when he talked about Sandra. As for me, I put the drink down and reached into my pocket for a couple of antacid tablets. My gut was on fire, reaching its worst point in a long time. Anxiety did that to me. So did impatience.

"No." He looked up. "I realized it that night. When I saw her. Dead."

A hush fell over the room. It was real to me now. More real than it had been sitting in the basement of the public library combing through files, reading photocopied pages of a diary I had invaded more than read. The silence broke with the sound of the register delivering cool air in a room that had suddenly become hot and small.

Charles drained his glass.

Kenny and I exchanged a glance.

"You don't need to ask," Charles said, dragging his hands down his face. "I'll get there. Just give me a minute."

We did.

Finally, the silence must have gotten to Charles, because he plunged in. "My second mistake, you see, was telling Sandra what I'm about to tell you." He stared at Kenny. "It's why divorce papers were found on her desk, and it's why the vacation plans were underway. She'd refused to go away with me, but I was sure—so certain—I could change her mind."

"Your so-called happy marriage was doomed over…uh, this girl named Nancy?" I asked, careful not to use her last name. Neither Coop nor Aaron had revealed her name, more out of respect than from hope that it could be kept private. Had anyone warned Nancy's parents? Someone was going to go on national TV and call attention to a cold case with the hopes it could be reopened.

"It wasn't so-called. We were happy all those years." Charles stood and paced back and forth. "That was no myth. She was exactly as she appeared for years and years, right up until the night at Café Brauer. The public Sandra and the private Sandra were the same person."

My thoughts switched to Zach, and the facts I was withholding. It was just as well that Zach couldn't come with me. I was hearing "what information had a way of coming out," and I was hearing it from Charles himself.

"Did you kill that girl—Nancy?" Kenny's voice boomed through the room. He'd even startled me.

"*No!*"

I knew Kenny's strategy in that moment. I agreed with it, and if he'd asked, I'd have recommended a bit of loud impatience to get to the core of what had gone on. Kenny had to get this not just moving, but focused. I doubted he believed Charles killed a girl and went on with his life. Leo, on the other hand…I wouldn't put it past *him*. Maybe Kenny wouldn't, either.

"But you knew she'd died. That's what you're saying?" Kenny prodded Charles.

"Just to get something straight here, Leo didn't kill her, either. At least I don't think so, at least not directly. He let her get drunk—or coaxed her to get drunk—and pass out. He probably stuck her in a basement at the frat house, thinking she'd sleep it off. Stupid…stupid," his voice trailed off.

"Wait, wait," I said, holding up my hand. "You were at this party? Didn't Aaron say otherwise?"

Charles waved me off. "Everything I know

about what happened at the frat house came from Leo, and the investigation afterward." He shrugged. "I know nothing first hand. I was alone that night. Out for a jog. That's why I saw what I saw. So, yeah, Leo told me that he found her dead in the basement. I believed him."

"Told you when?" Kenny demanded.

"I'm getting to that." Charles sat down in the chair again and held his head in his hands, muttering a string of unintelligible words, guttural sounds of anguish.

"Well, hurry it up. *I need to know*."

Well, well, my mild friend Kenny had reached his limits. Charles had pushed his lawyer too far, or at least Kenny wanted to leave that impression.

"Okay, okay." He looked up and stared at Kenny.

Reading the situation, I thought Charles had needed time to get it together, so he could force himself to meet Kenny's eye.

"God help me, I saw Leo carrying Nancy in a blanket. You see, we crossed paths while I was out for a late-night run by the river. He didn't expect to see anyone, so I startled him. Scared him. He told me she was dead. We argued about what to do. I grilled him about why he hadn't called a doctor in the first place back at the frat house."

"And?" I asked.

"The bastard claimed it was too late by the time he found her." He hung his head. "And it sure looked that way from what I could see. It doesn't sound reasonable now, but at the time, it never occurred to me he'd be lying about that. She was... lifeless."

Sighing, he added, "That's the best I can do. Over the years, I second-guessed myself, but not back then. I knew he could be the kind of guy the girls liked, a lovable jerk. At least at first. Then they'd catch on and the smart ones walked away from him. I didn't think of him as a guy capable of killing anyone. Not at the time."

"And you made a decision to stay quiet about the whole thing?" I asked, puzzled. Charles couldn't stand Leo, but he'd protected him. Why? What was behind the grip Leo had on him?

"I did." He shook his head. "Leo thought he was buying my friendship in some perverse way. But in hindsight, I know now that in reality, he was threatening me."

Kenny again stepped in. "We'll get to that. But, according to what you said, you ran into Leo before he actually hid the body."

Charles winced as he nodded.

My gut churned for the simple reason that the shame theme of this whole sorry story was about to surface.

In the next few minutes, we heard the dreary details of Charles hearing rustling on the embankment, watching Leo sliding down the steep slope that ended on the path where Charles was jogging. Their paths crossed in that moment, scaring them both. Leo had barely managed to hang on to Nancy's body. Charles could see her hair hanging out of the blanket. I thought of Zach talking about Sandra's hair hanging down over the stairs. Both images got to me. Somehow, the two women were victims of a couple of men behaving badly. Not directly, maybe, but they'd been caught up nonetheless.

"I was so stupid. Leo kind of manipulated me, you know…played on my fears. And my ambitions," Charles said, shaking his head. "We all knew Leo came from money. Daddy could be counted on to take care of his messes. I didn't have anyone to clean up after me."

"Did he threaten you?" I asked.

"Not until after I'd stood by and watched from the path while he went down another slope and hid Nancy's body in the tangle of trees and shrubs at the shoreline. Everything grew kind of wild below the path." His knuckles whitened as he tightened his grip on the arms of the chair. "It sounds unbelievable, but at the time, I thought I was protecting Nancy's reputation by letting Leo go ahead and hide her."

"But how did you think you could cover that up? What if someone had seen you?" Kenny asked, his face revealing incredulity.

"I took chances. You don't understand. As bad as I thought Leo was, I'd been following him from a distance all through college. I watched him, studied the way he walked, talked, sidled up to people and got their attention." He scoffed. "Oh, I was so fucking impressed. Leo had power, money, importance. Me? I had nothing…why do you think I ended up at Donaldstone? That place wanted me—it was like a courtship. They lured me in with a scholarship and then, as if protecting my pride, they signed me up for work-study, too. I had other jobs here and there, too, some on campus, some in town. It didn't leave much time for the fun and games, not like Leo and a lot of other guys."

"You mean Leo's money bought him self-importance?" I asked, my voice matter-of-fact. "And that swayed your willingness to watch him dump a dead girl at the edge of the river?" I suppose I hadn't minced words, but I wanted to be clear.

Charles let out a disgusted grunt. "Leo played on my vanity, telling me that he'd admired me, that he had connections through his family. If I wanted to go to law school, his dad could arrange an interview at a couple of schools. I went another route, but the offer was there." He ran his hands through his hair and cleared his throat.

Kenny and I sat through the silence. We could afford to give Charles time, to let him go at his own pace. The basic fact around which all the rumors circled was on the table.

"I worked my ass off in those years. I was still in high school when I took every AP class they let me. Even with a scholarship, I barely had enough money for room and board at Donaldstone. Living in a stinking dorm...and I do mean stinking." He was talking faster, louder, his emotions raw. "I was so fucking desperate. So close, just weeks away from my degree...I'd added classes so I could finish up by Christmas break. Free to go make my big mark in the world." He pumped his fist in the air. "What arrogance, huh?"

"Were Leo's offers that blatant?" Kenny still hadn't altered his astonished expression.

"Where did this conversation take place exactly?" I added, more interested in the facts than anything else. Emotions could wait. I'd process the motivations later. The question was how, or even if this scenario affected the case.

"Yes, that blatant...and he asked me to stand watch while he slid down that second embankment and left her. But mostly, he asked me to forget I saw him. I should have left him and run like hell. But, seeing him carrying her, knowing that Leo being Leo, if I refused, he'd claim he saw *me* on the path that night. He'd say he went for a jog to clear his head after the party. He'd find a way to put *me* in crossfire."

Charles stood and moved around the room, slapping the tables, gripping the backs of the

230

chairs, unable to stay still. "Yeah, the bastard scared me. Why not?"

"So, you thought Leo knew that you'd tried to date Nancy, but she'd turned you down?" I asked, trying to get a fuller picture of a young guy's fear. Ambitions and arrogance were powerful enough, but I sensed there was more.

"Leo said as much. He made some remark about me feeling bad about Nancy. Said she'd told him I'd asked her out, but she'd said no."

"Sounds like he was setting up a motive for you," Kenny said.

I agreed. It was a risk, though, to go along with that kind of scheme.

"So, you agreed to keep a lookout for those few minutes in exchange for keeping your mouth shut. He, more or less, threw you a bone," I said, "an IOU in the way of favors, but you had no guarantees that he'd make good on any of them."

"No, but it really wasn't Leo's candy I wanted. The thing is, I wanted him to forget he ever knew me. I didn't trust him. If the investigation zeroed in on him, then I figured he'd drop hints that I'd killed her. Deflect attention. No one could have sworn to where I'd been the night of the frat party. But they knew I wasn't there."

"You were confident about that?" Kenny asked.

"I was, but…I mean, how many people would be willing to swear that I hadn't wandered in, maybe left with Nancy. My roommates could have said I went on late-night runs. They used to razz me about it, like I was a guy who didn't sleep." His face scrunched up as if he were thinking hard. "You see, most of these guys had heard me talk about liking the river path, although I had a lot of routes. I changed it up for variety. When I stood there with Leo, sweat pouring off of me from the damp night and my run, it hit me that I was a sitting duck. As far as I knew, no one could vouch for anything." He stopped and stared at his feet. "That was the price I paid for keeping to myself so much. If it hadn't been for the volunteer stuff I signed up for, I'd have been labeled a loner—and we all know how scary that description sounds."

"So, the point is, Leo dumped Nancy's body, and no one came by, no one saw either of you." Kenny spoke the words flatly, as if this was the final word on the subject.

"And why was Leo so certain no one saw him leave?" I wasn't through asking the questions, no matter that Kenny, and probably Charles, wanted to wrap it up. Given what I knew about investigations and murder cover-ups, it seemed to me that Leo and Charles both had skated across some thin ice that could've cracked at any time and swallowed them up.

"I asked that over and over as we stood there," Charles said, nodding as if to assure us, "but he insisted everyone had either passed out or gone home. He knew about a way out of the basement that led through the woods to the river. The frat house sat on the edge of some kind of preserve. I knew the set-up, sort of, so it made sense…well, as much as any of it made sense."

Charles let out a ragged sigh, filled with regret. He could barely look at them. "I didn't see everything Leo did down on the shore, but he was only gone a few minutes, long enough to walk down the riverbank until he found a place he thought was hidden enough. That's what he said." He paused. "Even Leo, bad as all this was, wanted Nancy found eventually. He didn't want her parents not to know she'd died."

Real decent of him.

"What about the blanket?" I asked, my mind reeling with what could've gone wrong with this cover up scheme.

Charles shook his head. "I don't know. He didn't have it when he came back. He said he tossed it out into the river and watched it float away. Far as I know, it was never found."

Kenny had his own questions now. "And then you got your stories straight, I take it. You trusted him to keep his word?"

"Our stories were alike. Not much to remember or make up. I didn't go to the frat house and I went for a run. That part was all true." Charles paused. "The only made-up part was not seeing him."

"Why were you so certain Leo hadn't killed her?" Kenny demanded.

"At the time, sleazy as he was, that thought didn't cross my mind. It was all about saving his reputation, his future—and the fraternity's good name, such as it was." Charles had no trouble looking us in the eye when talking about Leo. His voice was confident and strong when he said, "He claimed that most people would assume she'd wandered off and made her way through the preserve and down to the river. Drunk and out of it. At the frat house, they'd blame themselves for not paying attention."

Charles smirked. "Yeah, sure, they'd worry for about five minutes. They were not a good bunch of guys. No wonder Leo wasn't worried."

"Drunk and out of it," I repeated, thinking of Nancy's parents arriving on campus, getting the news of her disappearance, and then her being found. "A rough image for the last impression the world would have of the girl."

Charles nodded. "Like I said, I didn't want Nancy to be talked about at all. I thought it would be worse for the memory of her if it was known she'd been dead in a basement when there was a party going on. Better to have people think she wandered off. Bad, but not as bad."

"If you say so," I said, unsure of how to compare the bad and worse in a situation like this. "Turned out no one was hunting for a killer anyway. The medical examiner didn't leave any room for doubt. No evidence pointed to any other explanation. The DNA was all incidental contact... just being around a bunch of people at the frat house. No semen, no bruising. Blanket fibers, but they had a dozen or so identical blankets in the frat house." When I'd come across that fact in the papers in the library file, it hadn't meant much. Now it did.

In some ways, this story reminded me of the case itself that had consumed us. No evidence except a body at the bottom of a staircase, no abuse, no sign of struggle. I hated ambiguous evidence. But that was often the only kind. The behavior of the two young guys itself was confusing.

"Since you claim to have liked her, seems like an odd way to act," I said, saving Kenny the trouble. He had to be neutral, tactful. I didn't.

Charles' jaw tightened. "Now you sound like Sandra."

"Is that so? Well, then, now is as good a time as any to tell us about your second mistake," I said, already more than a little disgusted by the sordid story. "We can come back to what happened when Nancy's body was found."

Charles went to the makeshift bar and held up the bottle, silently offering us a refill. I refused, and Kenny had barely touched his first. Charles fixed himself a short one and came back to the chair. When he sat, it wasn't powerful, successful, handsome Charles Marchand, but a guy whose shoulders drooped in defeat.

"I don't know which is worse," Charles said, his voice hoarse. "The pain of the past, of that night, knowing Leo had manipulated me, or the pain of telling Sandra about what happened."

"Why did you tell her at all?"

"Ambition...once again...my development business wasn't enough for me." Charles let out a cynical scoff. "I actually convinced myself that I could run against sleazy Leo Toland and win. And it was in his interest, and mine, to keep up the notion that we barely knew each other. We'd been doing it for years, and it was more or less true. Except for that one night."

Kenny waved him off. "Cut to the chase. Why didn't you keep your mouth shut?"

"Because the buzz about my political future had already started. You know, Lourdes Ponce was blogging and tweeting every day about the upcoming showdown between Leo and me. That new reporter, the politics girl at the *Trib*...what's her name?"

"Elayne Mertz," I supplied, although it had struck me funny that anyone named Elayne could be referred to as a girl, no matter how young. Elayne had been tracking the potential Toland-Marchand matchup for many months before Sandra died. There, I'd thought it again. Sandra died...not murdered, not killed accidentally. Died. I never could wrap my hands around the idea Charles was a killer. At least not a guy capable of killing his wife. I think that every human on the planet, even the popular Pope Francis and cheerful Dalai Lama potentially could and would kill under the right circumstances.

"Right," Charles said, nodding. "Elayne—she was on the story."

"So what?" Kenny asked, frowning. "There's nothing revolutionary about any of that kind of coverage."

"Unless you're Toland," I said dryly. Things were beginning to fall into place.

"Exactly," Charles said, appearing surprised that I'd understood what he was getting at. "And then Leo did something that scared the shit out of Sandra, and she doesn't scare easily. Uh, *didn't* scare easily." He shook his head again, his face a study in regret. "You don't know, you just don't know how much she put up with in order to have her charities, to have this public persona. A few years back, she had a stalker who managed to get through the security gate and right up to our back door." Charles gestured toward the back of the house. "Sandra came into the kitchen one morning and was greeted by a guy with a mask over his face looking at her through the window."

"I had no idea," I said, wondering if Wendy knew about that kind of incident. "Who else knew about that?"

"The police, of course. All they could do was recommend that she hire a body guard or two. We did use them occasionally, especially for the big galas, where fifteen hundred or two thousand people mingled, and someone could sneak up on her unnoticed."

Kenny and I were silent, both of us leaning toward Charles. Kenny wore his listening expression, and if I'd seen my own face, I'm sure it would have shown me alert and searching for kernels within his words, clues that maybe no one else had followed up on.

"She didn't want someone guarding her at her smaller events, like at the Café Brauer or one of her smaller luncheons." Charles' voice took on strength when he spoke about these decisions, and the ordinariness of them. "But a couple of years ago, an older woman, maybe seventy or so, showed up at a cocktail reception at the Hilton with some kind of so-called 'lady's gun'. It was pink and pearl-handled. Looked like a silly little toy, except it was real and tucked in her purse."

Kenny sighed. "What a travesty. I think I'll quit this business and become an anti-gun nut."

"You and me both," Charles said. "If I ever get a chance to run…oh, what the fuck am I talking about? My political days ended before they got off the ground. Anyway, this crazy gun slinger woman was working her way up to Sandra. But then she opened her purse and started reaching inside. Someone in the crowd, a man, spotted the gun and shouted to scare everyone into backing off. The woman ran, but didn't get too far."

Standing behind the chair, Charles whacked the top of the back cushion, his face red with anger. "Sandra drew crazies—and the envious."

"My assistant, you know, Wendy, who worked for Sandra, talked about that envy all the time," I pointed out. "But she herself came away from her time working for Sandra with resolve to succeed in *her* life, not try to copy Sandra's. Wendy saw other women aping everything Sandra did, right down to the kind of shoes she wore."

"Those people, those stalker types, have been investigated," Kenny said, addressing me, but ignoring a side trip into what Sandra tried to do for young women.

"I know," I said.

He'd filled me in on the police reports about

237

those stalkers, the street variety or those who tried to hide in cyberspace. They'd come up empty on all fronts. The masked guy at the back door was not a suspect, because he'd been serving a sentence for armed assault at one of the prisons downstate. The woman with the gun had been committed to a mental hospital in Florida, with her children appointed as her legal guardians.

I was waiting for Kenny to jump in and prod the conversation forward, but instead I saw him go still, as if finally patient with the unfolding narrative. I kept quiet, too.

Charles ran his hands through his hair. "A few weeks before the Café Brauer fundraiser, Sandra texted me at the office. She was at the cultural center to give the keynote to an international audience who were attending a training session in Chicago. They were all advocates for the disabled in their home countries."

Charles fell silent as he rubbed his eyes. Even Kenny had slumped back in his chair, prepared to give Charles some time. "At one point, a man Sandra described as good-looking and well-dressed, like a businessman or politician, approached her and *pretended* to engage her. He held out his hand, she said, flashed a big smile, like he was so happy to be meeting her. But while he shook her hand, he leaned in and said something like, 'Tell your husband to back off…things have a way of coming out.'"

"Uh, did she say what the guy looked like?" I kept my voice as cool and detached as I could manage, but my gut burned and churned inside.

Kenny frowned, no doubt wondering where that question came from. "Why do you ask?"

I shrugged. "No particular reason." I lied, of course, and added, "I was thinking about how he could be identified, that's all."

Great. Another thug in the picture. I had a question or two for Zach. Had he known about this visitor, the one who actually got the message delivered? I doubted it.

"As a matter of fact," Charles expanded, "she said something about him being tall, youngish, white blond, like a Norse god. She was joking, but I got what she meant."

Not Zach, that was for sure. He was neither youngish nor blond. The relief coursing through me was as surprising as it was real. I hadn't acknowledged the part of me that still didn't trust my brother.

"And I'm hearing about this now, Charles." Kenny glanced at me, as if acknowledging the numerous warnings I'd delivered about the boatload of crap Charles was hiding.

I kept quiet. I could have jumped in, maybe gotten up in his face and confronted him. Another lie of omission. But I waited. He seemed to have more to say. Hell, he might even disclose it on his own.

"It wasn't important—"

"The hell it wasn't," Kenny's voice thundered through the room. "Besides, *I'll* decide what's important and what isn't."

The crestfallen expression on Charles' face made me *almost* feel sorry for him. But when it came to Charles, I'd had that feeling before. *Why?* I asked myself that question often. Maybe because his wife had died, and no one knew exactly how. He was sitting in his own house, granted a big, fancy one, but with an ankle bracelet that tethered him to law enforcement and kept him restless, straining to get all this over with. Yeah, he lied. But it was difficult not to see him as a fundamentally decent sort.

"Finish your thought," I said. "Tell us what happened next."

Charles came around the back of the chair and sat down. "There's not much left to tell. That night I told her the whole story, starting with who Leo and I were in college. His money, his power. I told her about Nancy and how she didn't like me much and went after Leo. I described Leo's money and implied power, and my own lack of notoriety in school. Keeping to myself more than most of the students. I described exactly what happened at the river."

"And?" Kenny demanded.

Charles' face was red, sweat beads forming on his brow. "She told me I was a stranger. She paced back and forth in this very room and said she didn't *know* me. She acted like I'd covered up a murder, and was, to use a legal term, an accessory after the fact. At the very least."

Kenny and I exchanged a quick look. Good thing the trial *wasn't* about that old case.

He flopped back in the chair. "We had lived a lie, according to her. That's why she *demanded* a divorce. End of discussion. Ergo, the appointments with the lawyer. She wasn't wasting a minute to show me exactly what she thought of my past. She was enraged because the two of us had always operated by a code, our ethical code."

Charles kept on talking, but closed his eyes and rubbed his fingertips across his forehead. "She knew the way I did business and how I treated people who worked for me. I admired the way she conducted her philanthropic missions…and I do mean that as a plural. It's why it worked between us. It's like we got to have our passions and live well and share the best parts with each other."

Kenny got to his feet and walked to the make-shift bar. He exchanged his drink for a fresh glass and filled it with water from a pitcher on a tray. "She wanted a divorce because of that one secret? Because you'd never come clean?"

Charles thrummed his fingers on the arms of the chair, still red-faced and looking ready to burst. "Damn right. It was all about living a lie. *One mistake.* Putting Nancy's parents through days and weeks of hell. This wasn't an ordinary mistake, not in Sandra's eyes. It was big. I know that. She called it a moral failing…sounds formal, but she was right."

A hush fell over the room again.

Kenny drained his water glass. "I'm hungry."

I glanced at my watch. Granny's banana pancake would likely be my next meal. I had no appetite, maybe because I was queasy, or maybe it was because Charles had given me a glimpse of something inside him I didn't like to see. Oh, I didn't doubt he'd loved Sandra, but I could see in my mind's eye the fight at the Café Brauer carrying over to home. Her running up the stairs, him going after her. Arguing in the bedroom, the derision Sandra directed toward Charles. Her hatred of Leo. Accidents happen. Don't they?

"What have you got around here?" Kenny said.

With a shrug, Charles said, "Not much. But let me see if I can nuke a pizza or something."

Charles went into the kitchen, which meant crossing through the foyer and living room and the dining room, too. Out of sight, maybe out of earshot.

"Not to change the subject or anything," Kenny said, "but given what we've got, let's get ready for jury selection. Mirror jury to help us understand the real jury for sure."

"Based on what they've got and you've got, this trial could be over in less than a week." Cause of death was not an issue. The whole damn case boiled down to three words: *pushed or fell*. If it hadn't been for the public argument, there never would have been an arrest or a trial.

"I can't put him on the stand. If we probe into the reason for the fight, we open up a cold case in a little town on the river, for chrissake."

"Well, at least we know why Sandra reacted to Leo the way she did," I said. "I guess I understand Charles booking a trip. Hell, trying to make it up with her, hoping she'd forgive him. It's not unusual behavior."

Kenny nodded, "And he probably would have agreed not to run against Leo."

My phone buzzed. The text from Wendy was short: *If u can, CNN now.*

I picked up the remote and turned the TV on. A mother of all TVs, it spanned half the wall. I closed my eyes against an image forming of Charles and Sandra shutting out the world on some nights. They probably sat side-by-side on the couch and propped their feet up on the coffee table, maybe watching a movie and eating popcorn. Or, they settled in for a political debate. Regular stuff. Home alone.

"Go get Charles...now," I said, pressing the local number for CNN. There he was, Coop with Aaron in a replay clip. I pressed the record button for Charles, so he could see it all from that point in the interview.

Charles came into the room when the news anchor, Mary Patton, turned to Coop, who was live on the set. "So, when asked to react, the governor of Illinois, Leo Toland, issued a statement. Let's listen. The statement appeared in writing along

with some B-roll of Toland: *Charles March-*
and, currently awaiting trial for the death of his
wife, and I were acquaintances during our time
as students at Donaldstone College. Yes, indeed,
during those dark days when the young student
was missing, we were united as a campus in
searching for and ultimately mourning the death
of one of our classmates, a girl I knew socially. It
was a terrible tragedy, and like every other stu-
dent on our campus, I cooperated fully with the
investigation. Since graduation, I have crossed
paths with Mr. Marchand, usually in connection
to Sandra Marchand's public philanthropy, which
is why I was present at the Café Bauer fundrais-
ing event that took place on the evening prior to
Mrs. Marchand's tragic death. As I've said be-
fore, I was and will continue to be a supporter
of many of Sandra Marchand's good civic causes
and charities.

Not a word about the election, but then, what did
I expect? Leo had lied, but we'd already known
that. He had no reason to come clean. He'd gotten
away with everything he'd done.

The writing disappeared, and the anchor ad-
dressed Coop. "I'm wondering if you'll comment
about the reason any of this history matters now.
Do you believe there's a connection between the
governor and Sandra Marchand's death?"

"No, I'm not saying that," Coop said, "but I
was curious about the death of a young student,
and the Illinois governor's reluctance to acknowledge even a small link between himself and Mr.
Marchand. Why are we just hearing about their
connection now? Aaron Nagasaki, a journalist
then and now, has told us what he knows. The
young girl's diary mentions both men in entries
written shortly before she died. Her death was

ruled as alcohol poisoning. I'm curious why the governor has distanced himself from Charles Marchand, his old classmate."

What the hell? Nothing like making the link sound dangerous.

"That sonofabitch," Charles shouted at the TV. "Leo scared Sandra, and now he's acting all innocent. His statement is filled with lies. And I'm the only one who knows exactly what he did."

Feeling cold and harsh toward both men, I said, "For all the good that does you. You know exactly what you did, too."

"Don't you think I know that? Don't you think I'd like to shout out the fact to the world that Leo sent a thug out to scare Sandra, that he carried a dead girl to the river bank and left her there." He closed his eyes and tilted his head back. "And I helped him cover up what he'd done."

Still not done, he pointed to the TV screen, where an ad for a diabetes drug droned on. "But what the hell is this? Leo makes a statement full of half-truths and lies, and there's not a damn thing I can do about it. Meanwhile, my wife died and women in this city—and all over the damned country—think I killed her! I can't call out that bastard, Leo. I can't tell anyone why she hated *his* guts."

He flopped on the corner of the couch. "And after more than twenty good years, I suspect she hated me, too."

"If the so-called businessman thug hadn't forced the issue," I asked, "would you have ever told Sandra about what you did for Leo the night Nancy died?"

Charles cast an "are you crazy" look my way.

"Never. I planned to go to my grave with that secret. It's the single most shameful thing I was ever involved with. I lived with it. I stuck it in a compartment somewhere I stashed secrets." He thumped his chest over his heart. "And I don't have that many. Months and months would go by without ever thinking about that night, Leo, or Nancy. Meanwhile, I learned to live with myself, and become the kind of person I'd always intended to be, a builder not a destroyer. If I had decided to unload my guilty conscience, I'd have hunted up a priest."

Silence.

I could hear Charles inhale and exhale. Kenny stared at Charles. I still had questions.

"Running against Toland was sure tempting fate, wasn't it?" I asked, a little in awe of the audacity of it.

Charles shrugged. "He's fucking up the state. Besides, I assumed he'd leave the past alone. It wasn't in my interest to talk…and not in his interest to expose what he did."

"But there was fallout," Kenny pointed out. "Since we're putting it all out on the table, Leo did think it was in his best interests to threaten you through Sandra."

Nodding, Charles lifted his hands in a gesture of surrender. "What a price…"

"Charles, I know this is bleak, but…"

Kenny didn't finish the sentence because, I suspected, he had no clue what to say.

"Bleak? Yeah, that's a good word for it." Charles held his head in his hands again. "Do you have any idea what I wouldn't give to have that one night back? To jog the other way on the river path, to go to the gym and run on the indoor track? And if I had to do it over again, I'd tell Leo to go fuck himself."

Would he really? I wondered. Hindsight was a

valuable commodity. We all liked to be heroes in retrospect. I thought of a million things I could have done for my client Joey Haskell…starting with not taking on his appeal. I put my hand on my chest beneath my breastbone, where heartburn was rearing its head. Joey had a way of doing that. Sometimes it felt like he was reaching out from the grave, magically making my chest and gut burn as a form of revenge.

Charles puffed out his cheeks and blew out the air in one long breath. "I didn't kill my wife, but that doesn't mean I'm not responsible for her drinking too much that night."

Kenny looked thoughtful. "For what it's worth, based on what most everyone says, seems you did the right thing at the fundraiser. You got her to leave, you prevented a confrontation with Leo. You can't count people's drinks, not even your wife's."

"She didn't handle alcohol well," Charles said, his voice lowered. "That's the real reason she almost never had more than one drink. Her blood sugar would crash sometimes. She always had some kind of hard candy in her handbag or a cookie or something."

"Really?" I asked. "Was she hypoglycemic? You know, intermittent low blood sugar? She wasn't diabetic or anything, was she?"

Charles shook his head. "No, nothing like that. The doctors always said it was just some quirk with her."

Wendy had never mentioned any of Sandra's quirks, either because she didn't know about them or respected her privacy.

In my mind, something else lingered. And it went by the name of Zach. In all this conversation, the shock of knowing that Charles had withheld information about a threat made to Sandra and hadn't mentioned another stranger showing at the door stayed with me. Now I wondered if any of it would matter.

Chapter Eighteen

After a couple of slices of pepperoni pizza, we'd called it a night. We actually called it a night before we split up the sorry-looking frozen pizza. A great equalizer, microwaved food. It looks the same on paper plates in a two-million-dollar townhouse or an apartment in the projects. I kept that thought to myself.

We pivoted off of going over the same old ground when Kenny asked me to update him on what would come next as we prepared for the trial.

"Oh, yeah, a trial," Charles said, letting out a bitter laugh. "In the midst of all this, I almost lost track of what this is about. So, tell me, Matt, what will the million-dollar mirror jury do for me?"

I laughed back, although not bitterly. "We'll try to come in under a million."

By the time I got home, Maude was whining at the door. I quickly got her leash and took her outside. Maybe I'd sleep a couple of hours before I headed to Granny's. The Potash case was supposed to be my focus—it had to be. We'd had our mock trial, and in our version of events, Leann and her team had won…big.

I walked Maude around the block, past a couple of new renovation projects that were part of bringing my neighborhood back, as some called it. I guess I did, too. Others considered all the restorations, even the simple fixing up of the fixer-uppers, part of a grand scheme to displace people from apartments they could afford, pushing them out of my neighborhood and into a pre-gentrified one, a loaded term in itself. Reality bites. It was tough to see communities displaced, but was it better to let buildings crumble and decay?

Crumble and decay.

Interesting that those words came to mind. When I'd first visited Charles in prison, I might have used those very words to describe him. The gray pallor, hair cut too short, the faded orange jumpsuit with its fraying seams.

As his trial date grew closer, I hated knowing that the decisions I'd made, my research, or really, Wendy and Rick's legwork, my recommendation of a mirror jury instead of a mock trial, would to some degree determine what would happen to Charles. I hated it. Half the time I regretted answering Kenny's calls. In my worst moments, the vision of Charles growing old in prison, maybe dying there, kept me awake at night, or if the images came in my sleep, I'd open my eyes in a panic and a cold sweat.

In my own hidden places, I had a good feeling about this, despite Charles' secrets, omissions, and cover-ups. I'd had a chance to confront Charles about Zach's knock on the door the night Sandra died. I'd taken a pass. Why? I couldn't say. A couple of times, I opened my mouth, ready to drop the information. But something held me back. It was like an arm wrapping me in a chokehold, delivering a message that the time wasn't right for me to come clean over what I knew.

Once home, I settled Maude in her bed and I climbed into mine, expecting not to sleep at all. That's why waking up to the sun coming through the slats of the mini-blinds surprised me. I couldn't remember a single dream. Good.

I showered and dressed in a rush. In a rush to get myself a deep dish banana pancake.

I promised Maude I'd be back to get her, but she looked skeptical. I was convinced dogs were able to communicate disbelief. Maybe not all dogs, but Maude could. I'd left her alone for hours the previous day and night. She wasn't used to being treated like a dog who lived in an apartment whose owner occasionally visited. She was a creature on the go.

Once I got to Granny's, I waved to the familiar faces and claimed my table, ready to read my newspaper, but knowing Christina and Alexandra would have other ideas.

Christina came to my table first, no cigarette in hand, though, and no drink, either.

"Hey, Granny, what's missing and why?" I asked.

"Had a big scare last night. Nothing for you to worry about, though."

I did worry. "Might as well spill it, because I'll put you under the hot lights and interrogate you until you give me the details."

"Just a quick trip to the ER…chest pains and all that. The doc, or one of those not-quite-docs, told me that my heart was okay, for now. Indigestion, maybe my liver's getting older faster than the rest of me. But it's the smoking that's going to do me in."

I smiled to myself. Finally, somebody, a physician's assistant, it sounded like, put a little scare into Granny. It was about time.

She pushed up the short sleeve of her black blouse. "Looky there, Professor, ever seen one of these?"

"Nicotine patches? You bet I have. Many a friend of mine quit after a box or two of those. I think they're better than the gum. People get addicted to chewing that nicotine gum. Upsets their stomach, too." I squeezed her arm. "You stick with the patch."

"I will," she said with an amusing sneer of disgust. "But they're taking all the fun out of my life, these docs. I guess it's worth stickin' around to find out what the jury says about Sandra's husband." With her chin, she pointed up to the mounted TV screen. "I gotta watch the people on TV to find out anything around here. You won't toss any juicy tidbits my way."

I laughed. "You better take care of yourself. This would be a much-diminished world without you in it."

"You flattering Mom again?" Alex asked, moving in alongside her.

"I'll do whatever it takes," I teased, "to keep her around a long time…except violate my professional ethics and tell her all my clients' secrets, of course."

"That's okay. Your guy, that Cooper fella, is Mom's new TV boyfriend. He's keeping her on her toes. She can't die until all the cold cases from the last fifty years are solved."

"I'll be sure to tell Coop," I said, hoping this would be the end of the discussion. Granny never had believed that I nothing to do with Coop and Aaron's interview. I could deny it as an outlandish suggestion, but she wouldn't buy it.

I gave Alex my order, just as a formality, and the steps of my morning routine continued. Polish off the pancake, fetch Maude, go to the office, see what Wendy and Rick were doing with our new attitude survey for Charles, talk to Leann about Potash, walk Maude, and worry about Charles until it was time to sleep, and get up and drive to Granny's for another pancake and start it all again.

That morning, Leann called just before going into court. She was a confident attorney, a good advocate, but never cocky. Because the work Wendy had done on the community attitude survey matched the profiles of any number of people in the jury pool, she'd seated her dream panel. Every one of them had an obvious or subtle interest in heart health, their own or someone else's. Fudged data on a blood pressure drug, especially suppressing side effects, had a way of alarming regular people, the millions like me, who counted on a drug to be as safe as possible. I took those magic acid pills, and I didn't like the idea that medical professionals suppressed risky side effects. I wanted relief, yes, but not at the price of some outlandish side effect…like death. We needed a jury with attitudes like that, and it turned out that wasn't hard to assemble.

Potash hadn't been pleased with the demographic pool, but they had to deal with reality. Part of that reality was the many people who had a low opinion of Big Pharma right out of the gate. It gave the plaintiffs in these drug company cases an advantage.

"Every night this last week," Leann said, "I drive home thinking I'll get a call saying they want to talk. I only wonder how high the opening number will be. They know what we have, and they aren't thrilled with the jurors for obvious reasons. Older married women, men on the verge of middle-age. People likely to have a drug prescribed to control blood pressure, regulate blood sugar, lower cholesterol, thin the blood… you know the cluster of the stuff that scares the average Joe."

"I agree with you. I think Potash will try to minimize—every way they can—their complex relationships with universities and the major medical centers. Somehow Big Pharma paying doctors to test their drug tends not to sit well," I said, sounding like the professor Christina and Alex thought I was. My voice rose from the intensity behind my conviction about that little term "conflict of interest" in medicine. "If nothing else, this case is exposing the dark underbelly of institutional and academic medicine."

"Be nice if the case could change it."

"Come on, Leann, that's not our job," I said, trying to be realistic, "but industry people are bound to notice. Even the top tier medical associations are finally questioning the ethics of paying academic docs to test their billion-dollar drugs."

"I know, I know," she said. "The fact that they're not trying to settle and keep their name out of the news disturbs me. I'm always worried I might have missed something, data waiting to blow up the case."

I assured her that was unlikely, and we ended the call. With that hand-holding portion of my day behind me, I called Wendy into my office so we could go over our plans for the Marchand mirror jury. I'd chosen a mirror jury over a mock trial, because this wasn't the kind of case where we'd change course based on what our mock trial jurors said about the evidence and witnesses. That worked for trials where we had leeway, choices about what to present, what to leave out. A luxury, sometimes. But most everything the prosecution had, and Kenny had on Charles' behalf, was already baked into the cake. We couldn't invent new evidence. All we could do was adjust our style a little bit here, a little bit there. We had to try to tilt the subtle things, like how Charles behaved when they showed the medical examiner's photographs. Not that I believed in manipulating body language.

Well, maybe I did, sometimes. For a good reason.

In Charles' case, I didn't think he could create an inauthentic response to the visuals of Sandra at the bottom of the stairs or a close-up of her head wound.

Meanwhile, we had to pick the actual jurors… soon…and then match the mirror jury to the reality of who we had to convince. One person, a hung jury. It took all of them to convict.

"Based on your interviews," I asked, "are we better off with men or women?"

"We avoid young women at all cost. The older the jury the better," Wendy said. "But youngish guys tend to believe this kind of tragic accident can happen. Women are less inclined to think that."

"Kenny has lined up character witnesses—not difficult to do." I wondered how much what they had to say would count in the end. "Jordan Hayes, Sandra's half-sister, will testify, and a couple of Sandra's close friends will say they saw her in the six weeks or so prior to her death and she never mentioned divorce."

"Age is the biggest factor," Wendy pointed out, waving a sheaf of printouts. "Not race, and income only marginally, although it's true across the board that people think money buys justice and rich people are not held accountable for their behavior. Well, at least not in the same frequency as the middle- or lower-income people."

"No surprise there. So, let's use that and try to get a few wealthier types on the jury."

Wendy nodded. She made no move to end our meeting, as she normally would. Instead she stared across the desk and said, "So?"

"So? What do you mean?"

She threw up her hands in frustration. "For one thing, how is Charles doing?"

"He's doing as well as you would imagine. Hopeful on some days, miserable on others, terrified. Missing Sandra—a lot."

"I may have misjudged him, Matt. I realize that."

I thought a minute and finally said, "I actually think you'd like him. I saw nothing, and have uncovered nothing, to lead me to believe otherwise." That was true, if I overlooked his one so-called youthful indiscretion.

"You can't tell me more than that?" She grinned, knowing the answer.

"Your expression says it all," I responded. "Without violating any privileged information, I can tell you that Kenny got some clarifications about Leo and Charles. Once this is all over... we'll see."

I stood, a reliable way to end a meeting when there was nothing more to say. I had somewhere to be. I pretended to glance at my watch and act surprised by the time. I grabbed my jacket, and said, "I've got to get going. I have a meeting to get to."

Wendy stood, too, and gave me a pointed look. "Another meeting you don't have on your calendar, at least in the day planner Janet and I use to keep track of you."

I cast a pointed look back. "Speaking of that, you and I have a meeting with a potential client next week. A couple of other things Leann's partner is taking on might involve us." I smiled. "Tell Rick and Janet we can't have any more slacking off around here."

She gave me a weak military style salute. "Yessir, I'll be sure to send the message."

"On the serious side, I'm glad we have Rick. Irons in the fire, so to speak."

I left feeling good about the small team I'd assembled. Despite all the frustrations, and sometimes, even a degree of despondency, there was something about the Marchand case that felt like coming home. Too much so, maybe, but I couldn't deny it. Even within the aura of verdict fear, there was something undeniably exciting about the adrenalin rush of beginning a trial when so much was at stake.

I had no time to either revel in my cheap thrills or dwell on the fear eating holes in my stomach. I headed to the Lakeview Market and found Zach already sitting in our usual booth, thumbing through the *Sun-Times*.

I'd called this particular meeting. Instead of dreading that we'd run into each other and have an awkward, stumbling two-minute conversation, I'd begun to look forward to seeing him. I had something on my mind; sort of a plan. I couldn't talk about any of it. Not yet.

We ordered our usual grease-laden burger platters. Come to think of it, the biggest meals I had lately leading up to Charles' trial were at Granny's and with Zach at the Lakeview Market. Everything else was on the fly, or so it seemed.

"What have you been up to?" I asked Zach after

our round of small talk greetings were over.

He drew his head back and narrowed his eyes into slits. "Whaddya mean?"

I let out a bark of a laugh. "I didn't mean anything bad by it." But, of course, I phrased the question just to get his response. It was what I expected.

He flashed a lopsided grin. "You know I can't be shootin' the shit about my secret life."

"What if you didn't have to?" I shot back.

His face went blank. "Huh?"

"I wonder how much longer you have to stick around where you are. When is the note stamped paid in full?"

"Why do you ask, little brother?"

"No reason," I lied. "But let's put it this way. If you ever had a chance to do something else, say if Leo lost his next election, and what he needed from you changed, or, I dunno, maybe went away, what would you do?"

Zach plunked his elbow on the table and rested his cheek in his palm. "I know one thing. Charles Marchand ain't gonna chase Leo out. Somebody else, maybe, but not your guy."

"True. But that wasn't the question."

"Let me think," he said, tapping his temple.

He took a few more minutes to ponder his future while the waitress brought our food to the table. Then, biting off one end of a French fry, he said, "I wouldn't mind private security detail. Maybe for candidates coming to town, or big bashes, like the charity shindigs are. Glitter and gold. I could easily get a group of guys—and some gals—together to hire out to someone like that Sandra Marchand, or big-shots coming into the city." He grinned. "I always think of your father talking about big-shots. He didn't hang around long, but I remember him better than my sperm donor papa."

"I guess that would make sense. You were old enough to remember my dear old dad better than I do."

Zach's reaction about what he'd do in the future surprised me, although there was a legit part of what he did for Toland. It wasn't all about delivering messages in the middle of the night. "You'd really keep doing this kind of work?"

"Yeah, but I'm not done." He grinned again. "I've got a two-part answer. I only got through part one. You see, I liked the contracting work, while I could do it. Maybe I couldn't have my own setup anymore, but I like bringing shabby things back to life. We got a couple of churches out on the Northwest side need refurbishing and upgrades. I like the history part of these jobs. Those churches can spruce up their original stained glass windows, but people like modern bathrooms, not the ones with worn out floors with broken tiles circa 1930."

I detected passion coming through as he kept talking. I laughed to myself. I enjoyed hearing him talk about bringing historic churches back to their former glory, and the city had a lot of those buildings. At the same time, it was almost unbearably sad that a long-ago mistake had kept him trapped in the shadow of a powerful man. I stored away his answer to revisit at another time.

"By the way," I said, lowering my voice and scanning the room to make sure no one was near enough to eavesdrop. "Still no mention of that night, what you said. None." I wasn't violating privilege, since Charles hadn't said a word. If he had disclosed that missing piece of information, I'd have kept my mouth shut.

"He doesn't know that you found those journalist kids, well, not kids anymore, does he?"

"No." I left it at that, and for the rest of our lunch, we avoided business, his or mine.

We both paid in cash, but he picked up his newspaper, prepared to finish his beer and give me time to get back to my office and not run into each other.

"It won't be long now," I said when I was ready to slide out of the booth. "The trial, I mean."

"Yeah, I got that. And, uh, good luck."

I nodded. "I'll be in touch."

Out on the street walking to my office, it occurred to me that something had changed between my brother and me. It was almost as if we were brothers again...almost.

Chapter Nineteen

Not long after I hired Rick, he compared the themes he created for his games as akin to trials, which in his mind were the ultimate in depicting battles of good versus evil. At the time, I almost went into law professor mode and delivered a lecture about the lines separating good and evil aren't always so steadfast—or even discernible. I'd tell him that being innocent of a particular crime doesn't tell us much about the quality of the person or offer insight into guilt or innocence in another crime.

I liked Charles—there was something about him I'd admired all along. But why did I have a positive impression of him? Maybe because I admired his building projects, his preservation attempts, and Sandra's life reflected well on his. On the other hand, I was a keen observer of human nature. I knew Charles was neither a perfect human being or necessarily incapable of giving his wife a shove when she was ranting at him after he revealed his worst secret to her.

As we approached Charles' trial, I wondered about the real crimes he might have committed, like withholding information from his wife, violating relationship rules, but not the law. Or, the big one, standing silent while Leo hid a body, which was at least a felony, a conspiracy by definition. No matter how you put it, that was one bad mistake. But was it a crime? Should he be punished? His life ruined? Those kinds of questions raced around in my head sometimes, especially because in many ways, they were useless. Charles' life was already in shambles—even if the verdict went our way.

Unfortunately, most people think trials are like movies and plays, or miniseries or weekly dramas, where the crimes are well-defined, as is innocence. A few trials are more like sitcoms, or a classic farce, but probably not as many as most of us would prefer. Like a good stage play, trials *do* have opening acts and a cast of characters, rising and falling action, a twist here, a turn there, a few surprises, a crisis or two, and the wrap up scene, and maybe an epilogue.

On TV or the stage, all the dry stuff is condensed or pumped up to keep viewers excited. In modern trials, especially the complex ones, science is an equal partner alongside the fuzzier eye-witness testimony. The bigger roles that labs and forensic science play, the less useful the notoriously unreliable eyewitness testimony has become. That's an upside, but graphs, charts, and scientists in general are challenged to keep jurors awake during their testimony.

When Charles' trial finally started, Kenny wasn't happy with the jury. Well, neither was I. Too many youngish women and those on the edge of middle-age, too few older men. We tried. We used our challenges. We skidded into our second-best profiles. Just like any other trial of local renown, it was difficult to find people in Chicago without an opinion. It was impossible to find anyone who hadn't heard of Sandra Marchand. It's easy to blame a jury when things go bad, but evidence—and undeniable facts—matter, too. Hard evidence was sketchy in the first place.

Wendy and I were in the courtroom the second and final day of jury selection. Judge Lyons, who'd been on the bench when I was still handling criminal cases, liked to keep things moving along. She had a reputation for being fair, but fast. She openly showed disdain for showboating and posturing. She held special contempt for attorneys moving along at a languid pace and keeping themselves in the spotlight. Just because we had hundreds of potential jurors didn't mean Lyons intended to hear from every one of them. She had a reputation for being tough, and indeed she was.

The courtroom was packed, with a feed into a room reserved for the press pool. The crime reporters were joined by, and competing with, the people on the politics beat. What a bonanza for political junkies and the politicians they followed. This case couldn't escape the link with the stained image of Illinois politics and what looked like the certain destruction of a political career that had barely lifted off the ground. That's what happens when potential candidates end up arrested and charged with crimes before the voters have their say.

Assembling the mirror jury was easy enough. That job was clearly defined, and we paid the folks for their time, especially if they were unemployed or retired. Our secret jury was a good mirror image of the group we had for the real event. Once the trial started, we'd interview these men and women at the end of the trial day and see what they had to say. And we'd adjust accordingly, if we could.

Ho-hum…that's the technical description for the first day of trial. Two brief opening statements, with lead prosecutor Artie Okulek focused on about 80 percent on the motive…the impending divorce, the bad night at Café Brauer, and Charles' ambitions. I couldn't fault him.

Kenny's intro to the jury repeated a couple of key facts, mainly that no evidence, not a shred, he said, showed anything approaching proof that a murder had taken place.

The second day, we heard Charles' 9-1-1 call, the police report, and medical evidence. No argument anywhere on either side. Yes, Charles was distraught, in shock, but not inebriated. And, as any worthy medical examiner would say, it wasn't his job to determine how the injury that killed Sandra occurred. That was the job of two opposing attorneys.

Kenny asked very few questions, only those necessary to establish uncertainty about how the head injury occurred. In a case like Marchand's, the less time the medical examiner spent on the stand, the better. Although the details weren't definitive, it wasn't hard to picture a struggle or a push—or both—resulting in the fall that left Sandra dead.

As for Charles' reaction, Kenny kept a hand on his shoulder while he sat stoically, grim-faced, and at times with his hands folded over his mouth. He shifted in his chair when the forensic team and the medical examiner's photos were projected on a large screen. I observed a few jurors wincing.

I watched the day play out firsthand in the courtroom, and then again, on the recorded version we watched later in my office. Wendy interviewed the mirror jurors, and in spite of having a good impression of Charles, the prosecution team won the day. Not that Artie Okulek could take credit. It's hard for the prosecution not to win the first day of a murder trial, where the jury was presented with the evidence that a death had indeed occurred.

From the witness list, we saw Okulek's conventional set up of the way to argue a murder. Motive was next, presented to make it possible that the scenario offered fit their theory of the motive and the act.

On the third day, Steve Dale, the Chicago pet expert and also director of the no-kill shelter, was called to the stand to confirm facts of the event, which had brought in several hundred thousand dollars. Despite what Charles had initially maintained, Sandra's charities hadn't dramatically suffered in the previous, economically leaner years. That was an assertion made to Kenny and me, and easily blown.

As others on the scene that night gave their take on the mood, Sandra's behavior, and Charles' attempts to hustle her away, it occurred to me that we were in for one more surprise. Everyone who testified had seen Sandra at other events. Each witness expressed dismay and even disbelief with what they'd seen, from Sandra throwing back a glass of champagne with obvious anger to her high-pitched laughter as the evening wore on.

Even more mysterious, at least to our mirror jury, were Sandra's failed attempts to hide her seething contempt for Leo. Short snippets of cell phone videos were shown to these individuals, none of whom offered any statements that countered what the video demonstrated. The moment of Sandra's hot anger at Leo was there for all to see, and a couple of witnesses admitted to being jolted by it when they witnessed it at the event.

Their stories hadn't changed from the interviews detectives had conducted within days of Sandra's death.

So, in terms of setting up motive, we had alcohol, rage, political rivals, and a husband last seen almost dragging Sandra out the door and packing her into their Lexus. No one knew what went on during the ten-minute drive home. No one else saw either one of them again that night. Well, almost no one, but only Zach and I knew that—and probably Leo.

On the fourth night, I sat in the conference room, posing questions to our secret jurors, not surprised by the comments we heard back.

"I haven't heard the other side," one guy said, "but it sure looked like Sandra wanted to get rid of her husband, and he got rid of her first."

An older woman nodded. "And tried to make it look like an accident. He didn't count on all those people seeing their big fight that night."

Big fight. Was that how it came across?

"Oh, I don't know," a young woman said, "maybe she just fell. I fall when I drink too much."

Reasonable doubt, and based on common assumptions or experience. Our evidence, in the form of character witnesses, and booked airline tickets and a hotel room, would work with preexisting reasonable doubt.

Once our phony jurors had gone home for the night on the fourth day, Wendy, Rick, and I sat around polishing off what was left of a pot of decaf coffee.

"Are trials always this dull?" Rick asked. "I kind of had the idea that good versus evil was battled out in front of a rapt audience…the jury of our peers and all that."

I chuckled. "That's what everyone thinks. But

what you're describing is more like politics. It's why I follow elections. You know, the debate fights, the foot-in-mouth ailment, the accusations hurled between candidates claiming to be friends."

I let out a mock sigh. "As it happens, I'd been looking forward to someone challenging Toland. Could have been Marchand, and he could have won."

"But to answer your question," Wendy said, "the civil cases are even worse in some ways. They are data, data, data, and a little more data. On the other hand, you can be surprised. Sometimes we see the effect of one mistake—or a conspiracy of lies—on individuals. Real people. But with Marchand, the prosecution has its theory of the case, and we poke holes in it. It comes back to reasonable doubt."

"The fact is," I said, having decided to put the truth out there, "if it hadn't been for the Café Brauer fundraiser and Sandra's public scene, this would have been ruled an accidental death. Investigators would've seen a couple who had plans to take a vacation, and trouble in paradise would have been explained away as a rough patch in a long marriage. Even if she'd been drinking at home, Sandra's blood alcohol level wasn't enough to raise eyebrows, but was probably enough to make a fall plausible."

About to jump out of my skin, I got up and stood behind the chair and took hold of the leather across its back. "The fact is, that's very likely what happened anyway. It's the *only* explanation that matches the whole set of facts within the house itself. It's what Charles says must have happened, even though he didn't see it. Besides, there is nothing to indicate that Charles is anything other than who he says he is."

Almost nothing.

Wendy looked serious, but then she smiled. "You're probably right."

"Wait," Rick said, "nothing so far is making that case."

"It's not our turn yet," Wendy said, rolling her eyes. "Trials may be boring as hell, but you still have to be patient. You weaken what they have on the other side, and then you wait your turn."

I laughed. "You really need to go to law school."

She responded with a one shoulder shrug. "Been thinking about it."

Good for her. If she wanted to take that path, I'd help her make it happen, as long as she didn't desert me anytime soon.

The trial should have gone along and followed its logical path in key areas: cause of death, plausible motive, closing argument. Artie Okulek had other ideas, in order to help put the last nail in the coffin.

I groaned. I really was turning into Janet.

Kenny greeted me on morning six with the news that Artie planned to call one additional witness. None other than Governor Leo Toland. Of course, the lead up to the news didn't unfold dramatically, like it did on TV. No suspenseful theme music, just a phone call. Kenny did what lawyers in this position often do and said he was blindsided and needed time to prepare, meanwhile demanding that Artie prove relevance.

The teams met with the judge in chambers.

Okulek was prepared. "It was public knowledge that the defendant was going to enter the political arena and challenge the current governor in the next election. We have on tape Sandra's behavior toward the governor, and the distanced way in which the two men behaved toward each other. We believe he offers additional information on the state of mind of the deceased."

Kenny lost the argument, which centered on the 200 plus people who also had information. It was a weak argument, but it was all he had. And damn it, we couldn't put Charles on the stand and lie— or tell the complete truth about Leo and Charles as classmates.

We met with Charles that night, again in the den. Naturally, no matter how smart a client is, the first impulse is to insist he tell his own story. They all think they have great power to win over a jury—sheer force of personality.

It didn't take long for him to simmer down because of the can of worms it threatened to open. It galled him, though, that he ended up in the defendant's chair while a guy he could barely stand to look at, and whose ethics and style he disdained, would be in the witness box.

"We won't know exactly what we can ask," Kenny warned him. "If Artie opens up the past, then we can, too, but that's a risk."

"It's doubtful they'll probe too deeply into college days," I said, rubbing the back of my neck, which had stiffened with tension from the stress. "I don't get why they want to open the past up for review, so to speak. What the hell are they thinking? They watch CNN, too. They've heard about Aaron Nagasaki-Hanson and Nancy."

The size of the room seemed to shrink as Charles paced, his nervous energy changing the air in the small room. This shouldn't have blindsided any of us, but it did.

"It's not in Leo's best interest to bring up Donaldstone or Nancy or any of it. If it comes up, he has to lie," Kenny said, "because if he tells the truth, he walks into a case against himself. No joke."

I took my phone out of my pocket and pretended to scroll through it like I'd missed a call. "Um…I have to take this. I'll be right back."

Kenny frowned, looking like he wanted to say something, but I'd left the room before he had the chance. I stepped out the patio door in the kitchen and onto the back deck. I punched the number I used to reach Zach when I needed to talk to him right away.

He picked up on the second ring. "I thought I'd hear from you. Was going to try you in a few minutes."

"What's up with Leo and the testimony? Do you know what they've prepped him to say?"

"Nope. All I know is he's pissed. He was slamming around his office, yelling at his aide about having nothing to offer. He knows nothing, according to him."

"Really…maybe that's a bullshitting act. I smell a surprise coming our way."

"No. I know the bastard well enough by now to see when he's caught by surprise. He fought this. All he's hoping is to look like a good citizen doing his job in the interests of justice. That's horseshit, but he's spent most of the day getting himself wound up and ready. Gotta have that script right. That's 'cuz he tells so many lies. I told him that he had to be cool, you know, chill."

"You said that to him?" Why did that come as such a surprise. I thought of Zach as a kind of trusted shadow figure, not a confidant.

"Yeah, he listens to me about that kind of thing. It's part of my buddy-buddy stuff. The guy doesn't really have any friends. He's fucked over everybody, so instead of friends, he has people in little boxes he pulls out and uses when he needs them. His wife spends as much time in Florida in the winter and Wisconsin in the summer as she can get away with."

"Great. Remind me to avoid all criminal trials in the future, will ya? You know, if you hear me talk about some criminal case that sounds interesting, lock me up until I get over it."

Zach laughed. "You got it, little brother."

I went back inside the townhouse surprised by what I'd said to Zach. I talked about the future, like he and I would have one. Together.

Chapter Twenty

Leo didn't look any better in person than on television. I had called him doughy before and that was accurate. A well-tailored suit and an expensive haircut couldn't make him look any better. When Artie said, "The State calls Governor Leo Toland, your honor," all eyes in the crowded courtroom watched Leo walk up the center aisle to the witness box, where he, like everyone else, took the oath.

Like hell he'd tell the truth.

Artie dispensed with the trivia, the easy stuff. He confirmed his presence at Café Bauer on the date in question. He confirmed his presence at other fundraisers for the shelter, and other events Sandra held. In response to a question about a gala, organized by Sandra, benefitting the Fine Arts Council, Leo described it as a typically well-run event that his wife insisted they attend every year.

"Were you aware that the defendant, Charles Marchand, was considering a run for governor, which meant challenging you in the primary election?" the prosecutor asked.

Simple question. Leo said yes, that he'd heard the rumors.

"What was your reaction to these rumors?" Artie asked.

Leo shrugged and a smug expression took over his face. "I didn't think much about it. The election was still several months away. I had… *have*…confidence that voters recognize the progress we've made in our administration."

"Did you have a primary challenger?"

"No, I did not."

"What is your relationship to the defendant, Charles Marchand?" Artie asked.

"I'd call him a casual acquaintance. We don't have a relationship to speak of." Leo sat ramrod straight, looking at Artie and the jury, finally glancing at Charles as he answered.

I could have read something into the passing acknowledgment, but that would have been subjective based on what I knew.

"You and the defendant were classmates at Donaldstone College in Birchwood, Illinois, were you not?"

"We were."

Leo knew how to testify…close-mouthed. Yes or no answers, short phrases, not going a millimeter beyond what was asked. Perhaps he was trained to testify, perhaps he'd had a lot of experience being deposed through the years. Either way, he had the marks of a good witness.

"At that time, were you friends, fraternity brothers, perhaps, involved in the same activities?"

Leo's version matched Charles' story of their non-friendship, with only a few occasions during which their paths crossed.

Sitting behind him in court that day, I sensed Charles' fear rising, building second by second, becoming heavier and weighing him down. In my mind, I willed him to breathe. Kenny wrote a note on the legal pad in front of him and pushed it toward Charles, who read it, and sure enough, he inhaled deeply. We needed Charles to look cool, unfazed by the presence of his nemesis in the courtroom. Talk about a life flashing before our eyes.

I went back in my imagination to a riverbank and a pact between two young men worried about their futures. Charles' decision that night had finally come back to haunt him, and in a force so strong it changed his life.

Artie touched on Nancy Bayless. Briefly. Almost as if he was satisfying the public's curiosity. In a matter of a minute or two, Leo affirmed knowing Nancy and dating her, noting her presence at the party at the frat house, and being interviewed about her death.

"Were you and the defendant interviewed by both law enforcement and student journalists about your knowledge of Nancy and her death?"

"As I recall, we were in the same group of students who had been called in for interviews."

More like back to back interviews...the way that suited you. And Charles.

Artie, bone thin and more stooped than the average guy in his fifties, walked back and forth in front of the witness box. He was a jumpy prosecutor, almost never sitting, always on the move, distracting jurors with his tendency to wander around in the small sphere he owned at the moment.

My heart raced, along with my burning gut. A great combination, palpitations and acid. Surely, Artie wouldn't bring up the diary. But where was he going with this? The diary reflected poorly on Leo, but not on Charles. So the girl had turned Charles down for a date, called him a nice guy.

That was his big crime. Leo wasn't so nice.

"Is it true that the cause of Nancy's death was ruled as alcohol poisoning?"

"Yes, that is my understanding."

"According to the police reports, Miss Bayless' body was found on the banks of the Mississippi River not far from the fraternity house. It was never determined how her body came to be in that location. Is that your recollection, Governor Toland?"

"Yes."

"And that's why it's still considered a cold case, isn't it? Because the medical examiner believed she had died elsewhere and her body had been moved to the location at which it was discovered several days later."

Sonofabitch.

All this was completely irrelevant. Kenny had to be careful. Artie was smart. Somehow, he was going to pivot to Sandra and her anger, and leave a lingering impression of an unsolved crime that Charles was questioned about.

"I assume so," Leo said. "It was a terrible event. The campus was in shock over our classmate's death."

A gamble there. The gamble being that Kenny would want to ignore this, not point out that Leo had dated Nancy. None of it was relevant, but Artie made it so, based on the two men's hostile attitude at Café Brauer, presented as some kind of trick to pit the men against each other and somehow upset Sandra. Leo knew Charles wouldn't challenge any of what he said. The last thing Charles wanted was to contradict Leo on the Nancy Bayless issue.

"Other than a common sorrow over this young woman's death, did you and the defendant have any other dealings on campus?"

"No. We did attend, by invitation, a Donald-stone commencement one year. Both of us had been asked to speak. You see, I was familiar with Sandra's work and I was invited to her public events. If Charles was present, we exchanged a casual greeting. My time was focused on my life in public service, and he became a builder in the city. Our paths didn't cross, except over Sandra's charity work."

At the mention of Sandra's name, Charles shift-ed in his seat, breathing deeply again. He folded his hands on the table.

I was stuck on Leo's choice of words. *Public service*...my ass. Using a casual term like "build-er" for Charles, without any elaboration? What was that for?

Artie pivoted to the night Sandra died. No, Leo had never seen her so angry or drinking so much. Leo was completely mystified.

The video clips came next. Could Leo explain any of what he saw? Artie hit the pause button, freezing Sandra's face as she stared at Leo, hos-tile, her eyes filled with hate.

But that's not the place where the next question focused.

"Were you aware that Sandra Marchand had an attorney draw up separation papers?" Artie asked.

"No, I was not aware of that."

"Did Sandra speak to you that night?"

Leo paused and glanced at the jury. "Yes, we exchanged a few words, but she'd been drinking more than usual, so I didn't take her seriously."

"Can you tell the jury what Mrs. Marchand said?"

"Well, her exact words were, 'You won't have Charles to challenge you for your precious office.

I've seen to that.'"

That brought a gasp or two rippling through the courtroom. The reason for calling Leo as a witness finally made sense. The Bayless case had been on TV, and sure enough, Leo managed to link them.

Standing in place, Artie asked Leo about Sandra's demeanor when she spoke.

"She was distraught, angry, just as she appears in those video clips. She was sarcastic. Not like herself."

He sounded so reasonable, like he cared. Who did this crooked governor think he was kidding? Answering my own question, I realized he'd just fooled a lot of people with his phony concern.

"Did you say anything to Mrs. Marchand in response to her remarks?"

"Yes," Leo said.

"Can you tell the jury what you said?" Artie remained still, barely moving a muscle. I knew he didn't want to distract the jury or anyone else.

"I said, 'Sandra, stop drinking that champagne. You've had too much already'."

"Those were your exact words?"

"Yes."

"What happened next?" Artie shifted position, closer to the prosecution table, a subtle signal that he was bringing Leo's testimony to a close.

"Sandra laughed, real loud, and then gulped down the rest of the champagne in her glass. She turned away and headed toward Charles. She pushed the empty glass into his chest, and that's when the defendant hustled her out the door. I never saw her again."

No gasps this time. A hush settled over the room. No further questions.

Judge Lyons recessed for lunch. That bought us time, but not much. He hadn't done much damage.

I hurried into the conference room with Charles and Kenny so we could talk in private over a quick sandwich lunch.

Kenny's legal pad looked like a maze of boxes and arrows and starred points. My notes usually looked just as meaningless to unschooled eyes, but I knew Kenny had his own way of deciphering his code and turn them into a coherent train of thought.

"How bad is this?" Charles asked. "I never heard anything Leo said to Sandra. How do we know he's not lying?"

"We don't," I said, "but that's not the point."

"He's left the jury with the impression that I killed Sandra so she wouldn't interfere with my political career." Charles let his head flop back in an uncharacteristic gesture of helplessness. "At first, she was so excited about a campaign. It wouldn't interfere with her charities and causes, and might even have helped them." He shook his head. "She really enjoyed meeting new people."

"That's the impression Wendy passed on to me," I said. "She easily pictured Sandra stumping for you downstate and in the neighborhoods here. She was clever and charming."

Charles rubbed his face in obvious fatigue and stress. "We had fun with it, you know, until… well, you know what happened. But before that, we'd talk for hours about how difficult, but exciting, the campaign was going to be. She seemed so sure I'd win." He scoffed. "I thought my chances were good, too."

"But then she turned on the idea. That's the part we can't bring up," I said. "Damn."

"Leo doesn't have any way to know what I might ask him about Nancy. He doesn't know how much or little I'll ask." Kenny scrunched up his face in thought.

I stayed quiet, and so did Charles.

Finally, Kenny looked up. "It's a bit of a risk, but it might be all we have."

"What kind of risk?" Charles asked, his worried look intensifying.

"Let's just say it's in Leo's best interest to keep a lid on the past."

I tried to keep my voice casual, but this chance was too good to pass up. "Why don't you ask if Leo had any contact with either Sandra or Charles Marchand after the encounter at Café Brauer."

"Why?" Kenny asked. "What's behind it?"

"Nothing, I mean, no particular reason, except to establish he doesn't really know anything." Charles knew my fib, but Kenny didn't. "Let the question hang there, maybe make the jury and Artie wonder why you asked it."

Back in court, Kenny started slowly, with the tone of a little conversation between friends.

"When you first noticed that Sandra appeared upset, did you wonder about why that might be? Especially since her behavior was unusual."

"No," Leo said, "but I noticed the crowd was smaller than I was used to seeing. I wondered if perhaps her donations were down. I knew her to be committed to a group of no-kill shelters throughout northern Illinois. Her events had raised hundreds of thousands of dollars every year."

A little gamble... Kenny could have fed Leo that line. Of course, Artie objected on the grounds it called for speculation. And it did.

Judge Lyons wasn't so sure. Perhaps because she'd allowed Leo's testimony in the first place, she overruled the objection.

"Likewise, do you know the reason that Sandra might have decided that her husband's run against you was a bad idea? Any reason at all."

"No, I frankly assumed she was simply having a bad night. It's why I told her to put the champagne down."

Ha! He'd been afraid of Sandra. That much was clear. What if, in her semi-drunken state, she'd publicly accused him of sending a thug, disguised as a well-dressed business man, to threaten her? Leo didn't know how much of that sordid tale Kenny knew.

"Out of concern for her, you mean, her reputation?" Kenny asked.

"Yes, of course," Leo said, knitting his brows to appear concerned. "As I've said, I liked Sandra, and putting her husband's political plans aside, I considered myself one of Sandra's supporters."

Brilliant. Kenny was reminding our great public servant that he'd sent a goon to scare Sandra and by association, get Charles out of the race. Leo stumbled all over his words to leave the impression that he *loved* Sandra. I knew all the while he was hoping his secrets were safe. We had Leo dead to rights, but no one else in the courtroom knew it.

"Do you have any knowledge about the reason Sandra might not have cared to join the political fray? Was she *scared off* by the need…her perceived need…to be even more of a public person?" Kenny asked.

Leo shifted his weight. Left side to right side. He cleared his throat before saying, "I have no knowledge, but of course, candidates' spouses often do have that concern. It's true for office holders and candidates at every level."

Nice…embellish a little, Leo. Cover your lie. Keep talking.

I glanced at Artie. One knee was nervously

shaking under the table, like a tic he couldn't stop.

"Likewise, were you privy to any conversations Sandra and Charles might have had about her concerns, fears, and the like?"

"No," Leo said, "I have no knowledge of their conversations on any matter."

"Did you or your associates have any contact with Sandra after she left the Café Brauer the night of the fundraiser?"

Artie started to rise out of the chair. Instead, he held back. He didn't know what part of that he wanted to object to. Most likely, he didn't have an answer to the question. As for our side, we were confident Leo had lied.

I had a rush of unholy glee knowing how desperately Leo wanted to escape the courtroom.

Leo glanced at Artie, but seeing no signal *not* to answer, he skimmed his index finger across the space above his upper lip before saying, "No, I had no contact with Sandra. As I said, when she and Charles left, that was the last time I saw her."

Technically, correct. He had no contact. He never saw her again. The so-called associates? A different issue altogether. To him, but not to the law. He lied, and we could prove it, if it ever came to that.

* * *

The prosecution rested after Leo's testimony, as we knew it would. It hurt, we admitted, but overall, it was probably closer to a wash. Our thug of a governor lied, and now I took pleasure in knowing he hoped for an acquittal. Kenny believed calling the governor himself was the prosecution's way of grandstanding, adding heft to his case. Artie was no fool. He knew his case was weak.

Unfortunately, our mirror jury wasn't so sure. Even if all but two or three wrinkled their noses at the sound of the governor's name, it meant something to them that he was called.

That night, Kenny and I met with Charles at his home. Jordan Hayes, Sandra's half-sister, was the topic of conversation. Kenny's office had been working with Jordan, and because she was on the witness list, she wasn't allowed to attend the trial. Our chief character witness; and character was about all we had. Apparently, Sandra had revealed nothing about any problems cropping up between her and Charles, which was good. In fact, Jordan had some good stories about Charles' romantic side...the kind of stories that endear women to a man.

Our side's case was short, but not too sweet, because Charles crashed. Emotionally, that is. The leftover pleasure of knowing Leo had lied on the stand melted away that night.

"We've got nothing," he said, not once or twice, but again and again. Usually calm, sometimes impassive externally, but with a layer of confidence beneath the surface. Charles had lost most of that.

I didn't argue with him, because I knew this phase had to run its course. Panic attacks were not unexpected under certain circumstances.

Kenny wasn't so sanguine. He reminded Charles that he couldn't prove his innocence, not that he had to, but the prosecution didn't appear to meet their burden, either. No one, not the police or the medical examiner, could say how Sandra ended up at the bottom of the stairs. Even ol' Leo didn't implicate Charles, or hint that trouble had been brewing in the Marchand home.

And so it started. Our witness list was simple. A medical expert confirming the injury and ambiguous cause of the fall. From my perspective, it was inexplicable.

Two of Sandra's friends testified that Sandra had not given them so much as a hint that she was planning to divorce Charles. They testified that yes, she'd been excited about his political ambitions, but had changed her tune a few weeks prior to her death. The people who had seen her in the days before the night at Café Brauer heard her voice some skepticism about Charles' potential run, mostly because she didn't relish personal attacks from Leo Toland.

The testimony was consistent, and both women were concerned that Leo Toland had already begun undermining Charles and her, and that's why she was agitated—the word they chose at her fundraiser. Being close friends, they'd been concerned about Sandra for a couple of weeks.

One friend said, "I think she was afraid of the governor and what would happen in the run up to the primary election. I was present at the Café Brauer event. Sandra looked stunned to see him come in with his entourage. He was always on the guest list, his wife, too, at these events. It was routine to invite state reps, senators, and others. But she was taken aback when he showed up that night because of the politicized atmosphere."

Another friend said the same thing. Her purpose was to reinforce the previous testimony, and she did. "Sandra was afraid that Leo was so powerful, he could upset their lives to the point they'd never go back to normal."

Apparently, Sandra had been too afraid to provide specifics even to her closest friends. She really had been afraid, I concluded. She sensed what I did, that Leo would have stopped at nothing to get Charles out of the race. He'd already activated his well-oiled machine. Sadly, my brother had been part of it.

The mirror jurors liked what they heard. Wendy and Rick were happier than I'd seen them in a long time.

Mirror juror number 4 said he thought Kenny had implied Leo was hiding something. "The governor knows more than he's saying. Some of the defense lawyer's questions sounded a bit like a threat...maybe in a good way. I don't know."

A good start. Kenny's strategy worked at least for one person.

Mirror juror number 7 thought the case against Charles was weak.

Not so with juror number 9. He thought Charles flew off the handle and pushed his wife. Second degree murder, at least.

So, we still had work to do. The three of us sat late into the night after we sent our mirror jury home. I brought Maude out of my office, and she snoozed while Rick, Wendy, and I got a bad case of nerves watching Coop's show, recorded earlier. He hadn't moved his operation to Chicago, primarily because he was more or less sure this trial would be measured in days, not weeks.

As it turned out, it wasn't as sensational a trial as he thought it might be. In fact, he confided it was as mundane as many other criminal trials. The only element that saved it was the glamour and political intrigue surrounding it, and even that had not turned out to be especially exciting. Coop typically devoted about 12 minutes of airtime out of his sixty-minute show to the trial.

Rick had taken to calling Coop's show our evening brawl. This young game creator had grown on me, mainly because he said the work he did for my firm was way beyond interesting. A couple of times he called it *compelling*. His eagerness to help with whatever was needed didn't hurt. He was curious and picked up bits of information. But he wasn't keen on the legal shows with attorneys bantering, arguing, and some adding extra snark to their sound bites.

Coop himself thought the prosecution's use of Leo was a stunt, and that was good for an interesting ten-minute bout of harsh words back and forth.

"They're like actors," Rick said. "I can't suspend disbelief. Know what I mean? I don't like 'em for playing a role. They act like guilt or innocence doesn't matter. I create games, but I don't like when real life or death cases are treated like a game."

"Hmm...maybe trial law isn't exactly the place for you then," Wendy said with a smirk.

"Hey," I said, feigning hurt feelings, "you can't mean that. We use what we have, but we don't make stuff up."

"I'm just pulling your chain," Wendy said.

She yawned and got ready to leave.

I nodded to Rick. For reasons I couldn't define, I still didn't like the idea of Wendy going out alone to walk to the train station. Or Rick, for that matter. We were spending a lot of petty cash on cabs, Uber and Lyft.

"I'll come with you," Rick said.

Wendy rolled her eyes—at me. I couldn't fool her.

"Take a cab. Different day, same routine. I mean it," I said.

That night, Zach called, laughing. Gradually, he'd revealed his disgust for Leo and his petty corruption, his resentments, and Leo's way of leaving a lot of people owing him something. I had a feeling I knew what was coming.

"Leo thinks the prosecutor fucked him up."

"Artie?" That surprised me. "Why?"

"Shouldn't have called him in the first place," Zach said, "that's what he claimed. Because that gave your guy a chance to move in, make a liar out of him."

"He said that?" Was Leo that open with Zach?

"Nah, but he talked in code. He knows."

"Is he afraid?" I asked.

"Uh, too strong a word," Zach remarked, "but now he's hoping they let your guy off."

"He doesn't like the attention?" I could imagine Leo wishing Charles would disappear. Go back to his firm and pretend he never had thought about a political career.

Kenny lined up as much evidence as he could to show that a divorce was not in the works, but even more, Charles' feelings for his wife ran deep, and politics aside, never wavered. On the good side of the ledger, Charles had zero reputation as a womanizer. No sexual harassment charges or hints. No women coming forward to talk bad about him. That helped.

Kenny set the stage with the medical expert, evidence of the couple's booked vacation, and then he moved on to Sandra's friends and associates, and finally, Jordan, Sandra's half-sister, and even better, someone who loved Charles almost as much as she'd loved Sandra.

Jordan Hayes was an impressive figure on the stand. Older than Sandra, Jordan had the same classy look, not so much an aging beauty queen, but a graceful Meryl Streep, though with long red hair. Her equally classy husband, Joshua, came in with her and took a seat. Jordan wore a chic business suit and heels. She had the faintest hint of a southern accent, no doubt acquired in Kentucky, where she'd lived since marrying her husband, a big name in the banking world and in horse breeding. They had a home in Lexington, but the couple preferred their horse farm in the country. To each his own, I guess.

After Kenny established who Jordan Hayes was and got the jury engaged, he moved on to ask her about the first time she met Charles. Good or bad, we had a smart, elegant southern belle in our midst.

"I knew in a minute that Sandra was smitten with the handsome young developer," Jordan said, smiling at the jury as if on cue. "I was happy for her. And I saw in his eyes that the feelings were mutual."

Smitten…good word. It went uphill from there.

"Sandra and I spoke on the phone at least twice a week. We'd begun using Skype as well." Another pleasant glance at the jury.

She slowed down and looked at her folded hands when she added, "In our last conversation, we talked about plans for our next visit. We thought we might plan a weekend getaway to New York City, just for the two of us. We'd do that once or twice a year for theater binges. I guess we were lucky to be able to make plans like that."

"During that phone call, did your sister mention that Charles had decided not to enter the political arena?" Kenny asked.

"Yes, in that last conversation we talked about that decision."

I glanced at the jury. Each person was watching intently. All the faces were fixed with thoughtful expressions. Reasonable doubt, I told myself, *reasonable doubt*.

"Can you tell the jury the reason Sandra gave for the sudden reversal of Charles' decision?" Kenny asked.

Jordan turned her attention to the jury. "My sister had become frightened by, for lack of a better word, the process. She said Charles had decided that the attacks on him—on her, too—would become personal. She feared for his safety, you see. She mentioned the additional protection they'd both need. A couple of people she didn't know had already approached her and made various kinds of remarks. One day at Macy's, which Sandra and I still considered to be Marshall Field, the original store name...we didn't like when Chicago lost its identity...a total stranger came up to Sandra and said in a loud voice that her husband would never beat the sitting governor. So, of course, Sandra was upset that people she'd never even seen before would have that kind of easy access to her. And if she got that level of attention, then surely Charles would, too. She'd had experience with stalkers before."

Good. Fear. The questions first to Leo and now Jordan gave validity to Sandra's fears. I had a feeling it was going to be a good day.

The testimony continued. Jordan laughed off the idea of a separation. She was certain once Charles dropped the idea of running for office, their lives would have gone back to normal. "Sandra's threat to leave would have been based entirely on her fear of people that she called 'crazies'."

"So, you said your sister was familiar with stalkers. Can you explain?"

It was a matter of public record, and these stalkers had affected Sandra deeply. She feared for her wellbeing—and Charles', too. It was an area Kenny could open up. Allowing that history to come out, it helped mitigate, or at least we hoped it would, the testimony establishing that there was no sign of breaking and entering at the townhouse the night of Sandra's death. Although we had no evidence that anyone managed to get into the Marchand home, we hoped to open the door to even passing thoughts of the Marchands' vulnerability. Ideas are hard to remove from people's minds, just as testimony that is supposedly stricken from the record never goes away.

Kenny asked the key question, "What did you think when you learned Charles was accused of Sandra's murder?"

"I laughed… I mean, the very idea was absurd to me. Then I quickly realized I had to take the accusation seriously. I agreed to testify obviously," Jordan said turning to address the jury, "and because of that, I've had little contact with Charles since Sandra's funeral. Otherwise, I'd have been in the courtroom every day."

Stop, stop…enough. Even a good witness tends to meander, talk too much. Kenny gained what he needed to.

Artie decided to forgo cross examination.

Not surprising. I gave him some grudging respect for that choice. What was to be gained by grilling a grieving sister, who loved the defendant, but knew nothing about the night in question? So far, the trial had lasted six days. Total.

The defense rested.

Chapter Twenty-one

A little later in the morning than usual, I was polishing off my deep dish banana pancake when Christina hurried to my table. She pointed to the mounted TV screen where, sure enough, the "Verdict Watch" box in the lower right corner of the screen had been changed to "Verdict In." How could the media know before me?

At that moment, my phone buzzed. Kenny.

It buzzed again. Wendy. I smiled wryly at her text. *Janet will take good care of Maude while ur gone.*

In verdict watch mode, I'd taken Maude to the office first, where I knew Janet would take charge.

I put cash on the table to cover my check, and with a final nod to Christina and Alex, who had joined her mother, I left. As much as anyone, those two women, who I never saw in settings outside of the restaurant itself, knew more than anyone how much this trial had affected me, before I'd even agreed to join the team.

With Maude taken care of, I went to the courthouse and stood against the back wall. I could've made my way to the defense table, but I held back. I felt sick, and an aversion to being caught in a crowd had become part of my escalating fear.

We'd done everything, but even though our mirror jury had a couple of holdouts for acquittal, Leo, and Sandra's stalkers and her fear hadn't been enough to get us a wave of changing opinions. By the time I nodded at Charles and Kenny in the courtroom, the best I could hope for was a hung jury. Even that sent the acid burning in my gut.

I saw the back of Jordan's head from her place behind Charles. Judge Lyons took her time going through the rituals, but when it came time for the verdict, Jordan reached out to touch his shoulder as the word was spoken.

Guilty.

I was the coward in the next scenario. In the midst of the noisy response from the courtroom, I left, putting off the journalists who wanted a quote, ignoring calls from Coop, Wendy, and Rick.

Out on Dearborn, past the Picasso, I hailed a cab and gave the driver the address of my office. Then I texted Kenny. I'd see Charles later that day. I couldn't face him inside the courtroom. Later in the day was the best I could do. Charles would be put back in custody, not in his comfy den at home with pizza boxes in front of us and a full pot of coffee nearby, or a late-night shot or two of bourbon available.

I would have liked to go on home and hide, but I couldn't leave Wendy and Rick to huddle in front of the TV, and Janet to mind Maude alone. I owed them my presence. I owed them an upbeat, "it will be okay" attitude, because I could assure them Kenny would file an appeal. Great. Good for us. I'd stay only long enough, a decent interval though, to be ready to buck up and contact Kenny, and then I'd face Charles.

Once again, I swore off criminal cases. Deep in my bones, I was certain I couldn't handle a failure of this magnitude ever again. There were no two ways to look at it. I'd failed Charles…and Kenny, and Jordan, and in a way, I'd failed Wendy and Rick. No one else knew it, but I'd even failed Zach. I'd had plans for him.

Once I got to the office, I stood by the reception desk and took a deep breath. I waved off an offer of coffee from Janet, but gestured for her to join me in the conference room, where Wendy and Rick already sat.

I flashed back to the day Sandra's death was announced, which had been so devastating to Wendy. She looked almost as devastated over a year later. Rick seemed confused, much like a first-loss-response I'd seen on attorneys' faces all my life. They win a few cases early, but inevitably they lose and can hardly believe it.

Only weeks before, Potash had caved and accepted a multimillion-dollar last-minute settlement demand. Rick's elation had been palpable. Data had won the day. Skilled lawyering had taken advantage of every opening, and Leann's clients were elated, too. Rick had been a part of it and it felt good. Now this loss was worse than he could have imagined.

"There's not much to say," I told them. "All we can do is look to the next phase. The appeal."

"But on what grounds?" Wendy asked, her tone plaintive.

Good question.

"Well, I'll talk to Kenny. I haven't had time to think about it."

"What a fucking disaster," Rick said, wincing like he had a headache.

"You want to work in this office," Janet said,

her voice firm, "you gotta get used to having some calls go against you."

"Easy for you to say," Rick snapped. "You're not sitting in a cell right now."

The kid hadn't even met Charles, but he came off as embittered.

"I think it's too early to get over it," I said, looking at Janet, but intending to include all of them. "This one is tough. It's not numbers—money—it's a guy living in a jail cell."

"How I feel today is not where I started," Wendy said. "I don't think he did it."

Rick nervously tugged at his chin and sheepishly offered an apology to Janet. "I didn't mean to bark at you."

Janet smiled over her sparkly reading glasses she had perched on her nose. "I know that. We all get a little raw around here on days like this."

With the air cleared, we sat at the table for a couple of hours and hashed through the trial. I listened to them, they heard me out. We could second guess ourselves all day, or we could be completely unfair and critique Kenny's decisions. None of it felt just.

In truth, I don't know what I would have done any differently. Inside, I second guessed everything, every word of our surveys, every juror we seated, every juror challenge we passed up.

Still keeping up a stoic front, I told Janet to send out for Chinese from a new place called Little Wok that opened up down the block.

I managed to push a serving of spicy garlic beef around the plate and eat some fried rice, which was tasteless to me. All the while, Joey Haskell was taunting me in my head. I'd failed him, and now I'd fucked up again and failed Charles. I could hear Joey's voice reminding me that at least

Charles wasn't dead.

Small comfort. A guy growing old in a cell.

Finally, it was time for me to go. To see Charles. Kenny had arranged it.

I dropped Maude off at home and set out for the county jail. If I was gone long, I'd put a call into Samantha the dog sitter to be with Maude. It always gnawed at me when Maude was left alone for too long. The parking deck was just as bleak, the lawyer-prisoner room was just as stark, old, and grimy.

Charles was mourning all over again, only this time, he'd added hopelessness to his mix of feelings.

"I'm so angry I can barely talk," he managed to say in a hoarse voice.

I knew that sound. I'd heard it from Joey as his execution drew closer. Now I heard it from Charles. His throat had almost closed from the stress—if he'd had a heart attack right in front of me, I wouldn't have been surprised.

I nodded, avoiding cheap words. Besides, better to let him vent.

Holding his head in his hands, Charles said, "I suppose you're going to tell me not to worry, that the appeal gives me another chance…blah, blah, blah."

"No, man, I'm not going shovel a bunch of shit at you. Of course, you have another chance with an appeal, but I know that can't help you now. All I can say is that we did our best. Kenny is the best there is."

He nodded. "I know."

"If it's any comfort to you, we had some people on the mirror jury who were with you most all of the way. It was a couple of jurors, for what it's worth, which isn't much at this moment. But

293

there may be something we get out of the de-brief that sheds some light that can help us on the appeal." I slapped my thighs and stood. "Damned frustrating."

I left Charles to what I hoped was his temporarily miserable life, but I couldn't drum up optimism. I'd been around long enough to understand that no new evidence was going to suddenly appear, like a rabbit out of a hat.

On what grounds could we appeal? Wendy had asked. I had no answer for her. None. We needed a miracle. I didn't believe in miracles.

* * *

The next morning I went to Granny's, where Alex brought my breakfast in silence. Wasn't I beginning to feel like one self-centered bastard? They were tiptoeing around me, afraid to stir up my feelings or say something to make the situation worse. Christina made her rounds through the restaurant, greeting her customers, and being a cheerful presence to other people who, like me, had come to count on her. She carried a mug of coffee in her hand, and at one point, I watched as she put the mug down and lift her sleeve to show off her nicotine patch.

Days had gone by and I hadn't even asked the woman I called my Granny how it was going with her resolution to quit smoking. That realization left me feeling empty and sad. I needed a resolution of my own. Like maybe contact my friends, the people who had been so patient with me. I'd avoided so many friends during this miserable trial and had even minimized my conversations with Alex and Christina.

I had a mailbox filled with emails, a phone filled with voicemails and texts. When I got to the office I tried to greet everyone like a normal day was underway.

Janet handed me a padded manila envelope. "This arrived about ten minutes ago."

I looked at the return address. A newspaper in Minnesota? It could wait. Maude stayed with Janet and I went into my office and began scrolling through the texts and listening to the phone messages. Kenny, wanting to talk. Zach, telling me he was sorry, and on it went.

My eye kept going to the envelope until finally I muttered, "What the hell?" I ripped into it. I laughed out loud. I might have known.

How had I missed the connection between a newspaper in Minnesota and Aaron Nagasaki-Hanson? The cover note was handwritten and clear.

Thought you'd be interested in the water quality story. I've been working on it for over a year. Wrongdoing, lots of lies, cover ups and even falsifying water quality numbers. Class action suit is in the works. Something your firm might look into???

Multiple question marks in scribbled notes always made me smile. Aaron meant business. And maybe, even in my muddled mind, the idea of taking on this kind of case had a glimmer of appeal, as much as any case did that day. An escape route from what I'd just been through. Public service, I thought, my version of it. Wendy and Rick would love it. Could I pay them? Ah, what was I thinking? What we got paid from Potash could keep us going for a while. Marchand's fee, too, was a contribution to solvency.

In the midst of my reverie, Janet knocked on my door. "Better come see this, Matt," she said. "It's important."

I didn't doubt it. Maybe it was the serious look on Janet's face. Not a cliché or smart remark in sight.

I followed her into the conference room. On one side of the screen was an ambulance in front of what looked like automatic doors into O'Hare airport, and on the other side was a photo of Jordan Hayes waving off reporters outside the Daley Center.

"What the hell?" I asked. "What happened?"

"She's dead, at least according to the reporter," Wendy said. "Jordan's dead."

A reporter soon replaced the image of the ambulance. I recognized him as Danny Colman from one of the local stations. He stood with a young woman at his side.

"I have a person here, Diana Briggs, who was on the scene at the time. Mrs. Hayes, of course, had just testified on behalf of her brother-in-law, Charles Marchand. Only yesterday he was found guilty of his wife's murder. Mrs. Hayes and her husband, Joshua, were returning home and about to board their flight, when, from what we understand, she collapsed and lost consciousness. Ms. Briggs, can you tell us what you saw?"

Danny Colman looked like a contemporary of Jordan's, later middle age. Diana Briggs could have been his daughter, and more to the point, the young woman was clearly shaken, but like many people, eager to talk.

"I think many of us saw her fall to the floor. She was standing with her husband. He began to shout about calling 9-1-1. He repeated it over and over.

Then he shouted something I don't understand. He kept saying, 'She has HCM, HCM, HCM.' He knelt over her, patting her face, telling her to open her eyes. Then the paramedics arrived. I couldn't see much after that."

"Based on what this bystander—and others—have reported," Danny said, "when the paramedics arrived, they tried to revive her or keep her breathing. They understood the nature of the condition."

"Well, I'm not sure of the sequence or what happened. Airport security pushed us all back," Diana said. "I was told the flight would be delayed several hours, so I left the gate and came down here. My seat hadn't been called. Before I left, I saw her husband collapse next to her and then the paramedic covered her body."

Diana's voice quivered when she spoke those last words. And why not? I knew, too, that it was tough watching someone die.

Wendy and Janet were silent, and so was I. I was racking my brain for what HCM stood for. Must be some kind of medical condition or device, maybe. I remembered when she'd had a heart attack right after Sandra's funeral.

Of the four of us, only Rick had turned his attention elsewhere.

"Holy shit," he said. "HCM is Hypertrophic Cardiomyopathy. A cause of sudden death. Congenital. Gotta have a gene for it. Athletes drop dead from it."

"Wait, wait, wait…go back," I said. "What was that you said about there being a gene for it?"

"Yeah, it says right here you can test a person's blood for the gene. It's like a marker in the blood. Some doctors want young athletes tested for it, or they want it looked for when determining cause of death." Rick flopped back in the chair. "Huh, I wonder if…"

"I'll check with Kenny," I said, thinking that someone had to let Charles know what happened. Did he even know Jordan died? Who would tell him? It would be one more blow.

Something was off about this situation. I just couldn't put my finger on what.

I texted Kenny. A couple of minutes later, he called, and I stepped outside the conference room to talk.

"I'm heading over to the jail," Kenny said. "I want to tell him about Jordan right away. You want to come with?"

"Yeah, I'll meet you there. But listen, while you're gone, have someone from your office look up something called HCM. It's a disease. Have them send you the links so you can see it on your phone or pad. I'll explain later. We'll send over what we find on our end." I ended the call before I could be bogged down with his questions.

"I'm going to see Charles," I said, sticking my head inside the doorway. "Rick, you keep looking, and Wendy and Janet, you start combing through whatever data Rick finds. Organize the file, pick out the highlights, and text or email me the summaries."

"Do you think? I mean, is there something… you know…here?" Wendy didn't fill in the nouns and verbs, not her typical style.

"I don't know. That's what we'll find out."

"Well, Maudie," Janet said, looking fondly at the fifth member of the crew, if I counted myself, "we've got work to do holding down the fort, but don't worry, I'll take you out for a walk."

I don't know if it was a hunch or rational thoughts and facts lining up, but there was something important about Jordan's death. What if Jordan had been on a stairway and had collapsed? What would the death have looked like? A body found at the bottom of the stairs. An unexplained death. An accident the only explanation, under most circumstances, unless there was a public argument, a little too much alcohol, and a political rival showing up. Oh, and that little matter of separation papers.

My mind raced along and came back to those initials, HCM. I thought back to the last time I'd heard about a young kid, a high school basketball player, who had walked off the court when a timeout was called. He'd had trouble breathing, he was weakened, and his teammates helped him down to the floor, where he died, never regaining consciousness.

What if? What if?

At the parking deck, I spotted Kenny turning into a parking space, and I pulled my truck into the spot next to him. I squashed my own hunches, and followed Kenny's lead. We were silent as we went through the process all lawyers have to go through to see their clients. Kenny pulled out the stops to get us in right away, even though the trial was over and the sentencing hearing was several weeks off.

As it turned out, Charles had heard the news, so when Kenny and I saw him, he was ashen, looking almost as bad as he had the first day I'd seen him when his grief for Sandra had been fresh and raw.

As if he didn't quite catch on to the possible implications for himself, he was filled with regret. "I never got a chance to thank Jordan for coming here, for standing up for me the way she did. If I'd known she was still at risk, I'd have told her not to come."

"You couldn't have kept her—or Joshua— away." Kenny knew that first hand. He had prepped Jordan and commented on her ability to communicate her feelings for Sandra and Charles.

While they talked, I checked some summaries Wendy sent. Sketchy, but they did the job.

"Hey—they can check for the gene in Sandra's blood," I said. "They had the same father, but different mothers."

"And he died of cardiac arrest," Charles said. "He'd been brought back once before, just like Jordan, and had defibrillation, but it failed."

"Did Sandra ever say Jordan had HCM?" I asked.

"No, but Jordan herself said she had a complicated heart condition, but that it was under control."

"I'll call the medical examiner's office," Kenny said, "just to be sure they preserved the samples."

Charles covered his eyes. "It's like I'm back in the middle of the night, being wakeful, and seeing her on the stairs. It never occurred to me. No one ever said she could have that kind of heart condition."

Another text from Wendy mentioned stress.

"Look, Charles," I said, "we don't know if any of this is going anywhere, but with Jordan and the athletes I've read about, and based on what Wendy and Rick found online, stress can be involved. When Jordan had her first episode, Sandra had died. A defibrillator saved her that time. And then, Jordan's second attack came a day after you were convicted, but they couldn't bring her back."

I looked at a summary that included a fact Rick had found and explained it to Charles. "There's a move to try to get the medical examiner to check for the gene in cases like this. It goes unnoticed much of the time, and people with a strong family connection should be tested for it. That's the latest thinking. The point would be to try to prevent a cardiac arrest."

Charles ran his hands down his cheeks, a move of exhaustion coupled with frustration. "I'm afraid to hope, and besides, it's depressing to think of Sandra and Jordan dying that way."

"I understand," Kenny said. "I'm not going to offer hope. But what I will do is take this through the steps."

"You'll have to be patient," I added.

Charles smirked. "Fat chance of that happening."

It hadn't fully sunk in he'd be in jail for as long as it took to see if our new clue took us anywhere.

* * *

The seasons changed.

Charles walked out of the jail a little grayer, paler, tired to the bone, but free.

I had almost nothing to do in that phase, except for having hired Rick in the first place. Rick, who wasted not one second identifying the acronym, HCM. It was up to Kenny, but the way my office buzzed about it day after day, anyone would have thought my life depended on the medical examiner, and Judge Lyons following protocols to re-open the case.

Artie Okulek fought us every step of the way, but that was to be expected. On the other hand, Kenny and I agreed that the judge thought the case against Charles was, at best, weak. Listening to reason, she ordered the blood tested.

When the test came back showing Sandra carried the gene, Judge Lyons ordered a hearing, and in the end she vacated the verdict, which meant Charles was released. It also meant that Artie could retry him, but the way the judge explained her reasoning, only the foolhardy would take Charles back to court. The scientific evidence made it clear the case against Charles had officially fallen apart.

Charles was freed that same day. Kenny picked me up and took me with him to bring Charles home to his townhouse. I told myself I'd help to fend off the press, but more than anything else, I needed to come down from the high that exoneration triggered. Exoneration? A strong word. A *vacated* verdict leaves room for the diehard doubters to doubt.

We couldn't completely walk away from the reporters who had covered the trial, including some national press. With Charles standing behind him, and me watching from outside of the shot, Kenny thanked everyone involved, and threw in the moon and the stars, too. He mentioned Sandra and Jordan, and went on a little long about courts and justice and the system working in the end.

When Charles stepped to the microphone, he kept it simple. "I tried to have faith that the truth would come out, but it was difficult. A day doesn't go by that I don't think about my wife, Sandra, and now I'll also think of her sister, Jordan." And then he thanked Kenny and me.

We made our way to Kenny's car and he managed to maneuver through traffic to the house. I didn't stay long, though. After fighting our way through more reporters gathered on the sidewalk outside the front steps, I was worn out.

Charles soon started taking calls from his business partner and friends. Some wanted to come over, but Charles asked them to wait. "Tomorrow morning. Come then…I'll be here all day…Let's have dinner…Next week…Great…Thanks…I'll see you soon."

He repeated that a dozen times in less than half an hour.

"You're going to have a lot of dinners out," I said as I got to my feet.

"You leaving?" he said.

Nodding, I looked at him and at Kenny. "I need to check in with Wendy and the others. By the way, Cooper Julien texted me. He wants you on his show."

Charles groaned.

"He's a serious guy, Charles." I paused. "Uh, more to the point, I owe him a favor. Your interview will pay my debt."

"Oh, yeah?" Charles asked. "And what's that?"

Smiling, I shook my head. "It will keep. I'll tell you another time."

Charles walked me to the back where I could walk down a couple of side streets and get to a main street where cabs were plentiful.

"I can't thank you enough," he said, putting his hand on my shoulder.

I put up my hands in protest. "You could thank me if the jury had acquitted you. It didn't."

"Still. You believed in me. Your team started the research rolling."

As we shook hands, I said, "They're a good team all right. The new kid, a computer game designer guy, is the one who latched on to HCM first and started gathering all the facts."

He gave me a sidelong glance. "I hope you pay the nerd enough."

I laughed. "In due time."

I arrived at the office in time to sit with Wendy, Janet, and Rick to catch the end of the local news. The anchors had already covered Charles' story. I was feeling good enough that I didn't care. I'd told them I was taking them all out for a dinner in the neighborhood, but no one was inclined to rush out.

"What's next, Matt?" Rick asked, swiveling in the conference room chair, as if restless and looking for something to do.

"I'm not sure. We have a couple of medical device cases on the books. Maybe they'll go to trial, maybe not. We'll see. I'm thinking about something a bit more civic-minded."

"You mean like a corruption case. That would be a criminal trial." Wendy looked puzzled, but not disappointed.

"Maybe. I'm thinking public interest." I filled them in on Aaron Nagasaki-Hanson and the information about the poisoned water and cover up.

Before I got the whole story out, Rick started typing and searching, and was soon uttering profanities over what he found. "Sue their asses, I say."

Wendy sounded excited. "Meaning…that case has *meaning*."

As for Janet, she shrugged. "In for a penny, in for a pound."

She didn't know why the other three of us burst out laughing.

"Before we leave, I've got a call to make. I'll be maybe two minutes," I said, coaxing Maude into my office, where she could sit tight until I came back for her after dinner.

I closed my office door and called Zach. I got his voice mail, so I was brief. "Lakeview Market. Noon tomorrow. And thanks."

Assume Guilt

As I walked down the street with my three companions, I realized my gut hadn't burned all day. I smiled. Maybe the calm would hold all the way through the next day's deep dish pancake at Granny's.

Epilogue

I waited until, as Janet would say, the dust settled, before showing up at Charles' door, unannounced, one evening when icy air was once again blowing through the city. It made us pull our hats a little lower on our heads to cover our ears. I'd been feeling lighter in my gut and my heart than I had in a helluva long time. I was ready to take another step, the last one to finally end the case that had led me to change a few things in my life.

Charles and I still had something to settle between us. On a hunch, I'd withheld the last searching question, still not understanding why. I'd done it all the way through Charles' case. I'd banked my secret information, allowing it a little time to earn some interest. Now it was time for the payout.

I parked my truck down the street, then walked up to the front door and rang the bell.

I would have liked a cell phone photo of that look of pleasant surprise on Charles' face when he opened the door. I was high on his list of heroes. Not that I didn't give my team, especially Rick, a lot of credit—he got a fulltime job out of the deal.

"Matt. Good to see you."

"Uh, I should have called first, I suppose. Is this an okay time?" I looked past him, wondering if he was alone. No reason he should be, though. He was a free man, back to work, and contemplating a run for an open Congressional seat. At least that's what I'd heard.

He opened the door wide and gestured me inside. "I'm watching a Bulls game, thinking about life. The fact that I've got one. I'm still not used to it, strange as that might seem."

Looking into his face, his eyes darkened for a second, but then he smiled. I guessed he'd probably not finished grieving for what he'd lost.

He led me through the living room and into the same den and TV room I'd been in before. He went to the makeshift bar. "What can I get you?"

"That bourbon you keep on that counter is just fine…neat."

"Neat it is." He poured a couple of fingers of the dark liquid into two tumblers and handed me one before sitting in an easy chair across from the corner of the couch where I'd parked myself. Same place I'd claimed before and during the trial.

"So, what brings you by?" he asked.

"I've been sitting on something for quite a while. Over a year now. I need an answer to a… let's call it a lingering question."

A frown worried his face. "What is it?"

I leaned forward. "Look, let me be straight with you. You don't need to be afraid. This can't hurt you now."

He cocked his head. "Which is a not so subtle way to imply it, whatever *it* is, could have hurt me before."

I took a sip of my drink. "We asked you a shitload of questions. *I* asked a bunch of them more than once. You told us some lies. I knew which ones, too, even way back then."

Charles jerked his head back. "Hey, what's this really about? Are you accusing me of something?"

I wanted to do this my way. "You told us about a well-dressed thug scaring Sandra. But then you lied when you told us you barely knew Leo."

"I *did* barely know him."

"A technicality. You never revealed anything voluntarily. That's the point. Later, we found out why. But one secret you kept goes back to the night Sandra died."

Charles frowned, as if searching his memory. A flicker of recognition flashed in his eyes.

"I see you're remembering now. You know, the man who showed up and talked about a message but reassured you that he hadn't seen anything?"

Charles gulped back half of what was left in his glass. I did the same.

"So?" I opened my hand, as if offering him the floor.

"At first, I forgot about it. I mean, when I was arrested and you and Kenny came to see me and posed the questions. That night was a blur. I opened the door and thought the EMTs had arrived, but it was some guy. Then, before I could think too much about it, the ambulance showed up." Charles skimmed away moisture gathering on his upper lip. "Too late. And I was too late."

"So, your excuse for the lie is your faulty memory."

Still frowning deeply, he said, "I didn't spill anything about Leo until I had to. You were right about that."

After he was freed, and the trial was over, I'd told Charles about snooping around, finding things, little things that could matter. Charles knew about the diary and how I put Cooper Julien on alert about it. How I let him bring out the information that could have helped.

"But even then, when I was putting all that out on the table, you still left out the little detail about the guy at your door."

Charles stood, and like many times before, he paced. "When I thought about it, after Sandra's funeral, I figured Leo would back off. He got what he wanted. I couldn't run against him."

He stopped and spun around to face me full on. "Wait a second. When did you find out about that guy?"

Knowing I was being kind of sarcastic, I pressed my fingers to my temples as if struggling to remember. "Hmm…let me see. Let's just say it was before I met you."

His face scrunched in confusion. "If that's the case, why wouldn't you have said something?"

"I sat on it, like I sat on everything else, hoping that maybe you'd tell us first."

"A test," Charles said bluntly, "and I failed."

"Something like that. I was more intrigued by *why* you held back so much."

He leaned against the easy chair and folded his arms over his chest. "How did you know about that guy anyway?"

"You really want to know?"

Charles raised his arms in exasperation. "What the hell kind of question is that? You think I like this?"

Seeing that Charles thought I was playing games, and I was, and that I was still angry with him, which I wasn't, I decided he finally deserved a straight answer. "That guy is my brother."

I didn't need a cell phone picture of Charles'

face. Shock coupled with disbelief.

"Half-brother, to be accurate."

"Your brother works for *Leo*?"

I snickered. "Didn't see that coming, did you?"

"No, I sure didn't."

"His name is Zach. We have different, but equally lousy fathers. Sperm donors, figuratively speaking. Zach's older. Got into some trouble years ago. Leo pulled some strings that got him out of it. But Zach paid a price for the help."

"Tell me," Charles said, showing curiosity now. And I did.

I related the details of Zach's contracting business and his arrest for fraud; how Leo, a guy with big ambitions and limited scruples, made a deal that kept Zach free—for a price. Lifetime loyalty and ready-made gofer. I guess that he saw my brother was a smart guy.

"It was a deal with the devil, but it kept him out of prison, and employed on what eventually became Leo's special security detail when he was elected to state office. Zach made a living, not what he liked, but what the deal forced on him."

I explained that I hadn't seen Zach during all the years I'd taken on criminal cases and death penalty appeals. "We were like strangers. Now and again, he'd call, usually because he'd read something in the news about me. I never called him. It was like an agreement, you know."

Charles nodded in understanding, listening.

I admitted that we'd been more or less estranged, mostly because of Zach's ties to Leo. "I wasn't aware of exactly what he did for Leo, and I didn't want to know. Leo is exactly as sleazy as he appears. He sent Zach for the middle-of-the-night visit because he could trust him. Leo had seen you that night at Café Brauer, knew you could still run against him, regardless of what Sandra said, and that's why he sent a second message."

"Why did your brother tell you?"

It took time to gather my thoughts. "He saw— he heard—the buzz about my firm coming on- board with Kenny. He came to my office, just like I showed up here. My employees had never seen him, so they didn't know who he was. They still don't. We talk in code on the phone and meet away from the office. The thing is, he told me what he saw when you opened the door. He saw what you saw."

Charles' expression turned quizzical. "So your brother—Zach—he's the same guy who scared Sandra that day at the conference?"

"Uh uh…no. Believe me, my brother doesn't match the description of the handsome Norse- god businessman at that conference. Don't get me wrong. He's a not a bad-looking guy, but no one has ever called him handsome. I asked Zach about it, but he couldn't identify the guy who scared Sandra. He speculated that he was probably a campaign operative of some kind." I shrugged. "Zach maintained he was in the shadows a lot, sniffing out people for Leo, but according to my brother, our dirty governor had other people to take on the heavy lifting. Zach was more public. On the state payroll and all that."

"Typical Illinois state government."

I nodded. "Zach acted like a spy for me for those months. He told me about being on duty that day you were at the Donaldstone graduation and you got that honorary degree. You and Leo were good at hiding any hint of a past."

"I never imagined such a connection," Charles whispered, "and like I said, I all but forgot about that guy who showed up when I'd called 9-1-1."

I took one last gulp to polish off my drink and settled back on the couch. "Here's the thing. Zach's raised his two kids. They're in college now. His wife has her own hair salon. To be blunt, he's paid his debt to Leo."

Charles tilted his head, showing his curiosity. "Why are you telling me all this now? You were aware of it before. Why open up an old wound and put me on the spot like this?"

"I want a favor...let's say a little something for my silence you didn't even know about."

Charles' face darkened. "Hey, Matt, I'm thinking of running for Congress. You know I can't be—"

"Wait," I interrupted, lowering my voice. "I'm not headed towards anything improper here...not at all. I'd like you to offer Zach a job."

The relief on Charles' face was almost comical. "Well, I may need some security staff, pretty soon as a matter of fact. Or an advance team, even though it's local."

"I was actually thinking of something more in your business. Like I said, he was a good contractor. He was a project person. He liked restoration, too."

Charles grinned. "Do you mind if I talk to him? See what he wants, you know, give him a choice?"

I smiled and shook my head. "Can't argue with that. Whatever you do, I'd appreciate it. I don't want to hurt the guy's pride, though. I can't bullshit him, either, like this was some idea you pulled out of the hat." No, Zach would hate that. "I want to be upfront. I have to see if he thinks he can extricate himself easily. But it looks like Leo isn't going to run anyway. There might be nothing left for Zach to do for him."

"Consider it done," Charles said. "There'll be

something. I am serious about Congress. The seat is going to be open, so it might be now or never."

"I was one of those eager to see Leo challenged. There were a lot of us."

Charles exhaled, finally appearing relaxed, even content. "So, what's next for you? What cases are you taking on? You've gotta be in demand now, big time."

"Since you asked, I'm taking a look at water."

"Huh? You mean water we drink?"

I nodded. "Remember Aaron Nagasaki? Now Aaron Nagasaki-Hanson."

His eyes widened in surprise. "The journalist, from school. He interviewed me. Yeah, I remember."

"As it happens, he's quite the investigative reporter. Aaron works for a small weekly, but he's discovered lies, a cover-up scheme, falsified water quality numbers, and hush money changing hands—and that's just for starters. It's all about politicians and their corrupt appointees. The citizens of a little town in Minnesota are paying the price. I'm thinking of signing on for the class action suit."

Charles' mouth fell open. "Wow…that sounds fascinating. Must be hard, though, to take on a case like that." He flashed a lopsided grin. "You know, hard on the bottom line."

I laughed. "*Everyone* says that."

As if he caught the joke, he laughed. "So that drug company you worked with and I are philanthropists now. Don't worry, I'll get your bill paid."

Feigning a look of innocence, I shrugged.

I stood, ready to leave Charles to his Bulls game and political career. As I headed out, I turned my head back towards him. "Your words, not mine, but your money could go to worse causes."

I left with Charles laughing. I wished him well.

As I walked to my truck, ready to get Maude and take her for a walk, my mind drifted to the lowlifes who screwed up that town's water. "We'll get 'em, Maude."

It would take time, but so what, I liked a challenge. I was up for another one now.

Acknowledgements

Books do not get completed solely through the work of the author. It takes a network both related to task and emotional support that brings one across the finish line. I've written many nonfiction books but in this first fiction effort, I needed years of support from so many to see this project through to publication.

Authors who don't begin by thanking their parents for the gift of life are too caught up in their own talents. I would not be where I am or accomplish what I do without the lifelong love and support of my parents, Seymour and Sandy Lisnek. My mom left this earth this past summer after a valiant battle with Alzheimer's disease, a horrendous challenge that science must work to conquer. My memories and her spirit will both guide and inspire me always. Through the difficult times and challenges, my parents never failed to believe in me and know I could accomplish whatever I wished to do. The support of my family, kids Alexandra and Zachary, their Mom, Janet, and my brother and sister (the concept of sister-in-law is to me, a mere technicality because I could not love her anymore!) Rick and Judy Lisnek all provided the emotional support I needed to see this and every project through to the end.

The pet lovers will appreciate that I derive spirit from my wonderful four-legged kids, Matthew and Myles and dearest Mertz and Maude, who left this realm before the completion of the book.

As close as family, I couldn't make anything happen without the full support of Diana Briggs who has covered for me for over 30 years so I can attend to business. My thanks for over 20 years of assistance to the wonderful Nancy D'Andrea and of more recent years, Samantha Salzinski (and her Greta), who also edited this book, and Anne Marquez, all of whom babysit so I can have a life. Thanks, too, to Marc Matlin, Denise, Marco, and the team at Chicago Dog Walkers for their flexibility and assistance always; to Oscar Usky Fabian for insuring I'm always relaxed, and to Adel Madi and Toshia Lee for keeping me looking my best above the neck. And thanks to Nona Valladeras for her caring support of my parents and for making fabulous adobo mani.

My colleagues both in front of and behind the cameras at WGN-TV are always supportive of my efforts, and especially my News Director Jennifer Lyons and Assistant News Director Sandy Pudar, who are especially understanding. I owe my job and ongoing success to former News Director and warm-hearted man, Greg Caputo. The burden of doing a nightly show is eased through the work of my hard-working Producer, Jordan Muck. Special thanks to Executive Producers Aline Cox, Monica Zack, and Dom Stassi; Producers Mike Wilder, Samantha Julien (whose talent for producing rivals her incredible skills as a master baker!), and Rob Roper, who always have my back. Directors and friends Steven Novak, weather team members Jennifer Kohnke and Bill Snyder, fellow anchors Monica Schneider, Micah Materre, and my dear retired friend Mark Suppelsa (greatly missed, but he's happily living off the land now, all of whom are supportive in so many ways outside of the professional realm. And with thanks to my nightly TV crew of Bill "Butter" Crane, Joe "Wingman" Pausback, and Brian "jolly" Holiday, as well as John Szweikowsky, along with my IT expert and friend, Lee Rivadeneira, writer Chas Hayes, and Producer Jaime Elich. And a shout out to anchor Larry Potash, without whom I would not likely be working at WGN-TV.

Similarly, my Comcast TV family is so unendingly supportive of all the projects I pursue. Thanks to my *Newsmakers* co-anchor Ellee Pai Hong for lots of fun and covering for me when I have to depart early, even if you do get your choice of which side of the set to sit on. In a category all her own, Rebecca Cianci my producer, joined with Richie Foresman, Fernando Garron, Nancy Bayless, Amy Hanson, Freddy Prigge, Aaron Nowakowski, Matthew Leslie, Artemus Okulek, and Gary, Kenny, Eric, Jerry, Coax, and the rest of the gang. Thank you guys for the fun and support. And for years of fabulous makeup and brows care, the amazing makeup artist and friend, Brenda Arelano. Also, my friends at Broadway in Chicago (especially Eileen LeCario) and Margie Korshak, Inc., including Margie and Amanda Meyer, my thanks for all your work!

I appreciate my partner and friend, Richard Gabriel, jury consultant extraordinaire and the entire team at Decision Analysis, Inc.

To my agents at National Speakers Bureau: Brian Palmer, Don Jenkins, and Susan Masters for sending me around the nation and world.

To my accountants Greg Schultz and Bob Blackmun for making sure I pay the bills and keep the IRS at a distance.

The support of friends like Reverend Arnold Pierson, Wendy and Michael Marchant, Theresa Ehrhart, Pam Baumgartner, Kay and Haskell Pitluck, Linda and Michael Baden, Cindy Raymond, David Rittof, Al Menotti, Steve Rubin, Marlene Rubin Brown, Steven Gan, Raphael Sangel, Nikki Calvano, Danny Colman, Richard and Melanie Conviser, Marie Grabavoy, and Allen and Leann Almquist. Plus, special thanks to my favorite "celeb" friends: Kathy Garver (TV's "Family Affair," movies, author, and so much more) and fabulous designer to the stars (and me, too!) Mark Roscoe of Roscoe Coutour and JoAnne Fakhouri for her PR assistance. My thanks to you all!

And to Virginia McCullough. Your talent for writing and editing knows no bounds. This project has been in my head and being for years. It has undergone many start-over revisions, but you have gotten me through it all with meticulous detailed guidance that developed and shaped the plot line, got these chapters into existence, and forced me to keep going when I wanted to hang it up. I thank you Virginia. You are a writer's writer and no words of thanks do justice to honor the extent of your contribution to this book.

And finally, thank you to Brittiany Koren and the team at Written Dreams Publishing who believed in this project, took it on, and made sure it got into the hands of the person reading these very words.

—PML

If you enjoyed *Assume Guilt*, watch for the next installment of the series in Winter, 2019 or try these other mysteries from Written Dreams Publishing.

Assume Treason

A Matt Barlow Mystery

Paul Lisnek

It's a presidential election year, but other than following a few of his favorite candidates in state races, it's all routine cases for jury consultant Matt Barlow and his team...until the whispers about a prominent politician turn into headlines suggesting treason.

When an arrest is made, Matt follows the matter closely in the headlines but doesn't give much thought as to who he believes. Until...the phone rings...and Matt has a decision to make. Does he enter into a political bombshell of a matter that has international implications? The decision could be risky for Matt and his career, but also for the stability and future of the country.

Matt's used to representing the underdog, but in this matter, just who is the underdog?

Land Sharks

#HonoluluLaw, #Triathletes & a #TVStar

Katharine M. Nohr

Young attorney, Zana West, is assigned the perfect case for a triathlete— a lawsuit filed by Brad Jordan, a man who claims he was paralyzed during the Honolulu Olympic triathlon trials. As an added bonus, Zana's television crush, Jerry Hirano, the star of "Fighting in Paradise" by night and attorney-by-day playboy, represents another defendant in the case. Jerry insists upon date-like evenings with her to discuss the investigation.

Clues mount up, but Jordan's attorney, Rip Mansfield, a shark in an attorney's suit, takes every opportunity to harass Zana. To make matters worse, she's always one mistake away from being fired and she's stuck working with her boss's mini-me, Lucas Rossi, who would rather play video games than help with pre-trial discovery.

Will Zana be able to figure out the truth before the case goes to trial?

Death Nosh

A Noshes Up North Culinary Mystery

Mary Grace Murphy

People are dying in the pleasant community of Bayshore, Wisconsin. The police think it's the normal passing of senior citizens. But Nell Bailey, food blogger and restaurant reviewer, has a different opinion.

Someone is sneaking into houses, committing murders, and escaping without a trace. How can Nell convince the police chief to take her theory seriously?

Surrounded by mouthwatering meals, Nell struggles with her weight as she visits restaurants, and blogs about their delectable dishes. She strives to conquer her stress-eating as the death count rises.

To further complicate her life, Sam, her gentleman friend, isn't acting very gentlemanly. His plans for the two of them don't include Nell investigating any more murders. Can she hold her own against two men, Sam Ryan and Chief Vance, who are so accustomed to doing things their way?

About the Author

Paul Lisnek's world includes television, jury consulting, and politics. These worlds converge in this, Paul's first work of fiction (following 13 published books of non-fiction). Paul is the political analyst for WGN-TV and hosts a live nightly TV talk show, *Politics Tonight*, seen on CLTV in Chicago. He also hosts *Broadway in Chicago Backstage, Newsmakers,* and *Political Update,* for the Comcast Network. He anchors a podcast for WGN Radio called *Behind the Curtain* which can be heard at WGNPlus.com.

Paul holds a law degree and Ph.D. in communication from the University of Illinois at Urbana. He is a jury trial consultant with Decision Analysis, Inc based in Los Angeles. His firm has worked in notable cases including O.J. Simpson, Whitewater, People vs. Phil Spector, Heidi Fleiss (Hollywood Madame), Casey Anthony (Tot Mom case), and People vs. Kwame Kilpatrick (Mayor of Detroit). Paul has taught at the University of Illinois, Loyola University Chicago, DePaul University in Chicago, and Pepperdine University's Institute for Dispute Resolution. He is a national lecturer for BarBri Bar review and speaks at conferences, corporate meetings and for government entities around the nation and world, including dozens of lectures each year for future leaders who attend the National Student Leadership Conference (which he helped found).

The Museum of Broadcast Communication in Chicago hosts the Paul M. Lisnek Gallery which is a permanent exhibit honoring Paul's life and career. Learn more about Paul's books at www.paulmlisnek.com and www.paullisnek.tv and follow him on social media.

CPSIA information can be obtained
at www.ICGtesting.com
Printed in the USA
FFHW021508171218
49915244-54526FF